THE ELEVENTH FLOOR

ALSO BY SHANI STRUTHERS

EVE: A CHRISTMAS
GHOST STORY
(PSYCHIC SURVEYS
PREQUEL)

PSYCHIC SURVEYS
BOOK ONE:
THE HAUNTING OF
HIGHDOWN HALL

PSYCHIC SURVEYS
BOOK TWO:
RISE TO ME

PSYCHIC SURVEYS
BOOK THREE:
44 GILMORE STREET

PSYCHIC SURVEYS
BOOK FOUR:
OLD CROSS COTTAGE

PSYCHIC SURVEYS
BOOK FIVE:
DESCENSION

PSYCHIC SURVEYS
BOOK SIX:
LEGION

PSYCHIC SURVEYS
BOOK SEVEN:
RISE TO ME

PSYCHIC SURVEYS
BOOK EIGHT:
THE WEIGHT OF THE SOUL

BLAKEMORT
(A PSYCHIC SURVEYS
COMPANION NOVEL
BOOK ONE)

THIRTEEN
(A PSYCHIC SURVEYS
COMPANION NOVEL
BOOK TWO)

ROSAMUND
(A PSYCHIC SURVEYS
COMPANION NOVEL
BOOK THREE)

THIS HAUNTED WORLD
BOOK ONE:
THE VENETIAN

THIS HAUNTED WORLD
BOOK TWO:
THE ELEVENTH FLOOR

THIS HAUNTED WORLD
BOOK THREE:
HIGHGATE

THE JESSAMINE SERIES
BOOK ONE
JESSAMINE

THE JESSAMINE SERIES
BOOK TWO
COMRAICH

REACH FOR THE DEAD
BOOK ONE:
MANDY

REACH FOR THE DEAD
BOOK TWO:
CADES HOME FARM

CARFAX HOUSE:
A CHRISTMAS GHOST STORY

This Haunted World:
Book Two

THE ELEVENTH
FLOOR

SHANI STRUTHERS

Authors Reach
www.authorsreach.co.uk

ISBN: 978-0-9957883-4-3

For Rob – It had to be.

Acknowledgements

There's no way writing is a lonely process. Not only do you get to meet a whole host of wonderful characters that you've just created, there's practically an entire army behind you! Thanks so much to my fantastic beta readers for all your help and encouragement; I'd be lost without you all. In no particular order these include Rob Struthers, Louisa Taylor, Lesley Hughes, Sarah Savery, Rumer Haven, Veronica McGivney and Corinna Edwards-Colledge. Thanks also to Jeff Gardiner for his editing skills and Gina Dickerson of Rosewolf Design for the front and back cover and interior formatting. The dream team!

Foreword

If you've read the first in this series – The Venetian – you'll know that novels in the *This Haunted World* series are all standalone stories, set in the world's most haunted places and blending fact with fiction. The Eleventh Floor is no exception. I may have changed the hotel name and location slightly, but this hotel exists, and I had the pleasure of staying there in 2016. When I say pleasure… I can't reveal too much more without giving certain plot elements away, but again much is drawn from fact with fiction weaved through it. And actually, it really was a pleasure to stay at this hotel; it's charming, unique, lost in time, as special as I'm trying to portray. One day I'll go back.

Prologue

The building of THE EGRESS – an extract from a newspaper in 1921:

A NEW Hotel for Williamsfield!

No city in the state needs a modern hotel more desperately than Williamsfield. Are we equal to the occasion? Will we have this New Hotel?

This is a civic enterprise, the biggest project Williamsfield has ever undertaken, it means more business, more social life, more visitors, and more dollars for those who live here!

The New Hotel is YOUR hotel. It is a part of the community because WE, the community, will build it. All of us, joining together to boost our city, to make it somewhere people will want to visit, putting Williamsfield on the map!

Grand but accessible, formal but friendly, it is

somewhere to celebrate every type of occasion; a social center, a gathering place. From diplomats to downtown workers, all are welcome! Once visited, never forgotten, it promises to be a very special place indeed.

Chapter One

From the driver's seat of her rental car, Caroline leant forward to turn the radio up.

"We…e…e…ll," the deejay said, dragging the word out as far as it would go, "it's going to start getting very dramatic out there very soon. I'm not sure who amongst you remembers the Great Appalachian Snowstorm of 1950, but what's in store looks set to rival it!"

Caroline swore. "Shit! A snowstorm. Seriously?"

It was mid-November, she was in Pennsylvania en route to the town of Williamsfield, and so far, the weather had been fair to middling. She'd landed in the US seven days before and had spent time in Upstate New York, just below the Canadian border, visiting family members she hadn't seen since her late teens. Yes, there'd been rain, quite a bit of it, and certainly it was cold, but a snowstorm? That was the first she'd heard of it. How long was it supposed to last? Not long, surely – one or two days, three at the most? What a blow if it was the latter! With only a week left, that would seriously disrupt her schedule.

Instinctively turning up the heating, she continued to listen.

"Back then, the National Weather Service recorded 27.4

inches of snow in Pittsburgh – a record that still stands. But the question is, folks, for how long? Many other areas in the state of Pennsylvania at that time saw at least thirty to forty inches. Public transportation was crippled, the mail delivery stopped and industry all but ground to a halt. And you know what? We think we're more equipped to handle extreme conditions nowadays, but I'm not so sure. I reckon the only thing that's gonna fly when the white stuff hits is the Internet!"

The deejay laughed heartily, clearly enjoying the joke he'd made. And well he might, sitting in his safe warm studio, putting the fear of God into those like her, travelling America's vast highways; those long, long roads that seemed to carry on forever, so different to the more cramped, often crowded roads she was used to in England.

"Oh, would you believe it, here it comes, bang on cue," she muttered as the first flakes of snow hit the windscreen, the wipers smearing them against the glass. She glanced at her Sat Nav, there was another fifty miles to go before she reached Williamsfield; the plan being to make a brief stop at the Egress Hotel on the outskirts of town just to have a look at it, this hotel she'd heard so much about. After that she'd find a stopover that was more central, close to bars and restaurants, and shack up for a night or two or however long she had to. If she put her foot down, she might be able to keep the storm at bay, the thought of which made her smile: outrunning the elements, or at least giving it a shot.

Making the most of the weather as a news item, the deejay introduced listeners to a guest, a woman, her voice old, gnarled almost, as well it might be, considering she was someone who remembered the great storm he'd been talking about.

"It was beautiful," she informed them, a wistful sigh escaping her. "Everything was cloaked in white and the silence... I swear you coulda heard a pin drop."

The deejay and the old lady – Betty Jean Ramsey – laughed together and even Caroline raised a smile.

"I was getting married the week it hit. I always did pick my moments! And Paul, my husband-to-be, had some miles to travel to church, miles I didn't think he had a hope in hell of making as I stood at the altar and waited...and waited...and waited."

Clearly well versed in the dramatic arts, Betty Jean paused for effect putting Caroline on tenterhooks. "Come on, Betty, did he make it or didn't he?"

"Betty Jean?" the deejay prompted.

Still there was silence, stretching into two seconds, into three... Into four...

"He made it!" Betty Jean declared at last. "But he had to walk a fair amount of the way. And he was cold, so cold he was shivering, poor soul, his teeth chattering so much he could hardly say his vows. But he was determined. He told me later on that night that no damn storm was going to stop him from making an honest woman out of Betty Jean!"

Again there was much laughter and, as the snow started to fall in earnest, a thin layer quickly covering the once lush countryside but not yet claiming the asphalt in front of her, another similar story of devotion sprang to mind; one that involved her parents.

They'd been caught in a storm too, in this very state, in the nineteen eighties – 1983 to be exact – when another weather front of note had swept across northeast Ohio and northwest Pennsylvania. A Valentine's Day blizzard that was also their wedding day. Unlike Betty Jean, it was her British father, Tony, who'd been waiting at the church for his American bride, Dee, to reach his loving arms. And he'd waited and waited too, breaking into a cold sweat at the thought of not making the woman he loved most in the entire world his, to have and to hold on this most romantic of days. Oh, how he'd loved her, how she'd loved him – their feelings towards each other never failing to shine through, at least not in Caroline's memory. Displaying the same kind of grit that Paul had, Dee had also made it to the church, not on foot – although Caroline was sure she would have walked if she'd had to, wedding finery and all – but driving a Chevy C10 Pick-Up commandeered from a willing neighbour. She'd got to the church, marched up the aisle, and said 'I do'. Later, unable to travel the two-hour distance to the suite they'd booked in the Pocono Mountains for their honeymoon, they'd gone somewhere closer instead – the Egress, a few miles outside of Williamsfield, and stayed there for the best part of a week.

"Such a nice hotel," her mother had said, her expression always dreamy whenever she talked about it. "It was quaint, you know, that English kind of quaint, everything so nice, so proper, so grand. It had class, real class, and the staff were my idea of great too, always there, on hand, but never intrusive, giving you the space you needed."

At this point her father would always interject. "It's an interesting building granted, but Dee, you're wearing your rose-tinted glasses again. The hotel was faded, run down, it had potential, but somehow, maybe because of the location it's in – a forgotten location, nothing much around it –

that potential was never quite realised. A shame really, because a lot of effort went into it, I think. As for the staff, they *were* nice, but you know what? They always looked jaded to me, as tired as the hotel."

Her mother had started laughing; it was such a girlish sound, the tinkle of her laughter. "To be honest, Caroline, we hardly ventured out of our room, our corner *suite* – room 210, on the second floor. See I remember the number, of course I do, I'll never forget it. I had everything I wanted right there in those rooms, in that hotel. The world outside simply failed to exist. We did eventually make it to Mount Pocono, although it was some months later, when the weather was on the up, but I'm honestly glad we spent our honeymoon where we did. Faded or not, there's something so...*special* about the Egress. I've never been anywhere else like it before or since. We should go back, Tony."

"Relive old times?" Tony had smiled at her indulgently.

"Why not?" And then she'd given a shake of her head. "I can't think why we haven't."

After their marriage, they'd moved back to England, to the Hammersmith area of London to be precise, so that Tony could take over the running of his family's building firm from his father. They'd made a good life in England, producing Caroline nine months after their marriage and then Ethan two years later – who now lived in Canada with his wife and two children. Work had taken over, and what with the rigours of kids and life in general, that's why they hadn't revisited. Or was that strictly true? wondered Caroline. After all, they'd been to America a few times while she was growing up, doing as she was doing now, catching up with friends and family members, but somehow the hotel never made it onto what was always, admittedly, a packed agenda. In truth, Caroline wouldn't be making a detour to visit it now if her mother hadn't mentioned it yet again as she lay dying in the hospice the previous year.

Her eyes becoming as blurred as the windscreen, she wiped at them. It still hurt so much to think about her mother's final days.

She had looked so fragile, lying amongst sheets and pillows that were not as white or as soft as Caroline had wanted them to be – like a child that had been ravaged or starved for an eternity. Dee adored her two children. She'd been an amazing mother, the very best, but losing Tony two years prior had floored her. That's when the rot had set in, that rot being cancer, a strain of the same disease that had felled her husband.

As she drove, Caroline was aware of voices on the radio still, and bursts of continued laughter, but her memories effectively drowned them out.

"Such happy days they were." Dee's voice had barely been above a whisper, forcing Caroline to lean closer so that she could hear. "Just me and Tony."

Taking her skeletal hand, Caroline had stroked it. "You and Dad were so lucky to have found each other." That they had, never ceased to amaze Caroline – two people from two different continents meeting in a diner one day, their eyes locking, their souls *knowing*.

Dee had nodded, the gesture barely caught.

"Loved him," she said.

"I know, Mum, I know you did."

"Loved you and Ethan."

The fact that she was speaking in the past tense, as

though she were dead already, had caused a tear to fall onto Caroline's cheek. "Mum." Her voice was as strained as her mother's. "Don't. I know it hurts when you speak."

So weak she'd been – the cancer in her breast spreading like a bush fire.

"I wish I had more time."

That was something Caroline wished too, fervently. Ethan was due to arrive later that evening. He was flying in from Calgary and she only hoped he'd make it in time.

"Such happy days," her mother repeated.

They had been; a happy life spent together, all four of them. And now that life was being snatched away. Dee was so young still, as her father had been – both of them in their late fifties, no age at all. Why had he been taken? Why was she being taken too? She was needed here, this once vital and carefree mother. So damned much.

"The hotel, the honeymoon."

Caught in her own grief, Caroline hadn't been able to recall the name of the hotel her mother was talking about. She'd barely been able to think at all.

"Hotel," Dee's voice had grown insistent. "Caroline."

"Um…" It was a strange name, beginning with an E. "The Egress! That's it."

Incredibly, a smile graced Dee's face – the first in a long while. "Bliss," she muttered.

"It was just you and Dad against the world," Caroline forced a smile too.

"Against the world." Dee clearly approved of those words. "Should have gone back."

Yes, thought Caroline, *you should have.*

"Conceived there."

"Was I, Mum?" A honeymoon baby, for sure.

"Special place."

"It sounds it."

Dee suddenly gasped.

"Mum! Are you in pain? Shall I call a nurse?"

Again Dee's shake of the head was barely perceptible. "No, don't," she implored before having to rest again to catch the breath that rasped in her throat. "It's important, Caroline."

"What's important?"

"To love."

"Yes, yes, I know it is."

Dee's grip became firmer and she leant forward slightly. Caroline was stunned that she still had the strength to do either. "It's important," she reiterated.

"Mum, please, relax, stay calm, it's best you stay calm."

"Live, Caroline."

"I am, I will."

"Don't grieve for me."

How could she say that? Of course she'd grieve for her. Her father's death had wrenched her heart. now her mother's threatened to shatter it completely.

"Live. Love."

Two words followed by just a few more.

"Such a special place."

And then Dee's grip relaxed as she lay back against the overly starched sheets once more. She'd closed her eyes and never opened them again.

Ethan had arrived too late, but his presence was still welcome. He was a rock to Caroline, but of course he had a family to return to after the funeral and she had her job as a financier in the city – an environment she'd once found exhilarating, but which now seemed soulless.

Despite having turned thirty-three and with a wide circle of friends, she felt every bit the orphan she now was. There were plenty of people who loved her still but no one who loved her unconditionally. Would she ever find that kind of love again? Did it exist outside of immediate family? She honestly didn't know. Certainly, no relationship she'd had to date had served to enlighten her, but in truth she wasn't really *that* bothered. She was independent, fiercely so; it was something she prized. Men came and men went. More often than not, they went.

But connection – she craved it. She was human, after all. And that's why she was back in America, connecting to her parents' memory via Dee's relatives that were still living, reminiscing with them about her mother and the day she'd met a tall young man with the shyest of smiles who was on a sabbatical from England to learn about construction in America, principally the Amish way of building, which had fascinated him.

After leaving Upstate New York, where most of her family on her mother's side had moved to in recent years she'd returned to Pennsylvania, intending to stop and have a look at the Egress en route – hoping in some way that Dee was looking down on her and nodding approvingly. A stay at the hotel really wasn't necessary. Besides, recent reviews on *TripAdvisor* hadn't been that favourable. Her mother had said it was grand, her father had said it was faded. That was in the eighties. In 2016 it appeared to have deteriorated further, not many people recommending it as a place to stay. No, her mind was made up; she'd stay in Williamsfield proper, the city centre, that's where her mother's family was originally from and where Dee had lived her early life, surrounded by the green hills and the deep valleys of this spectacular state. She was sure to feel a degree of connection there too. After that, she'd push on to Mount Pocono – continue the pilgrimage.

She tuned into the deejay's voice again.

"Seriously, folks, the snow's settling in now, and it's only going to get worse. All the usual weather warnings are in force. If you don't have to travel, please don't. It's not worth the risk. I repeat, if you don't have to travel, stay inside, and wrap up warm. If you've got elderly neighbours or neighbours that live alone, keep an eye on them, make sure they're warm enough too. Look out for each other and stay safe. Above all, stay safe."

After delivering such sage advice a track was played – Simon and Garfunkel's *Homeward Bound* – clearly an attempt to drum his advice into the psyche. Once again Caroline looked at the Sat Nav; ten miles eaten up, which left forty more to Williamsfield, but only thirty-four to the Egress. Not that far, not really.

She pressed harder on the accelerator.

Live. Love
Such a special place.
Her mother's words the trigger that spurred her on.

Chapter Two

By the time Caroline reached the Egress her heart was pounding.

The snow – the blizzard; the storm; call it what you will – couldn't be outrun. If anything, she'd met it head on, watching with grim fascination as it turned the countryside around her oh-so-pretty, and the highways and byways treacherous. She had no choice but to press on, though, despite the deejay's dire warning. Between the first flakes of snow falling and the hotel her parents had honeymooned at, there was nothing. Absolutely nothing. A few roadside trailers perhaps, and some rather decrepit-looking bungalows tucked down roads that led off the main highway, but she could hardly go banging on a stranger's door seeking shelter for God knows how long the storm was going to last. She was determined to make it to the Egress, ticking off the miles as avidly as the Sat Nav.

Luckily there was hardly any traffic, with everyone clearly more aware of the impending storm than she was. But when she'd left Upstate New York this morning – in bright sunshine – there'd not even been a hint of snow in the air. She supposed if she'd gone to breakfast at the hotel she'd been staying in, instead of choosing to sleep in, she might have seen something about it on the news. But even the previous night, Violet, an elderly aunt of her mother's whom she'd had dinner with, hadn't mentioned anything. It really was as if it had swooped out of nowhere, picking on her, *just* her, toying with her, letting her believe she could make it out of harm's way before lashing out. Losing control of the steering had been terrifying, as she went zigzagging across the road at a speed of over forty miles per hour – a crazy speed under the circumstances, a desperate speed.

Caroline was not particularly religious, but she found herself thanking Jesus, Mary, Joseph, and all the saints that ever existed that no one else was on the road at that exact moment. She'd careered into a bank of snow, hitting the side of her head against the windscreen pillar and causing all the stars of the American flag to dance before her eyes.

You need to see a doctor, had been her immediate thought. *Get checked out.* But then more basic needs kicked in. *You have to get out of this storm, find yourself some shelter.*

The Sat Nav told her she had another five miles. She was so close and yet… What if she lost control again? *You have to drive. You can't stay here all night, on an empty highway.* No, she couldn't. She'd freeze to death, buried alive in her Kia Rio, to be found as stiff as a board in the morning. If the Egress was indeed the first hotel she stumbled upon, she'd be staying, and to hell with *TripAdvisor*.

Tentatively, she'd turned the engine over. Despite her fears, it had started immediately, causing her to release the breath she'd been holding. *Good car, you're such a good little car*, she praised, urging it to remain that way. Turning the radio off so that she could concentrate, the heating to max and the wipers on full, she attempted to back up. The wheels span uselessly at first, again igniting a spark of fear, as cold as any weather front, but then the tires managed to get a grip. Pointing the car in the right direction, she'd proceeded to drive. *Nice and slowly does it. Nice and slowly.* This mantra accompanying her all the way to the Egress, daylight fading by this time, night taking hold.

The hotel was down a road that led off the highway, sitting in its own parcel of land, the parking lot more empty than full, unsurprisingly. Keeping her goal firmly in her vision, she left the road and headed up a slight incline towards it, all but stalling the car at the entrance. It could stay there, she decided. She'd move it another time. This hotel, so beloved of her mother, this sanctuary of her parents that was about to become a sanctuary for her too, really did occupy a lonely position as her father had said, only a few farm-type buildings in the run up to it, all of which looked deserted. Downtown Williamsfield seemed like a world away. Would she be able to make it there tomorrow? How long was she going to be trapped for?

Trapped?

The weather had trapped her for certain but at least she'd made it to a hotel and not just any hotel either, one that was a part of her family history. She should stop whining and count her blessings; there were worse places to spend a night or two. And it was only likely to be a couple of nights, which wasn't such a catastrophe. There were such things as snowploughs in existence. Unlike the storm of the 1950s, governing bodies would ensure the wheels of industry turned as usual, or as usual as was damned near possible.

As much as she might want to, there wasn't time to

stand and admire the exterior of the hotel. No real point either as the snow and the darkness effectively masked it. Instead, she grabbed her case from the boot and raced from one shelter to the other, yanking open the doors to the lobby, having to struggle with them they were so heavy, but finally managing to gain entrance, and climb several stairs to reach reception. At the top she came to a standstill, panting as though she'd just completed a marathon, her light brown hair, still wet from the brief time she'd spent outside, plastered to the sides of her face.

"You made it then."

The words drifted towards her, no urgency to them at all.

Caroline lifted her head. A few feet in front of her, a sea of red patterned carpet separating them, was the lobby desk, a young girl standing behind it, and behind her there was a closed door, presumably leading to an administration office. About average height, pale skinned, and with black hair tied in a ponytail, the girl looked thoroughly bored.

"Yes. I made it. Just."

"Good. Not many do. Not in this weather."

"I'm not surprised!"

The girl shrugged and began flicking through a register as Caroline drew closer, dragging her case behind her.

"You haven't booked," the girl – a name badge identifying her as Raquel – stated.

"I wasn't intending to stay."

"Would you like a room?"

Caroline was incredulous. "I don't think I've got any choice! I can't go back out there."

Raquel's eyes latched onto hers. "You're a long way from home."

Caroline nodded. "If you're referring to my accent, yes I am. I'm English, although my mother is...*was* American, from around here in fact, Williamsfield."

"On vacation?"

"Yes, visiting relatives."

Her eyes were so dark, such a contrast to the green of Caroline's own.

"I'm just figuring out where to put you," Raquel announced.

"Are you busy?" Caroline asked, looking from left to right. They didn't look busy. In fact, she couldn't spot anyone at all; the lobby was empty of people, only a suggestion of movement in a large room leading off it, which looked to be a dining area.

"Busy enough," Raquel replied, again scrutinising her before reaching a decision. "I'm going to have to put you on high, I'm afraid, the eleventh floor – room 1106. There's renovation going on elsewhere in the hotel right now, quite a few rooms in the process of being updated. It's quiet on the eleventh floor. I'm directing most people there."

"No problem." Relief flooded through Caroline. Whilst Raquel had been pondering, she actually thought she might be turned away. That there was no room at the inn, so to speak; that she would indeed have to venture outside to battle with the elements once more. That last stretch into Williamsfield, it seemed so daunting. She decided to chance her luck further. "I don't suppose the corner suite on the eleventh floor's available, is it?"

"The corner suite? No! That belongs to Althea."

"Althea? Who's she?"

"She's as much a part of this hotel as the fixtures and

fittings."

"She *lives* here?" Caroline enquired further.

"That's right," answered Raquel, "she does."

"Fine… I… I was only asking."

"Room 1106 is yours. Do you have any more bags?"

Caroline shook her head, feeling weary all of a sudden – having to concentrate so hard whilst driving and the near crash were beginning to take their toll.

"I'll call the bellhop," Raquel said, stepping out from behind the desk to reveal a slender frame as she went in search of the aforementioned employee.

"There's no need—"

"It's what he's here for," she insisted.

Raquel's absence gave Caroline a bit of breathing space to look around. Her mother had described the hotel as quaint. To her that translated as outdated, perhaps even a little bit shabby? Was it so? Perhaps shabby was too cruel a word. Definitely there was a sense that it had once been more than it was, with the Art Deco features that remained holding a certain charm. A good-sized space, the lobby doubled as a lounge, a place to meet and mingle with other guests. It was long and narrow, with various pieces of artwork on the walls and framed pictures, which she would inspect at leisure later, as well as a couple of ornately framed mirrors that looked as if they'd come straight from the Chrysler Building in New York. Above two seating areas hung two very grand crystal chandeliers, in alignment. Below one of the chandeliers were three elegant sofas and two chairs, again Art Deco in style, and a little careworn. Underneath the second chandelier was a grand piano and more chairs and low tables – an ideal spot to sit and have coffee whilst perusing the morning paper.

Leading off from the lobby, to her left, was the dining room she'd spotted earlier, although the doors to it were partially shut, obscuring her view.

It wasn't a big hotel, by any stretch of the imagination; very unlike the Holiday Inns and Best Westerns she'd made use of so far on her trip. Not quite a boutique hotel either, though. Whatever. Her parents had been content with it, and she would be too. Oh, but she was looking forward to heading to the second floor; to the corner suite they'd shared. She'd stand outside it and imagine them as happy as they ever were, as excited, still so many years ahead of them.

"Here we are." Raquel was back. "Tom will show you to your room."

Tom stepped forward, his somewhat old-fashioned uniform making Caroline smile: a red jacket with gold buttons and brocade and dark blue trousers. All he needed was a pillbox hat to complete the look. She appreciated it. His clothes were a nice touch and she'd seen porters, or bellhops as he'd been called, dressed the same in other – albeit larger – hotels. In contrast to her sidekick, Raquel looked like she'd come straight out of the fifties, clad as she was in a black cigarette pants, black pumps, and a white blouse. Slick on a bit of red lipstick and she'd be a ringer for Uma Thurman in *Pulp Fiction*. They were two characters in a hotel full of character. *Charming*, Caroline thought again, *unique*.

Taking her bag, Tom led the way to an elegant, old-fashioned elevator, Caroline smiling her goodbye at Raquel, and Raquel turning from her, that bored look evident yet again. Pressing the button to call the elevator car, they both stood and waited, Caroline admiring a gold painted metal mailbox attached to the wall to the left of it. Tom caught her staring.

"That's original, that is," he informed her. A young man, probably in his early twenties, there was pride in his voice, in his entire manner in fact.

"What constitutes original exactly?" Caroline asked as the elevator opened to allow them access. Below their feet was an E for Egress encircled in a band of gold.

Before answering Tom leant forward, his hand hovering before a set of black buttons. "You're on the eleventh floor?" he checked.

"Yes, room 1106."

"Dead centre."

"Is it? That's good. I gather the corner suite is already occupied."

Tom laughed, a bit of a goofball sound, as her mother would have put it. "Sure is. That's where Althea lives. I always give a quick bow whenever she's near."

"Does she manage the hotel?"

"She takes care of it, yes."

Hence the bow, Caroline thought, amused at the prospect. "So, the hotel, how old is it?"

"It was built in 1922."

"The nineteen twenties? That explains your uniform."

"My uniform?" For a brief moment his blue eyes clouded. "I suppose."

"It's such a quiet spot here."

"There were other buildings once."

"What happened to them?"

"They got demolished. To make way for new buildings."

She was genuinely perplexed. "What new buildings?"

Tom shrugged. "I guess some things don't go according to plan."

Evidently.

"It's a bit of a hike from the city of Williamsfield, isn't it?" she continued, looking for an explanation. "People like to be closer to where there's more life."

Tom huffed slightly. "There are some who happen to like how peaceful it is."

"Oh, I'm sorry, I wasn't suggesting otherwise, not really. And I agree, it is peaceful."

He nodded, hopefully appeased.

The elevator – a relic from the 1920s too, she'd bet – chugged its way upward.

"Weather's awful, isn't it," she remarked, to pass what was taking an extraordinarily long time. "I wonder how long it's going to last."

"Who knows? It could be over in a flash; it could go on for days."

"What do the forecasters say?"

"Don't know. I never listen to 'em."

Nor had she, which is why she'd been caught out.

The elevator ground to a halt. Finally.

"Oh good, we're here," Caroline stated, getting ready to move forwards but Tom reached out a hand to stop her.

"This is the sixth floor. We don't want this one."

"The sixth floor? Really?" She could barely believe it.

"The elevator is old too," explained Tom.

"I'd guessed," Caroline replied.

"And it does have a tendency to get...stuck sometimes."

"Stuck? You're serious? Is there an alarm or something, in case it does?"

Not according to Tom. "But don't worry, it never gets

stuck for long. You just have to be patient, that's all."

"Patient? Right, okay." Easier said than done when you were the one confined. She found herself lamenting the fact that she was on the eleventh floor, if she'd been lower, she'd stick to the stairs. She might do that anyway if it proved too much of a problem.

"Is there another elevator?" she checked.

"Just this one."

At last they reached the correct floor. The steel doors cranked open and in front was a corridor that seemed to stretch forever, as endless as any American highway.

"Follow me," Tom instructed.

Beneath her feet was a variation of the same red carpet that had been used in the lobby. Either side, the skirting was clad in an unusual tile trim, which might have been fancy once but now many of them were chipped. Despite the walls lined with pale, slightly yellowing paper, they felt narrow, closed in, like a tunnel almost. Chrome uplighters, all in a row, lit the way, yet Caroline struggled to see properly. A glimmer of unease made itself known deep inside her. She longed for her room, where she could step over to the window, fling back the curtain, and remind herself there was a big wide – albeit wild – world out there. Here in the corridor it was just too claustrophobic.

Tom stopped at 1106 and inserted the key – not of an electronic nature, but traditional, made of brass to match the ornate Deco brass lock. Stepping aside, he let Caroline enter and she was pleasantly surprised to see how large the room was, comprising a living area with a comfortable sofa and a set of closed panelled doors behind which was obviously the bedroom and bathroom.

"This is lovely," she exclaimed. "Really nice."

Tom set down her case and smiled. "You sound surprised."

"No, well…yeah. The room size, it's very generous."

"The Egress prides itself on how spacious it is. You'll also find that each room is different, some subtly, some more noticeably, but all home comforts are included."

The way he said it had all the attributes of a sales pitch.

Doing as she had promised herself only a minute or two before, Caroline crossed over to the window and drew the net curtain aside. "It's got so much worse."

She sighed, partly impressed by the weather, and partly dismayed. From on high the vista should be impressive – the bright lights of Williamsfield twinkling in the distance perhaps, instead, it was a whiteout that greeted her, disguising even the blackness of the night. She'd reached the hotel in the nick of time and for that she was grateful, imagining herself still stuck on that stretch of highway, shivering in that tiny rental car, praying for someone to come along and help her.

She turned to find Tom waiting patiently by the door…*expectantly*.

"Oh," she said, realising what he was waiting for.

She dug around in her handbag until she found her purse, swiftly retrieving a five-dollar bill. "Here," she said, handing it over to him, "and thank you very much."

"Thank you," replied Tom. She guessed this would have been the point where he would have tipped his hat at her, had he been wearing one. She couldn't resist enquiring.

"Isn't there a hat that's supposed to go with that uniform?"

"A hat?" Again Tom looked taken aback.

"Yeah," Caroline said, smiling at him whilst gesturing to

23

her own head.

"Oh, I see, yes, there is," Tom confirmed. "It got lost, though, a long time ago."

"That's a shame. You'll get a new one perhaps?"

"Perhaps." There was no conviction whatsoever in his voice. "I'll leave you to settle in."

She thanked him again and walked over to the door. About to close it behind him she heard a sudden, rather startling, burst of high-pitched laughter. Curious, she stepped further into the corridor, initially glancing right, towards the corner suite, the room that was *always* occupied. Was it Althea responsible for such a noise? Quickly, she realised it wasn't coming in that direction, and looked to her left instead. A head appeared, poking out from one of the rooms further down – a female, definitely a female, with a shock of auburn hair. For a brief moment their eyes met, Caroline registering a whole range of emotions evident in the other woman: glee, but a *manic* kind of glee; surprise too – perhaps that someone had turned up in weather like this. Caroline started to smile politely in greeting but the head retreated, and the door slammed shut.

Bemused, Caroline looked at Tom. "Who's that? Do you know?"

"Another newcomer," Tom answered, a slight frown on his face. "She introduced herself as Elspeth."

"Oh right. I'm Caroline by the way."

Tom simply smiled at her.

"Are there many guests here?" She'd asked Raquel a similar question but hadn't got a clear answer.

"There's enough. If you don't mind, Ma'am…"

"Ma'am?" She was surprised he'd addressed her as such.

They'd been speaking in a fairly informal manner until now. "No, of course not, I'm sure you need to get on. Tend to all the other...*guests*."

"Dinner is served at eight o' clock in the ballroom," he told her.

"The ballroom? That sounds very grand. Where's that?"

"Just off the lobby."

So the dining room she'd spotted was a dual function room too by the sounds of it.

"Is there room service by any chance?" she asked. She fancied just kicking off her shoes, getting out of her clothes and into more comfy attire, catching up on some news, the weather forecast, of course, and the havoc it was wreaking across Pennsylvania. The more she thought about it, the more that idea appealed.

"Tom?" she prompted when he made no reply.

"It's best you come to the ballroom," he insisted, turning on his heel and walking away.

Chapter Three

In the privacy of her room, Caroline shook her head at Tom's insistence. *Okay, have it your way, the ballroom it is.* A wry smile crossed her face. *What clothes will suit such palatial surrounds, I wonder?* If indeed it was palatial.

She'd brought a pretty good selection with her, but it was mainly in the form of jeans, tee-shirts and jumpers – she wasn't really a dressy kind of girl.

Settling her case on the suitcase stand, she opened it and rummaged inside. There was one dress, which she hadn't in fact worn yet – a close-fitting black jersey dress, which ended just above the knee and had a V-neck. Retrieving it, she smoothed any creases with her hand and laid it over the arm of the soft brown leather sofa, added to it fresh underwear and kitten-heeled black shoes, the latter which she'd packed on a whim. She glanced at her watch. It was a few minutes past six, plenty of time to get ready – perhaps a little time to explore too, starting with her own room.

As she'd already said to Tom, it was a sizeable room, more like a small apartment. Certainly back in London, especially central London, studios didn't come much bigger. She'd never have guessed there'd be so much space. It seemed…*exaggerated,* somehow. The main light was as subdued as those in the corridor, so she turned on various lamps as well; none of them overly bright either. In the living area, in front of the sofa, was a low coffee table, a striking piece of furniture with a highly polished top – oak she guessed – making a mental note not to put any coffee cups directly down upon it. Under the window there was a writing desk and a chair, and also a flat screen TV facing the sofa, the only obvious gesture towards modernism. Immediately to the right of the main entrance was another door. She opened it, expecting to find a storage cupboard. To her surprise it was a kitchenette, compact but nonetheless boasting a white ceramic sink, tea and coffee maker, and a microwave. Delighted, she filled the coffee maker with water and switched it on. A cup of tea would be very welcome after what she'd been through, although she yearned for Twinings English Breakfast rather than the Lipton's sachet on offer.

The bedroom was next. Behind the double doors was another revelation. The bed was a real feature piece, enormous with an oak headboard, cream sheets, and blankets. Other than that there was a wardrobe and a dressing table. To the right was the en suite bathroom, which Caroline entered with high hopes. Not as glamorous as expected, it was actually rather basic, with a short tub that although clean was stained dark brown in places, particularly where the tap would drip if not turned off properly. Above the sink unit was an oval mirror – again it was nothing fancy, not backlit or anything, with a blue and gilt frame. Placing her hands either side of the sink she stared at her reflection. Her age was beginning to show. Not just that but the loss she'd suffered in recent years was apparent too, at least to her. She had a few lines forming around her eyes and dark circles beneath them, but it was actually the eyes themselves that gave the most cause for concern. Green with brown flecks in them, the same colour as her mother's, they had a look that was hard to describe. Haunted sounded a bit affected, but it was the only word she could drum up.

Go and turn on the TV, see what's happening in the world.

It was sound advice – anything to take her mind off her melancholy reflection.

Leaving the bathroom, she was about to go back into the living room when a piece of paper on the desk caught her eye; it was fluttering slightly, probably because of the air con. Picking it up, she found it was a welcome letter, printed rather than handwritten, but in an elegant script on cream vellum paper, an encircled E at the bottom of it.

As she scanned the content, her eyes grew wider.

To Our Guest,
Welcome to The Egress – a very special hotel!
We hope that you are granted peace and serenity while you remain under our roof. May those whom you love and hold dear be near to you in thoughts and dreams and, even though you may be simply passing through, we wish you nothing but good will.
All of us are on a journey. From birth till death we travel between the eternities. May these days be pleasant for you, helpful for those you meet and a joy to those who know and love you best. When you journey onwards, may your passage be a safe one.

For a moment all Caroline could do was stare. In every hotel she'd ever been in, never had she seen such a greeting. It was weird. Immediately, she berated herself for thinking such a thing. It wasn't weird…well, maybe just a little bit, what with all that stuff about travelling between the eternities, but it was something else too: special. That's how the Egress had described itself and that's how her mother had described it too, and in that instant, she considered them both right. Glancing around she found she was smiling. She hadn't been planning on staying here, but here she was and once again she was grateful. This was an establishment that seemed to care about its guests. Although perhaps the same couldn't be said of the receptionist, a young woman obviously bored with proceedings and not averse to showing it! Not wishing to be uncharitable, Caroline backtracked. Perhaps Raquel was having a bad day. Maybe she lived in town and couldn't get home tonight, the weather having trapped her too. Whatever the reason, it was no concern of hers. She was going to have that cuppa, dash off a quick text to Violet, in case she was watching CNN and was worrying about her, then take a long hot shower. The TV would be left on in the background, not only for news information but to counter the silence. Once dressed, she'd go to dinner, via the second floor and room 210.

* * *

At the elevator, Caroline paused. She really didn't fancy getting stuck in there, banging at the doors, yelling to be released, no one around to hear her. *Don't be so dramatic, you'll be fine!* A laugh escaped her. Perhaps she was getting a bit carried away. Of course she'd be okay.

Whilst waiting, she looked behind her, at the room

Elspeth had poked her head out of earlier – 1101. Would she be at dinner? If so, that might prove interesting. When she returned her gaze frontwards, she was surprised to see the elevator doors already open – there'd been no bell to alert her, as was the norm, no sound at all in fact.

Everything's so quiet, she thought, notwithstanding Elspeth's sudden burst of laughter earlier, as quiet as a world freshly covered in snow ought to be.

Entering, she selected the second floor. For a moment nothing happened and then it was as though the elevator remembered it had a job to do and woke up, closing its doors and travelling downwards, taking its own sweet time, as it had done earlier.

"At last," she muttered, slightly irritated. The elevator came to a stop, but one glance at the floor counter told her she wasn't on two but five. "What the…?" Was it really going to take this long to travel between floors?

The doors opened again, and a girl stepped in – a young girl with a fine head of thick black hair that obscured her face, Emo style.

Caroline smiled at her but was duly ignored. Instead, the girl turned swiftly to face the direction from which she'd come. Dressed in a lemon-coloured blouse and an A-line, knee-length blue plaid skirt, she also had on long white socks and a pair of black slip-on shoes. Although Caroline hadn't got a good look at her face, she guessed she was a young teen – fourteen or fifteen – one who stood completely still, not jabbing at any buttons.

The elevator waited as did Caroline…and waited. After a few seconds she at least could wait no more.

"What floor do you want?" she asked brightly.

The girl didn't answer.

"I'm going to floor two. Would you like the lobby?"

Still the girl didn't answer.

What's wrong with her? Is she deaf or something?

Immediately she chastised herself for being uncharitable again. What if she *was* deaf?

She decided to take matters into her own hands and pressed the lobby button for her. To her relief, the girl didn't object.

Once again it took an age to burst into life but floor two was eventually reached and Caroline skirted around the girl to walk down yet another corridor, one identical to the eleventh, the same patterned carpet beneath her feet, the same chipped tiles on the skirting, the same dull lighting, giving everything a shadowy edge. Before the elevator doors closed, she glanced backwards, intending to smile again at the mysterious child, but she must have moved to the side, as she couldn't spot her.

Mentally shrugging, Caroline continued onwards. There was not even a hint of any renovation going on, but she couldn't deny it was sorely needed. As she walked, she listened for signs of life behind guest room doors but couldn't hear a thing. Once again, the quiet unsettled her. As on her floor, there was a window at the far end of the corridor, net curtains obscuring the view, and to the right of that was the corner suite: 210. Directly opposite the corner suite was another door with an illuminated *Exit* sign above it – the stairwell. She'd use it to reach the lobby, fearing if she opted for the elevator again she'd miss dinner altogether. But first, there were memories to indulge in, those of her living, breathing parents, when they were young and in love. Turning back to 210, she laid her hand against the oak door. *Is this it? Is this where I was conceived, in this very room?*

How amazing if it was, the life that was hers coming into force a few feet away, in a hotel her parents had found themselves stranded in, just as she was stranded now.

If there was an occupant in room 210, Caroline sincerely hoped they wouldn't choose this moment to yank open the door to find her standing there. Not that she'd loiter for long. She wouldn't. All she wanted was a little time to remember – to connect. As there was no sound of life from within, no TV blaring, no coughing, no shuffling, no snatched conversations, she figured she was safe to shut her eyes briefly as memories dutifully flooded her mind. Her mother's smile: soft and beguiling. Her father's laughter – he was always laughing, except at the end when cancer had wiped all humour from him.

Think good thoughts, she reminded herself, only *happy thoughts*.

She tried, but it was difficult. Every time a good memory surfaced, a bad one raced to catch up with it – the tragedy of her parents' fate refusing to be denied. She was doing her best to obey her mother's last instruction, to embrace life, just as Dee had embraced life, squeezing every last drop from it, but grief had a habit of consuming her.

Unsurprisingly, her memories returned to childhood – they almost always did – she and Ethan in a park, her father pushing her on a swing, her mother chasing her brother down the slide, a family day out, simple, but joyful. Eating meals together around the dinner table, her mother cooked a mean spaghetti with meatballs and her father was a dab hand too, tending to create more exotic fare such as curries and tagines, telling them that they'd travel the world one day, eat such food in their countries of origin.

Live. Love.

Bedtime stories were another favourite memory; her parents keeping the ritual going until she was eleven at least, long after it had ended for most of her friends. She inhaled. Chanel No.5 – a scent her mother loved. She swore she could smell it now, as sweet as ever, then a more masculine smell: soap and cologne, peculiar to her father, and just as comforting.

"Sweet Caroline." That's what they called her. "Did you know there's a song about you?"

They'd played her that song many times, the gravelly voice of Neil Diamond always such a pleasure to listen to. For years she'd thought *Sweet Caroline* was written solely for her, was amazed, in fact, that Mr Diamond had gone to such lengths. How did he even know she existed? Certainly she couldn't recall meeting him. Only when she was older did she realise the truth – Mum and Dad, being Mum and Dad, hadn't wanted to burst her bubble.

Her eyes still closed, she started swaying to the tune, humming along to it too, still make-believing the song was about her.

Good times never seemed so good…

This felt good, listening to it again. It had been an age.

Listening to it…? Her eyes flew open.

"What the—?"

She could *hear* it, actually hear it, although she couldn't detect where it was coming from. Not from the room in front, it was more in the air around, the atmosphere, familiar notes that caressed her. The smells of perfume and tobacco, they had substance too – not just the wisps of memory.

She swung around; half expecting to see a man and a woman standing beside her – Tony and Dee – but of course there was no one, only an empty space. And the tune, her *special* tune, began to fade, but taking its time, as slow as the elevator.

Hardly daring to breathe, she listened until the very last note played, clinging to it.

The fragrances dissipated too – the *pungency* of them.

Caroline dared to breathe again, stunned at the power of imagination. It was as though she'd conjured her parents up! Was that a good thing? She pondered that question, but only for a moment. Of course it was a good thing. It meant in some way they were still with her. She laughed, couldn't help it, relief flooding through her. But, as wonderful as it was, enough was enough. She would hug the experience to her, not milk it. Turning towards the stairwell, Caroline pushed the door open. Just before it shut, she once again marvelled at the power of imagination. She'd caught another sound – tinkling laughter – her *mother's* laughter – coming from directly behind her.

Chapter Four

"Holy crap! That was a close call."

In the lobby someone else had made it to safety.

A man, with a good smattering of snow still clinging to his shoulders, was standing in the exact same spot she'd stood in earlier, the same bewildered look on his face. Although amazed to see him, Caroline couldn't resist looking at Raquel too. As she suspected, she looked bored, totally unimpressed. She even rolled her eyes at one point and sighed. Was she going to utter the same words?

Caroline had to suppress a burst of laughter when she did.

"You made it then."

Before the man could reply, Caroline jumped in – unable to resist repeating what she was sure Raquel would say next. "Good. Not many do. Not in this weather."

Both the man and Raquel turned their heads to stare at her – Raquel not in the least bit impressed by such mimicry, the man's bewilderment increasing.

Feeling her cheeks redden under the spotlight of their glare, Caroline cleared her throat. "I mean… It's terrible, isn't it? The snow. As bad as they said it would be."

She glanced behind the man as if to reinforce that fact.

The floor-to-ceiling windows were netted but she knew as well as he did what lay beyond, and what was yet to come.

"I crashed the car," the man said, capturing her attention again.

She gasped. "Did you? Are you alright?"

"I'm fine." He lifted one hand to his head. "Gave my head a good whack, though. Passed out, I think, but only briefly."

Horrified, Caroline hurried over to him, noticing Raquel doing no such thing.

"You probably need to see a doctor! There might even be one on the premises." She laid her hand on his arm as if to steady him.

"Honestly, I'm okay," he said, smiling at her concern. "I just…lost control, careered into a tree stump of all things." His smile became a grin. "I'll tell you what, you shoulda seen the tree stump! That'll teach it to pick fights. I'm David by the way, David Mason."

"I'm Caroline Daynes. Were you on your way to the hotel?"

"Yeah, I was. The weather turned kinda quick, didn't it? Got caught out."

She nodded. "I crashed my car too. Gave the side of my head a good bump."

"Jeez, are you okay? It looks like you might have some bruising."

Her fingers adjusted her fringe to cover any damage. "I'm okay. It's a bit sore, but nothing more than that. I'll live to fight another day."

"I'm glad to hear it, Caroline Daynes."

Their eyes held and then he broke his gaze to look around, giving her a chance to study him further. Taller than her – she was a little over five foot six and he was closer to six foot – David Mason was also dark haired, rugged, maybe even good looking, certainly there was a twinkle in his dark eyes when he turned back. "I'd better go and check in," he said. "I haven't actually booked a room yet."

"Dinner's being served in the ballroom," she blurted out. "That's where I'm going."

Immediately she could have kicked herself. Why was she telling him this? He might think she was hinting or something.

Luckily, his expression perked up. "The ballroom? Nice. Is it a lavish affair, do you think?"

"Gosh, I hope not, I'm hardly dressed for a lavish affair."

"Believe me, honey, you look great. So... I'll see you in there?"

"Sure," she said, feeling her cheeks burn. *Had* she been hinting? She supposed so.

Stepping aside to let him pass, she didn't venture far. Pausing at one of the tables nearby, and pretending to flick through a magazine, she was curious. Was Raquel going to spin him the same yarn about renovations taking place in the hotel? She didn't mean to be cynical, but so far, she'd found no evidence of any such work being carried out, despite the hotel's public spaces being in need of it. As for the elevator, that needed fixing too. Why was there only one in a hotel of this size anyway? There should be two at least. Whilst pondering this, she listened to Raquel talking.

"I'm just figuring out where to put you."

Again, she was delivering the same spiel she'd delivered to Caroline.

"Are you busy?" asked David and Caroline raised an eyebrow, that's what she'd asked.

Busy enough, Caroline thought, a split second before Raquel said it.

Although she didn't dare turn to look at them, to make what she was doing obvious – being nosey, basically – she'd bet anything that Raquel was scrutinising David right now, looking him up and down as she'd done with her, appraising him. *Any minute she's going to talk about placing him on high, on the eleventh floor. Wait for it, Caroline, wait for it…*

"There's a room available on the third floor. Not superstitious, are you?"

She swore under her breath. "Damn!" That'd teach her for being such a smart arse.

"Superstitious?" David questioned. "No, not at all."

"I'll call the bellhop."

Caroline sighed. So, he wasn't on the eleventh floor, like her, like Elspeth, and like Althea. He was on the third.

Not superstitious, are you?

That statement puzzling her, she closed the magazine and headed to the ballroom.

* * *

The ballroom was vast, not just in floor area, but in height too – at least two storeys high. Again Caroline was shocked, she simply would never have guessed at a room this big beyond the partially closed doors that she'd glanced through upon arrival. It seemed out of all proportion. She reminded herself that she hadn't had time to check the exterior of the hotel properly; she'd been so busy trying to escape the weather. Perhaps that was why she couldn't reconcile herself with the space inside because she hadn't yet got a sense of it from the outside. In the morning she'd wrap up warm, go out and get a good look at the Egress, try and put the building into some sort of perspective. She'd also check the state of the roads, see if any snowploughs had been able to pass through. If so, she could follow their trail into the centre of Williamsfield and explore the town that her mother had grown up in instead of hanging around here. She could visit the same stores, the same cafés, and the same bars. Sadly, her mother's family house no longer existed, as it had been knocked down years before to make room for yet another highway – a whole street of houses demolished, and the memories those walls contained obliterated, too.

But that was tomorrow, this was tonight. And there was dinner to be had.

Tables sat on a polished floor, a decent amount of space in between them. Only a few were laid – just over half – although all were covered with pristine, white linen tablecloths.

The first to arrive for dinner, she waited patiently at the entrance to be shown to a table. When no waiter appeared, she gave herself carte blanche to choose whichever she liked.

As she continued forwards the lights flickered. They were grand; a rival to those in the lobby, suspended from a ceiling that was white with gold detailing. She wondered if the storm outside might be responsible for the flickering, although to call it a storm seemed wrong somehow. A storm suggested banging and crashing, with windows juddering in their frames as the wind hurled itself against them. There was no noise at all in the ballroom, not even piped music – serene or surreal? She couldn't decide.

Coming to a halt, she selected a table that gave her a good view of the double doors. *Being nosy again, Caroline?* Perhaps, but whoever else was a guest at the hotel intrigued her. They were her fellow inmates, whether here by choice or stranded as she was. In particular, she'd keep an eye out for Elspeth and also the mysterious teen in the elevator.

And David?

Of course David. She was looking forward to getting to know him a little better, although certainly she didn't mind dining alone, she'd done it often enough. In London, during her lunch hours, she'd often grab a quick bite at one of the pubs or cafés nearby, and she'd often do it solo, relishing some time to herself. She'd lose herself in a good book or catch up on the latest tabloid nonsense. But tonight…tonight she wanted something different. It surprised her how much she *craved* company, and David had seemed so nice…

Pulling a chair out, it scraped against the wood of the floor; that sound at least reverberating. But then it would. This was a ballroom and the acoustics were bound to be good. When was the last time a ball had been held here? And who'd been in attendance, a celebrity perhaps, several celebrities, VIPs, and bigwigs? Like the rest of the hotel, if it was grand once, it wasn't now. Although certainly an illusion of grandeur clung to it, due in part to its scale. She counted five floor-to-ceiling windows, two on one wall and three on another. As in the lobby, heavy white net curtains obscured what was happening outside, as did pleated drapes, which hung either side of the windows, gold too, a pale, delicate shade, and kept in place with giant tassels.

Once grand – opulent even – right now she found the ballroom bordering on pitiful. Why weren't waiters buzzing around? Where were other guests? There'd been a few cars in the parking lot, so there must be some.

The unease of earlier was blossoming into slight panic when at last she caught movement. Thank God! People were beginning to file in.

A woman entered first, possibly in her mid-fifties, and alone. With her full figure and perfectly coiffured honey-coloured hair, she reminded Caroline of the movie stars of old: Loren, Lollobrigida, Bardot, those types. There was one difference, though. This woman didn't walk with confidence. She seemed nervous, in fact, a little lost; her glance bouncing off Caroline to settle on a table that separated them by a few feet. Caroline tried to catch her eye again, to smile in welcome, but the woman simply lowered her head, took a seat, picked up the menu and started to read.

Next came a man, younger than the woman, but not by much, in his late forties perhaps, and tall with rounded shoulders, his brown hair thinning on top. Slight of build, he looked as if he could do with extra portions tonight, and on his cheeks the markings of teenager acne were still apparent. Caroline wondered if he might know the woman, if he might join her, but he too chose a separate table, sitting at it and immediately pouring himself a glass of water, taking long draughts from it, his hands shaking slightly.

Elspeth! This had to be her – the giggling redhead. Caroline was surprised. She was not as young as her giggling suggested. She'd imagined a woman in her twenties, bohemian in style, with flowing skirts and lots of bangles. Certainly Elspeth was brightly dressed, in a green tunic that complemented her hair, but her skirt was short and tight rather than flowing and her patterned tights had a rusty hue to them, the same shade as the scarf that she'd tied around her abundant curls. She wasn't young, but she wasn't old either, although certainly she was trying to be younger than her years.

Whereas the woman had avoided Caroline's gaze and the man too to a certain extent, Elspeth seemed to blatantly seek her out. Growing hot and bothered under such scrutiny, Caroline prayed for a diversion, not at all sure now that it'd be interesting to deal with someone like her. Just the opposite in fact, it could prove draining.

Thankfully, Elspeth selected a lone table too. Caroline sighed in relief, noticing that other tables in the ballroom had filled up, either lone guests or couples sitting together, some talking, others busy perusing the menu. Not all tables were full, far from it, but where everybody had come from suddenly, she had no idea. Her attention must have been so wrapped up in the woman, the man, and Elspeth that they'd slipped in unnoticed. She didn't ponder it for long; after all, in a crowded room only certain people stood out. But still, she was intrigued. The teenager, the one from the elevator, where was she? Not here, not at the moment. Would she arrive with her parents, sullen still, lost in her own world as teenagers often were? Perhaps her parents had realised dining with their teen in tow would be a less than joyous experience and had insisted on room service. Or perhaps they were here, one of the couples, the teen having parked herself in front of the TV.

Another guest entered, another loner – a young woman, tall and slim with blonde hair close-cropped in a boyish style, but which was utterly feminine on her. She looked at no one, gazing ahead, *imperiously* ahead, Caroline thought. A *woman who knows she's beautiful and acts like royalty because of it.* An instant dislike for the woman flared. Not because she was jealous of her beauty, or her superiority – far from it. Caroline was comfortable in her own skin. This woman, though, there was something about her. Something...*unsavoury.* As she sat at her chosen table, a waiter emerged at last from his hiding place and rushed over to her, a marked difference to when Caroline had entered. But for a woman like this they'd make an effort – physical beauty being something that was worshipped in society, a prize to behold. Who cared what lay beneath?

"Well, hello again, mind if I join you?"

Caroline almost jumped out of her skin. Like the other diners who had simply appeared, so had David, standing tall beside her – his grin firmly in place.

"Oh, I'm sorry, did I startle you?"

"No. Yes. Um."

"Let's take it I did, then," he answered, laughing still. "I waved to you as I came in, but you seemed a little preoccupied with Princess Perfect over there."

"Princess Perfect?" she queried before realisation dawned. How embarrassing! If he'd noticed her staring, had anybody else in the room, not least Princess Perfect herself?

"May I sit down?" David asked.

"Of course, of course, please. I'd love it if you joined me."

Selecting a chair to the right of her, he eased himself into it.

"We look like mourners at a funeral," she remarked,

smiling too.

"Sorry?"

"The way we're dressed, you're in black too."

"Ah," he said, looking down at his jeans and shirt. "I suppose we do." Inclining his head towards Elspeth, who was engaged in rather loud chitchat with another waiter, he added, "I think there are enough colourful characters in here tonight."

"I think you might be right. How's your head?"

"Like yours, sore, but it'll heal."

"Hopefully. If we can escape this place tomorrow, you can always get checked out."

"Escape?" He looked bemused by her choice of word. "It's not a bad place to find yourself. I'm liking the company I'm keeping."

She could feel her cheeks colouring again. "I'm liking it too. Wine? Shall we order some?"

"Sure," he replied, summoning a waiter. "I tried to find the bar earlier, thought I'd settle in there for half an hour before dinner but no such luck. Drinks are served either here or in the lobby. Still, can't complain, at least they *are* being served."

"The lobby's a nice enough place to sit."

"It sure is. Ah, waiter, thank you, can we have a bottle of… Merlot. Is that okay, Caroline?"

"Perfect," she replied.

With the bottle brought out to them a few minutes later, Caroline asked David whether he was travelling for business or leisure.

"Business. I'm a salesman."

"A salesman?" she queried. He didn't look like her idea of a salesman. *Hey, Caroline, are you stereotyping, imagining*

44

someone older, overweight, balding on top, someone stressed, with a nervous tic perhaps, praying to God they're going to make their targets, selling their soul for a chance to exceed them? Perhaps. This man was far from stressed; he looked relaxed, as comfortable in his own skin as she was. "What do you sell?"

"Insurance."

"Insurance?"

"Health insurance. It's a big deal in America, don't you know."

"I imagine it is. It might be a big deal in the UK too soon enough, considering the state of our NHS." She inclined her head to the side. "I'd have thought most insurance is bought over the Internet now, the travelling salesman being something of a dying beast."

David shook his head as he poured into both their glasses, beautiful glasses she belatedly realised, with intricate etchings on them, crystal for certain. The dinner plates were also impressive, a gold band to match the gold of the ballroom encircling each one and an elegant 'E' in the middle, the same design as that on the floor of the elevator, and at the foot of the welcome letter – the hotel logo, obviously. Beside the plates, the flatware looked as if it was real silver, certainly knives and forks were heavy to the touch.

Having taken a sip, David answered her question. "I sell to major companies not door to door. And God knows I'm busier than ever."

Sipping her wine too, relishing its rich, deep flavour as well as its ruby red shade, she told him she was in America on holiday, glossing over the exact reasons why, stating instead that she was catching up with long lost family. "I was supposed to be staying in Williamsfield itself, my mother's hometown, but, of course, I never got that far."

"Your loss, my gain," he said, offering his glass to clink against hers.

As she did so, another feeling erupted in her chest, not unease this time, something far more pleasant than that – excitement? Perhaps. As he'd said, the Egress wasn't such a bad a place to be, not when there was company like his to be found.

Ordering their food, a garden salad to start, and then steak for him and Atlantic salmon for her, they continued to talk, a pleasant level of chatter also in the air around them. She was so engrossed in their conversation, so absorbed by David's expressions as he spoke, his dark eyes sparkling in the light of the chandeliers, that it took a minute to register two things: another presence in the dining room, that of an elderly lady, she looked as old as the hotel itself, frail but dignified. Assisted by a younger woman, she didn't walk in; she seemed to *glide* – taking her seat at one of the tables – the head table. She was clearly someone very special – the lady in the corner suite on the eleventh floor? She had to be.

The other thing that initially didn't have the impact it should have done was a scream. It was Elspeth. No longer sitting alone, Princess Perfect had joined her, a smile on her perfectly sculpted face as Elspeth continued to struggle, not screaming anymore but choking. Definitely choking.

Chapter Five

The blonde with the fuller figure was the first to reach Elspeth.

"Oh, honey," she was saying, doing her utmost to sound in control rather than panicked, "you're alright, we're here to help you. Just cough it up, that's it, cough it up now."

She and David as well as the balding man had also reached the redhead's side. A couple of waiters flew across too, but it was as if they hovered in the background, waiting for the guests to do something about it instead. Around her all chatter ceased.

"What is it?" David addressed his question to Princess Perfect. "Why is she choking?"

"I told her to look out for bones," the young woman replied. She had the same air of boredom as Raquel. "The fish is full of them."

"Bones?" Caroline queried. She'd had the salmon too and it was filleted perfectly. "Is there a doctor in the house?" Quickly she raised her voice, looking at those still sitting in silence, some of whom had turned their heads away pretending they hadn't heard her, not wanting to get involved, to have their night ruined. "Is one of you a doctor?"

She thought she saw David about to respond but, if he was going to speak, the balding man beat him to it. "I know the Heimlich manoeuver, I could try that?"

David nodded. "Go ahead," he instructed.

Elspeth was continuing to choke, her face almost as red as her hair, her eyes – they were blue, and pale, almost milky – bulging. Beside her, the woman that David had dubbed Princess Perfect, continued to look bored. Caroline wanted to grab her by the throat, to shake some concern into her. How could she do that, remain so cold when a woman was in distress, a woman who was sitting right beside her? And how come she was sitting right beside her? Did they know each other, after all? Only briefly did she glance towards the elderly woman, Althea – the woman who took care of this place – wondering what her response to the scene unfolding in front of her would be. Sitting with her hands folded together, her lips pursed – she looked...*horrified*.

Caroline turned back to the balding man. "I think you'd better hurry."

"Yes, yes, of course," he replied, almost as agitated as Elspeth.

Positioning himself behind her, he folded his arms around her torso, just below her breasts, and, with one sharp movement, thrust upwards. All waited patiently – no one daring to breathe whilst one of their party wasn't able to.

Nothing happened. Elspeth continued to choke, tears running down her face.

Come on! Come on! Caroline willed the man to succeed. He *had* to succeed. It was as simple as that. Again her mind turned to the fish that was 'full of bones'. Could one rogue bone left in Elspeth's dish really have caused this? It was just so…dramatic.

The balding man, beads of sweat breaking out on his forehead, tried a second time. He was shaking again, Caroline noticed, terrified of failure or rather the consequences of failure. To be honest, so was she. Again she found herself urging him towards success. Elspeth's life was in his hands – literally. As for her hands, one was clinging onto David's arm, and not gently either. No matter that she barely knew him, she needed his support.

Success!

Thank God!

Elspeth choked again, regurgitated almost, a ragged sound, as painful to hear as it must be to experience. Something flew from her mouth, barely caught by the naked eye, thin and silvery white, landing back on her plate ironically, to lie beside the offending fish.

His job done, the balding man stepped back, shaking as much as ever, and the concerned woman took over, hugging Elspeth to her ample bosom, stroking her hair, petting her, soothing her with a barrage of kind words. All the while Elspeth clung to her, trembling violently too, sweat having caused some of her curls to hang limply.

Caroline released David at last and he glanced at her, as relieved as she was, before holding out his hand to the balding man, who perhaps was the most relieved of all.

"Well done," David exclaimed. "Where'd you learn to do that?"

"High school." The man didn't smile as he said it, instead he looked weighed down again, any relief owing to his success short-lived.

David nodded, introduced himself.

"I'm John Cole," the man said in return.

Finally letting go of his hand, David turned to Elspeth. "Are you okay? Would you like some water?"

"Wine," she croaked. "Pass me the wine."

He did so and she gulped down several mouthfuls, the red liquid sloshing against her lips and her hand reaching up to wipe roughly at them.

"I'm Marilyn Hollick." The woman still holding Elspeth introduced herself.

"Hi, Marilyn," both David and Caroline said in unison, after which Caroline fixed her gaze on Princess Perfect. "What's your name?" she asked, a note of steel in her voice.

The young woman with hair the colour of ice and features that looked as if they'd been hewn from ice too, stood up – the scraping of her chair as grating as the scrape of fingernails on a chalkboard. "I'm Tallula," she announced. And with that, she flounced out of the ballroom, leaving those around her to stare in open-mouthed amazement.

* * *

Despite meals being only half finished, the ballroom started to empty, people's evenings blighted by what had just happened, the atmosphere no longer mellow but strained. Caroline couldn't help but be disappointed; she had been looking forward to a longer evening, not one that would come to such an abrupt end. Halfway through her meal too, as David was with his, their dishes looked less appealing than before. Caroline picked apart the remainder of her salmon but was unable to find any bones lurking within. Finally, the pair of them admitted defeat, pushing their dishes to one side.

After Tallula's departure, Althea had risen too, summoning the woman who was clearly her assistant and, once again, drifting from the room – a movement that was elegant for such an old lady, no hobbling, no bent back, no fits and starts – her dexterity was admirable. That she hadn't got involved during the choking fit surprised Caroline. Perhaps she could see that John knew what he was doing, and that's why she'd refrained.

Elspeth had continued to need comforting and, perhaps because of the wine that she continued to knock back, she'd started to ramble, her lips moving rapidly as she professed how afraid she'd been that she was going to choke to death, that she didn't want to die, that the thought of death was terrifying. 'What's out there', she kept saying, 'surely it terrifies you too?' Having abandoned their food, David, John, and Caroline had all congregated again around her table, doing their utmost to placate her but it was Marilyn who had the most success. What's more, Marilyn seemed *pleased* to have someone to fuss over, showing signs of frustration whenever anyone interrupted her efforts. Realising this, David and Caroline made their excuses, and left, David summoning a waiter to ask if they could have their coffee in the lobby.

There were still a few people milling about and Raquel – the tireless Raquel – was behind the desk, her eyes downwards as she flicked through something – a magazine or a book? Maybe even the guest register. Caroline and David were the only ones to take a seat in the lobby, after she had crossed over to one of the windows and pulled the net curtain aside, noticing as she did a tear in it that needed mending. As she expected, the snow was piling higher and higher, her car resembling a small hillock; one of two.

David came up behind her. "My car's the one next to yours."

"How do you know it's mine?"

"If you arrived in a panic like I did, you wouldn't have bothered going to the lot."

She smiled. "Well deduced."

"Coffee's here," he continued.

Turning around, she saw he was right yet again. The coffee had been placed on the table in front of the piano. There was no sign of the waiter who'd brought it.

"Shame there's no one to tickle the ivories," she said, nodding at the piano as she sat.

"I'll give it a go later, if you want?"

"You can play?"

"*Chopsticks*."

She pulled a face. "Everyone can play *Chopsticks*."

"Can you?"

"Even me."

"Hey, we can play a duet, liven up this joint!"

"I forgot to mention something."

"What?"

"I *can* play it, but badly."

He sighed. "Dammit, I forgot to mention that too."

She looked around her. Just as the ballroom had emptied, so had the lobby, apart from Raquel that is, disappearing into the office behind her once or twice before settling back at the desk. "This place could certainly do with a bit of livening up, I agree."

David, however, backtracked. "Actually, I kinda like how it is."

"So Tom was right then."

"The guy who carried my one bag to my room and expected five bucks for it?"

"The very same. He said not everyone wants to be in the thick of it."

"Well, three cheers for Tom. And really, it could be so much worse."

"How?"

"We could be stranded along with a busload of tourists, sightseers from Nebraska or something."

She frowned. "What's wrong with people from Nebraska?"

"You haven't heard?"

"No."

"Oh, they're a crazy bunch, the Nebraskans. You gotta look out for 'em."

Again he was teasing her, but she was enjoying it, enjoying his company full stop.

"So, Caroline from England, how long are you here for?"

"I've got another week to go, plenty of time for the skies to clear."

"Yeah, plenty of time, I'm sure. As someone who has American heritage, have you never been tempted to move here, give the good old US of A a go?"

"I'm happy in London. But… I do like it here, very much. Never say never, I guess."

"That tends to be my mantra too."

"You haven't actually told me, where are you from? What state?"

"This one, but closer to Pittsburgh."

Mentally she tried to calculate. "So, if Pittsburgh's to the west and we're next to Philadelphia, in the east, that's a fair distance you've travelled."

"Correct, nearly two hundred miles."

"And all in the name of sales."

"What can I say, I'm a martyr to the cause."

"You married, got any kids?"

For a second David didn't answer, instead he held her gaze. She wanted to close her eyes and hide, for the ground to open up and swallow her. Why had she got so personal so quickly? What business was it of hers, anyway? Damn it, her cheeks were burning again, as red as Elspeth's hair. "I'm sorry... I—"

"No," he answered, interrupting her. "I'm not married. Are you?"

She shook her head, embarrassment rendering her tongue-tied.

"Good," he said, his expression serious instead of amused. "I'm glad."

She had to change the subject. She'd burst into flames at this rate. Abruptly she turned her head to the side and pointed. "I noticed some interesting pictures on the wall earlier, photos of the hotel I think, in its glory days. Shall we go take a look?"

David nodded in agreement, amusement creeping back in as he realised how mortified she was, but it was a sweet amusement, she couldn't deny it. So far, she'd sensed nothing but sweetness in this man and that realisation made her smile too. *I'm glad*, he'd said, regarding her single status. She'd never been so glad either. She bit down on that smile, did her level best to stop it turning into a grin as wide as the state of Pennsylvania itself.

Together they rose and made their way over to where

she'd pointed, to the far left of the lobby desk. Black and white photos of the Egress were indeed gracing the wall, a few framed prints too, of more generic subjects: a vase of flowers, and a green valley with a river running through it. But none could hold their interest as much as the old photographs.

The Egress in its glory days, that's what she'd said, and it was an apt description.

One photo was of the lobby – no carpet on the floor this time but a series of intricate tiles instead, adjoining squares with black diamonds at intervals. Was it still there, beneath their feet? If so, would it ever be revealed again? The chandeliers gleamed in the picture, the furniture no doubt brand new plus there was plenty more of it; deep armchairs dotted around, and tables with Grecian-style urns on top of them, home to dramatic plants whose green fronds soared upwards. Grand. So very grand. There was a black and white depiction of the ballroom too, the tables set up very much as they were now, the same configuration, each table boasting a resplendent vase of flowers in the middle. There'd been a posy on their table too, but it was just that – comprising a small spray of carnations, and some baby's breath. Another photo showed the lobby desk with billboards standing either side of it – the print was too small to read properly, but she assumed they were welcome boards. Behind the desk was a wall clock, a fancy timepiece with a carved wood surround. She looked towards the desk. Was it still there? No. The wall was bare.

"Weird," murmured David.

"What is?" she asked, studying his profile as he leant in towards one of the pictures. He was handsome for sure, his personality a contributing factor.

"All these photos, there's no one in them. Have you noticed?"

"Really?" She redirected her gaze. "Oh, yes! You're right." The rest of the pictures in the gallery included a poster celebrating its 75th birthday, a close up of the entrance with two fancy cars from an earlier era parked outside it, and a bedroom shot – one with slightly more opulent fixtures and fittings than the bedroom she occupied, a corner suite perhaps. There was also an earlier construction shot, a building that was part demolished – the one that had made way for the Egress.

"I wonder what that building was?" Caroline mused.

David glanced her way, looked thoughtful too.

The poster was advertising an event, a celebration dinner in the ballroom – perhaps that's why, in the former photo, the ballroom had been laid out so beautifully, in preparation. It would have been more enticing if there'd been at least a few people in the shot, the staff perhaps, resplendent in smart uniforms, or guests relaxing with a drink.

"You'd think that a hotel such as this, when it first opened, might have attracted some people of note," Caroline continued. "Maybe not A-listers, but town planners, and the mayor. You do have mayors in America, don't you?"

"We certainly do."

"Normally hotels like to boast about stuff like that. There's certainly no boasting going on here."

"You know what, one of the problems could be its location. There's peaceful, and there's the middle of nowhere. As far as most people are concerned, even the main town of Williamsfield isn't on the map."

56

"And yet here we are."

"Indeed."

She straightened up, yawned widely. "Come on, I think it's time we went to bed."

He burst out laughing, surprising her at first, until she realised what she'd said. "Oh my God!" One hand flew to her mouth. "I'm so sorry, I didn't mean to imply anything."

"You sure?"

"Of course I'm sure!" she replied, feigning indignation. "It was said in all innocence, honestly."

"Dammit, and here was I thinking my charm and good looks had pulled off something truly spectacular." He shook his head, refrained from teasing her anymore. "You're right, though, it's been a hell of a day. I'm bushed."

Falling into step beside him, they made their way to the elevator, Caroline bidding Raquel goodnight, who in turn barely lifted her head to murmur the same.

Entering the elevator, Caroline sighed. "This thing, it takes forever to get to eleven."

"You're on eleven?" he asked, raising an eyebrow.

"Yeah, didn't I say? The top floor."

"Oh, right."

"What is it? You seem surprised."

"No, no, not really. I'm on three."

Something she already knew, thanks to her earlier loitering. "I hope it's not too noisy, apparently there's a lot of renovation going on."

"Really? I hadn't noticed. Would you like me to see you to your room?"

She couldn't help it, she snorted. "Are you being

serious?"

He held his hands up. "No ulterior motive in mind. I'm just being a gentleman."

"A gentleman? Well, it's very kind of you, but I'm a big girl now, I can find my own way."

"Ah, Miss Independent?"

"I like to think so."

"And I like to think I'm a gentleman. I'll ride with you to eleven first and then I'll go back down. I wonder how Elspeth is," he added, leaning in to select the relevant floors.

She'd been wondering the same thing. She wasn't sure what floor Marilyn was on, but perhaps she'd offered to accompany Elspeth to her room too. If so, she couldn't see the redhead refusing. She'd clung to the older woman as a child would to its mother. She also wondered what floor Tallula was on, just her luck if she were next door or opposite.

"We're here," David's words brought her back to the moment.

"Already?"

Disappointingly, the elevator was suddenly all brisk efficiency.

"See you tomorrow at breakfast?" he asked.

"Sure."

"Same table?"

She nodded. "Same table."

"Night."

He ensured the elevator doors stayed open as she stepped over the threshold and into the endless corridor. "Night," she replied, perhaps as half-heartedly as him.

Still he held the doors open, and she turned to say

goodnight again, their gaze holding. Eventually she had no choice but to look away, to face the direction in which she needed to go, to actually *get* going, to reach her room.

"Sweet dreams," he called out jovially.

"I hope so," she called back, wondering if she'd dream of him.

Chapter Six

Sweet dreams. That's what he'd said. But the dreams that plagued her were far from that. Instead, they were causing her breath to hitch in her throat and her hands to tightly clench the sheet that covered her, as her head thrashed from side to side.

She was in her room, she knew that much, her large, almost vault-like room. In some ways the dream she was having emulated reality, at least at the beginning. To reach her room she'd had to take the elevator, and surprise, surprise, it was playing up again, chugging and spluttering its way to the eleventh floor, as if it were all such an effort. An aeon seemed to have passed, but then the doors opened and she drifted, Althea-like, along its corridor, one that stretched on and on, the carpet beneath her feet more frayed than ever, the skirting more chipped, the paper on the walls distinctly yellow; not bright and cheerful like sunshine but as faded as everything else. How long was this going to take? Shouldn't she have reached 1106 by now? She'd passed so many doors, far more than there really were, but that was dreams for you – they distorted everything.

From behind each door she sensed movement: a

shuffling backwards and forwards; the low murmur of the TV or a radio; a cry of anguish that was quickly stifled. The latter had caused her head to whip around. Was it coming from Elspeth's room? Was she still upset after what had happened in the ballroom? If so, she should backtrack, go to her, comfort her as Marilyn had, but she couldn't stop drifting, past her room, perhaps Marilyn's, and Tallula's too, if their rooms were here. Another shudder. There was something about Tallula; not Princess Perfect – Ice-Cold Tallula suited her better. The way she'd sat beside Elspeth, not lifting a finger to help her, as if amused by her plight, was awful. Especially after planting the idea of bones in her head. *There were no bones. There were no bones.* The words kept going around and around. But there were. She'd seen Elspeth cough one up. Tallula had been right. Why continue to doubt her?

The end of the corridor – the corner suite – was still some distance away. She'd never reach it in time. Again, she had to check her thoughts. In time for what? There was no time, the absence of the clock over the office door in the lobby proved that. In dreams, time was meaningless. Also, if she did reach Althea's room, what did she expect to find there?

The dream fast-forwarded. She was in bed. There was a noise. Although silent outside, inside things were beginning to stir.

Things?

Thrown from her dream-like state, her eyes snapped open as she sat bolt upright.

What kind of things?

God, it was dark. She raised a hand and held it out in front yet couldn't see it at all.

My eyes will get used to the darkness. They'll adjust.

But the more she stared, the thicker the darkness became, confusing her further.

Was she actually awake or was she still dreaming?

She had to do something constructive, switch on the table lamp perhaps. Her hand reaching out, she was met with nothing. Where was it? Where the hell was it?

Another sound!

What the—?

A choking.

"Elspeth?"

But Elspeth had been saved. John Cole, the balding man, the *shaking* man, had saved her.

There it was again, faint, not as dramatic as Elspeth's choking had been, more of a cry.

"Who are you? Who's there?"

Her voice sounded hollow, and alone… So alone.

But she wasn't alone.

She knew that now.

"Who's in the darkness?"

Her eyesight must be adjusting because, despite how black it was, she started to make out shapes in front of her bed, people of all heights and sizes. It was just their outline, nothing more, no clue as to what their gender might be, but all had one thing in common: they were holding their hands up as if pushing against something, an invisible barrier, their faces squashed to the side as those behind surged forwards.

Were they seeking release? Is that what they wanted? They seemed desperate – that emotion also engulfed her; making her feel desperate too.

She brought her knees up to her chest, wrapped her

arms around them, and lowered her head, not wanting to see anymore.

"Get away from me! Get away!"

She didn't want these tortured souls anywhere near her.

"Get away, I said. Go on, go!"

Someone was whispering in her ear. "A special place… It's such a special place…"

A male voice, the words smooth and unhurried, no desperation in them at all.

Releasing her legs, she batted furiously at the air.

What's happening? Am I asleep? Am I awake?

Dammit, she couldn't tell!

And then there was tinkling laughter. *Familiar* laughter.

"Mum?"

It was that that distressed her most of all.

Chapter Seven

"Christ!"

Caroline woke up. Properly woke up. And she wasn't in darkness, far from it. A ray of light shone in between the curtains, dust motes dancing happily within it. It was morning. She'd made it. Had there been a break in the weather overnight? Although she didn't leap out of bed, there was certainly a hopeful spring in her step as she crossed over to the window. Passing the point where there'd been a wall, of sorts, in her dreams, behind which so many were trapped, she almost faltered. It had seemed so real, that dream, the desperation of those trying to escape – an invisible barrier preventing them. But what if that barrier failed, and they rushed at her, grabbed at her, started tearing her apart...?

Enough with the imagination! The snow, remember?

Remember? How could she forget!

Hauling the curtain back, supposedly deep burgundy, but pinkish in places due to sun damage most likely, her heart sunk further. The snow had stopped falling, but the sky looked ominous, dark clouds hanging in the sky, biding their time before the next attack.

"Shit!"

There was no way she'd be leaving the Egress today, no way at all. Where were the snowploughs? Where was anybody? The land below was deserted – no tracks in it at all.

Turning around, she had to blink several times. The brightness of the snow had temporarily blinded her, making the room seem dark again in contrast, the bed, the desk, and the wardrobe disguised within it. She sighed, fought against frustration, and remembered again to be thankful. She was stranded, but in a hotel, with plenty of food and drink, and people, including David, someone she'd already clicked with. She may as well make the most of it, get showered, dressed, and return to the ballroom where breakfast was being served. What other choice was there?

* * *

It was late, almost ten thirty. Most people had eaten breakfast, Caroline presumed, and departed already – but gone where? To their rooms? Some had been milling about in the lobby, where she herself had lingered for a minute or two, noting Raquel still in position, filing her nails as she stared almost blindly towards the main entrance. Caroline too had stared in that direction; she was determined to catch a breath of fresh air, even if she only got a few yards. She simply couldn't stay cooped up all day. She'd also taken the opportunity to check her phone to see if a return message from Violet had come through and was annoyed to find that the one she'd written hadn't even sent. She really should have checked that, not been so slapdash. The Wi-Fi too was dreadful, a couple of times she'd tried to log onto Facebook but had given up when it had taken too long, that little round circle whirling away. Not that she went onto Facebook much anyway, so it hadn't bothered her overly. But a text should get through easily enough. She pressed 'try again'. No joy, that time or the next. About to give up, it seemed to deliver at last. Good.

Despite Raquel's tendency to ignore her, Caroline had wished her good morning before entering the ballroom, the tables once again immaculately set, although the posies had been removed. David was the only guest she recognised and the smile he flashed at her told her he was glad to see her too. She walked over to him, to what had become their table.

"Okay to sit?" she asked, a tease in her voice.

"I'd be offended if you didn't. Sleep well?"

Seating herself, she wondered whether to tell him the truth before deciding against it. She had an urge instead to keep their conversation as light-hearted as possible, offsetting everything that had happened since entering Pennsylvania. Seven days, that was all she had left of her holiday with her chances of achieving all on the agenda she'd created looking less and less likely. Pretty much done with family visits, she'd so much wanted to travel to Mount Pocono after a day or two in Williamsfield, before heading back to Boston and spending a couple of days there, following the Freedom Trail perhaps – something she'd done as a kid and had thoroughly enjoyed – as well as shopping at the Faneuil Hall Marketplace, with its arts and crafts stalls, promenade and restaurants. It was as well all family commitments had been scheduled for the first half of her journey – she'd have hated to miss out on any reunions – and a blessing again that the second leg was more flexible. David was staring at her, his head to one side, clearly waiting for an answer.

"I slept great, thanks, and you?"

"Not bad," he replied. "Woke up a couple of times, you know, as you do when you're in a strange place. Unfamiliar noises."

"Yeah, I woke once or twice too." Except she hadn't, she was sure she hadn't, she'd just *thought* she was awake, her exhausted brain fooling her. Glancing around, she stated the obvious. "There's no Elspeth. I hope she's okay."

There was no Marilyn either to check with. Looking back at David, she could see he was concerned too. "Maybe she ate earlier," he suggested.

Or perhaps she hadn't bothered to come down at all, thought Caroline.

Breakfast was impressive, consisting of plenty of hot items stored in covered silver serving dishes. Although in recent months grief had curbed her appetite, it reappeared with a vengeance, as the smell of maple bacon, sausage links, home fries, and French toast became nothing less than tantalising. She caught David's amusement when she returned with her filled plate.

"I'm...hungry," she explained.

"Hey, no judgement here! I like a girl with a good appetite. You carry on."

"Don't mind if I do," she murmured, unable to stop grinning too. The food was every bit as good as it looked and smelt, and she was ravenous, trying to eat as delicately as possible, but somehow suspecting she was failing dismally. Her appetite being on the mend heartened her in more ways than one. Whilst part of her suspected she'd never recover from the tragic early deaths of both her parents, whilst it angered her still to think of the unfairness of it, there was no doubt about it, wanting to eat again, *enjoying* food, rather than it simply being a mechanical process, was a good sign. She'd eaten the previous evening at dinner, of course, and the food had been of a good standard, but there was something different in her this morning, as if something had dislodged. Could it possibly be grief, that all-consuming stage of grief anyway? Was she moving on at last, and here of all places?

"Let's go outside." The words were out as soon as she'd finished her last mouthful.

"You wanna case the joint?"

God, how his eyes twinkled!

"Uh huh, starting from the outside."

He wrapped his arms around his body and shivered. "It's gonna be cold out there."

"Where's your coat?"

"In my room."

"Go and get it and I'll meet you back in the lobby in half an hour."

"Lady, you've got yourself a date."

It was actually less than half an hour when they met up again. He had on the same overcoat he'd arrived in – thick tweed, classic in style, well worn – plus a scarf and gloves.

He noted her grey woolly hat with a bobble on top. "Fetching," he said.

"I'm glad you think so."

As they turned towards the entrance, Raquel finally showed a spark of interest.

"Going somewhere?" she asked.

"Nope, you just need to turn the heating up a little," quipped David.

His joke failed to raise a smile. "Good luck," was her only response.

"Thanks," Caroline answered, not sure if Raquel's wish was genuine or sarcastic.

David seemed to read her thoughts. As they walked, he leant across and murmured into her ear, his breath pleasantly warm. "She's definitely being sarcastic."

Caroline shrugged. In that moment she couldn't care less.

Snow had drifted upwards to settle at the entrance and David had to push hard against the double doors in order to open them. As he did, the blast of air was icy – as expected. Earlier, whilst she was getting ready for breakfast, she'd had the TV on again in the background. Continuing reports predicted there'd be a break in proceedings – as was evident – but not to be fooled by it, that another weather front was hot (or rather cold) on the heels of the first and looked set to be even heavier.

As Caroline stared ahead, she couldn't help but sigh.

David noticed. "You'll be on your way again soon, don't worry."

"Will I? I mean I know I've got a fair while before my flight home, but I've never experienced weather like this before."

"You get snow in England, don't you? I've seen the Charles Dickens Christmas movies."

"Sure, we get snow, but more often than not it's just a smattering. In Scotland it's worse but…not on this scale."

Gently he placed his hands on her shoulders. "Okay, let's put this into some kind of perspective. If you miss your flight—"

"Miss my flight? Are you serious?"

"Just hear me out. If you miss your flight, what's the worst thing that could happen?"

"I get into trouble with my boss?"

"But you won't lose your job?"

"Lose it? No, of course not. But deadlines must be met."

He inclined his head to the side. "How much do you love what you do?"

"On a scale of one to ten?"

"If you like."

She considered. "It used to be about seven but now I'd say four or five."

"Why's that?"

"What's the point of making money for people who've already got more than enough?"

"Can't take it with you, can you?"

"That's my way of thinking lately." If she didn't have bills to pay, the mortgage on her flat, she'd look for something else, something a little more altruistic. Maybe she'd do that anyway, although she'd have to move out of London first, and into the more reasonably priced suburbs. What an upheaval that would be, her shoulders sagged just thinking about it.

Noticing, he sought again to reassure her. "Caroline, you made it to safety, and so did I, that's the main thing. A couple of days from now and things could look very different, or," he paused briefly, "it could look the same. If it's the same surely your firm won't hold that against you. What do they want you to do, kill yourself in the effort to make it to your desk? I don't think so."

She pulled a face. "You don't know the kind of business I'm in. It's cut-throat."

"Maybe, but it's also a world away. This is our reality,

right here, right now."

"It sure is. The heaviest snow Pennsylvania's seen since the 1950s."

"Kinda pretty, though, ain't it?"

She laughed, appreciating his ability to lighten the mood.

"And of course there's something else you can do," he added, "but nearer the time."

"What's that?"

"Change your flight."

"Yeah, yeah, I know." It really was that simple.

Removing his hands, he offered her his arm instead and together they ventured deeper into the snow, stopping briefly at the hillock that was her rental car, so she could wipe away the snow from the passenger-side window and peer inside. It proved a fruitless task – underneath the top layer it was thick ice, she'd need a tough scraper to penetrate it.

"What are you trying to do?" he asked.

Admitting defeat, she straightened up. "I don't know actually. I suppose I just wanted to make sure it really is my car underneath all that."

If she expected him to scoff, he didn't. "It's hard to believe in something you can't see, isn't it?"

She glanced at him. "I think it's called having faith."

"Yeah, right, of course it is."

She was curious. "David, are you a religious man?"

"I...um... I'll tell you about it some other time."

His voice had an edge to it, something that hinted at a deeper person beneath the jovial exterior. She wanted him to tell her about it now, was suddenly impatient to know as much as she could about the tall, dark stranger before her, was about to probe further even when, in one swift movement, he gathered a handful of snow and threw it at her.

"What the…?" She was stunned.

"You didn't think we were gonna come out here and not have a snowball fight, did you?"

"A snowball fight? Right! You asked for it. You're in trouble now, Mr Mason."

"Promises, promises, Miss Daynes."

As quick as he'd been, she gathered a handful of snow too but already he was moving away from her, the depth of the snow requiring him to take comical moon steps backwards. Firing her first shot, it fell woefully short. "Damn," she swore before gathering another handful and taking giant moon steps towards him. If anyone was staring out of their windows at them, they'd think they were a pair of idiots, she was sure of it – their laughter raucous as he aimed yet another fistful. That hit her square on too.

Determined to wreak revenge, she managed to close the gap between them. But just as she raised her arm, her feet slid from beneath her, causing her to fall flat on her face.

"Aargh," her scream was quickly muffled.

Instead of helping, David continued to bellow with laughter and, despite the coldness of the snow being really quite crippling, she turned onto her back and lay there, grinning too. She felt like a naughty kid, one who'd managed to dodge the chores, and gone out to play instead. She hadn't laughed this hard since… She tried to remember the last time and couldn't. Without the constraints of work, of family and friends, of illness, she was free! Elated, she flung out her arms and her legs, moving them up and down, in and out.

At last he stooped to help her.

"Come on, snow angel, that's enough of that."

On her feet, they both dusted at her clothes.

"You wanna go in, get changed?"

"I'm okay, this coat is pretty waterproof."

Releasing her hand, he stood and looked at her instead. "So, it never snows like this in England?"

She shook her head. "Have you ever been?"

"To England? No, but I'd like to, one day. It's on the wish list."

"When the Thames freezes over perhaps."

His eyes lit up. "Hey, does it really do that?"

"You're kidding, right?"

"You're the one who mentioned it."

"It's a joke," she replied, but not without amusement. In fact, he amused the heck out of her. "The Thames hasn't frozen for decades, the sixties was the last time, I think."

"There you go, that's global warming for you."

"I suppose so. Although right now, looking around me, I'm tempted to believe the sceptics."

"Never believe the sceptics," he countered, relinking arms with her.

Veering towards the left side of the building, Caroline couldn't help but be struck again by the sheer isolation of their surroundings. In England, nothing was ever that far from anything else, whereas in America, there were giant swathes of empty space. She wondered again about the buildings that were supposed to have been built around here, the ones that were planned, but never came to be, and also about what was here before – the building that had been knocked down to make way for the Egress.

A few metres from the hotel, her legs aching from the giant steps they were having to take, they finally stopped and turned, her intent to survey the building she was staying in, to get a sense of how tall, how grand it really was.

"Like a lone sentinel," she mused, "that's what it reminds me of."

"Presiding over what?" asked David.

"Failed dreams," Caroline answered without missing a beat. She told him what Tom had said when they were travelling to her room and he nodded, not in the least surprised.

"This might have been the ideal spot once," he commented.

It might have been, the town of Williamsfield expanding to accommodate it, but it was a gamble – a *plan* – that, for some reason, hadn't paid off. And so it stood alone, on a highway leading downtown instead of being part of downtown proper. Not the only one of its kind. In this land plenty of lone hotels graced equally lonely roads. Even so, she couldn't help but feel a tragic sense of waste.

It *was* grand, she decided. Although snow clung to it, she could see the two upper floors were grey stone with an overhung roof. In contrast, the middle floors, being the major part of the elevations, were cream brickwork, but the grey stone kicked in again at lobby level. On top of the hotel, sitting perch-like, were huge red letters, storey height at least, spelling out THE EGRESS. Impressive, beautiful, it was a façade to be admired.

A silence that was almost reverent descended on them. It was companionable, though, no hint of awkwardness in it. It was a silence she found comforting, that allowed her to drift, just as the snow was drifting, as Althea tended to drift, falling deeper into it…

"What's that? Look."

Shaken out of her reverie, she asked David what he was referring to.

"There's movement on the top floor, in the corner room."

That was Althea's room, the woman she'd just been thinking about.

"It looks like someone's staring at us," he continued.

"Staring at us? Really?"

She squinted too, could see the outline of someone, one hand holding aside the curtain as he or she gazed outwards.

"Perhaps we should wave," Caroline began and then noticed movement at other windows too. Not on the eleventh floor, but the floors below, random windows, random movement, as if they were indeed an object of scrutiny. One figure in particular caught her eye, was it on the fifth floor, or the sixth? She would have counted upwards just to make sure if she could drag her eyes away, but she couldn't. She was transfixed.

The figure had both hands pressed against the window, its head turned sideways, as if he or she were pushing against the glass, trying to burst through.

The dream. It's like my dream.

"Oh God," she whispered. "What's it doing? What's that person doing?"

Once again their desperation was infectious.

Before David had a chance to answer, she managed to tear her gaze away, swivelling around to stare in the opposite direction instead. There was nothing, absolutely nothing beyond them, just a whole lot of whiteness. No end and no beginning. Except there had been a beginning once, she reminded herself: hers, in room 210.

"Caroline?"

She knew he was calling her, but he sounded so distant.

"Caroline!"

Finally she faced him.

"What is it," he asked. "What's the matter?" His hand was on her again, steadying her.

"The dream," she said and then her words died out as the clouds gave way and snowflakes spiralled downwards, a gentle flurry that would soon become a deluge.

"Dream? Look, you're shaking. You need to get inside, get some dry clothes on."

He was right; the cold had penetrated, her coat not resistant enough.

"Come on," he continued, and she allowed him to steer her back to the Egress, their bolthole, and their sanctuary, the only shelter that was available. All the while she kept her head low, not wanting to see again the figure that felt as if it was warning her.

Chapter Eight

Having returned to her room, and showered as well as changed, Caroline had lain on the bed, exhausted but fearing sleep. In the end she succumbed, waking more than two hours later, unable to recall if she'd dreamt at all. Even so, the first thing she'd thought of was the dream she'd had the previous night, that and the figure she'd seen at the window this morning. Was it just something her imagination had constructed? That was one explanation. There was no doubt she was tired, overwrought still from the events of yesterday, from finding herself stranded at the Egress for God knows how long. Rising, she'd freshened up once again before deciding to go downstairs to the lobby. Leaving her room, she'd pulled the door behind her, stepped into the corridor and that's when she saw Marilyn, on the eleventh floor too, hurrying to the room opposite Elspeth's: 1102.

"Marilyn, hi. Can I have a word please?"

At first Marilyn didn't respond. With her eyes cast downwards, she had the key to her room already in her hand and was about to insert it into the lock. It was only when Caroline called again, much louder this time, that she took any notice.

"Oh, honey, hello," she said as Caroline drew nearer.

The smile on her face seemed a little strained and, lifting her left hand, she began scratching at her neck as though an itch had started up.

Caroline apologised. "Sorry to disturb you. I was just wondering, you know…" she lowered her voice and inclined her head towards 1101, "…if everything's okay?"

"Oh, I see," replied Marilyn, straightaway getting the gist. "Perhaps it's best you come inside. We can talk in there."

"I don't want to disturb—"

"You're not disturbing me, of course you're not." She made a show of looking at her watch. "My, oh my, look at the time. Won't you join me for tea?"

Tea? Caroline was surprised. Most Americans she'd encountered preferred coffee. "Yes," she replied. "I'd love to." It'd be nicer perhaps than sitting in the lobby on her own, reading the magazine she'd been flicking through the day before.

Marilyn's expression was more genuine this time; she beamed at Caroline, seemed delighted that she'd agreed. Opening the door, she moved aside so that Caroline could enter first. Room 1102 was the same configuration as hers, something to be expected, but whereas hers was more traditional in style, restrained even, Marilyn's was somewhat vintage in feel with a patterned wallpaper instead of stripes, tiny flowers with accents of red and gold not clashing with the patterned carpet beneath her feet – the same as her room – but complementing it. *No mean feat*, Caroline thought, praising the interior designer. The curtains were floral too, and polished surfaces bore an assortment of knick-knacks, including several vases of various sizes and a dish with red and white striped candies in it. On a small round table, there was a tea service, comprising a pale green china teapot, and matching cups and saucers.

"Sit, honey, make yourself at home," Marilyn insisted, explaining that Elspeth had calmed considerably after such a 'shocking episode' and that 'she went back to her room for some much-needed rest, the poor darling.' Apparently, she'd not seen her today so far. Having told all, she excused herself and went to the kitchenette to boil water for their tea.

From the cushion-adorned sofa, Caroline continued to survey her surroundings.

Home. That's what this room looked like – as homely as Marilyn herself.

"It's nice in here," she remarked when Marilyn returned briefly to fetch the teapot.

"Isn't it?" she replied, all hustle and bustle. "More personal than all those modern hotels that have sprung up. It's not my usual room, though. My usual is being renovated."

"Really? Where's that?" Caroline enquired.

"On the ninth floor. But I mustn't complain, it's remarkably similar."

Finally, Marilyn came back for good, one hand holding the handle of the teapot, the other supporting it underneath. She placed it back on the table and beckoned Caroline to join her there, pulling out a chair for her and patting the seat.

Rising from the sofa to sit opposite Marilyn, Caroline watched as she opened the lid of the teapot and stirred before placing a strainer over one of the cups.

"Milk? Sugar?" she asked.

"Just a little milk."

She poured, her actions as neat as she was.

"Thank you," Caroline responded, duly taking a sip. Despite the fact that it hadn't been left to stew, she detected a slight bitter note.

"Darjeeling," Marilyn said, nodding enthusiastically, "my favourite."

"I like it too," Caroline replied. *Usually.* "So…you've obviously stayed here several times before?"

Pointing that out caused some of Marilyn's good humour to fade. She was an attractive woman still, impeccable even, her use of make-up really quite expert, making the most of her full lips and high cheekbones. Beneath the make-up, however, there were lines, scores of them, and in the blue of her eyes, sadness. Again Marilyn lifted a hand and started scratching at her neck, a nervous habit perhaps or a patch of eczema?

"My husband and I used to visit," she began, her voice initially curt. "We're from Illinois, it's such a flat state. That's why we love it here, the hills that surround it. There's so many opportunities for shooting and fishing, for getting back to nature, to the things that matter." A wry laugh escaped her. "Oh, how he loved the valleys around here, and the rivers that ran through them. For hours he'd fish, and I'd sit, happy to watch him. It's a graceful sport, isn't it, fishing? You have to be agile. After a while, I'd insist he come and sit with me. He never took much persuading. My picnics were no ordinary picnics, you see, they were really quite lavish; he could never resist them." Her laugh became lighter, as she started to relax, clearly enjoying such memories. "Afterwards we'd return to the

Egress, I'd take a bath, he'd make the cocktails. It's a man's job in my opinion, mixing drinks. There's a science to it." She inclined her head towards the drinks cabinet. "A Manhattan was my favourite, it's such an elegant drink. He preferred a Sidecar, said it suited the mood of the hotel. I don't know what he meant by that, perhaps that it was a popular drink back then, I never asked." Her voice trailed off. "As you can see, I tend to stick to tea nowadays."

Nowadays? Caroline winced. "Oh, I'm sorry, your husband, is he—?"

"Don't say it, please, I beg you." She held up a hand as if warding off evil. "It's such an ugly word, isn't it?" She took a deep breath before continuing. "Leonard passed. Two years ago. It was all rather sudden. A heart attack in the night. I woke to find him…" Her voice trailed off and briefly she screwed her eyes shut. "Dear Lennie, he'd complain about getting fat, you know, but he wasn't, truly he wasn't, he was just…cuddly. He loved my cooking and I loved to feed him; I adored seeing his delight whenever I tried a new recipe, although meat and potatoes, any variation on that, remained his favourite. I looked after my man; so many women don't, especially these days. Are you married?"

The question when it came was unexpected. "Um…no, no I'm not."

The idea of being single was clearly anathema to Marilyn. "Why ever not?"

"Because I haven't found the right person, I suppose."

Marilyn's eyes grew wider. "If you don't mind me asking, how old are you, honey?"

Caroline didn't know whether to be amused or offended. Her marital status, her age, they weren't details she necessarily gave out to people who were as good as strangers. Perhaps it was karma for getting personal very quickly with David. "I'm thirty-three," she said at last. Before Marilyn could say it, she added, "I know, I know, I'm an old maid."

Marilyn sat back in her chair, shook her head, and tried to deny it. "Oh no, honey, of course not. It's just unusual, that's all, to be single at your age."

Was it really? Caroline had never really thought so, but when she did a quick mental round up of her friends, she supposed the vast majority of them, if not married, were certainly involved in a relationship of some kind. Whether all of them could be described as *happy* relationships, however, was another matter, even those who'd tied the knot. For years, Caroline had sat and listened to complaint after complaint, to so much heartache and grief, that usually she felt nothing but relief to be on her own; had cherished that fact.

Marilyn had closed her eyes, her face becoming slack, or perhaps dreamy was a kinder description. "Finding your soul mate is so important. Lennie was definitely my soul mate."

"I'm glad for you—"

"We met in our late teens." Again Marilyn interrupted her. She'd opened her eyes to stare intently at Caroline. "I was eighteen, he was nineteen, and I knew right away that he was the one. He took a bit more persuading, mind, wanted to be one of the boys for a bit longer, but I'd set my sights on him, and eventually he buckled." She sighed. "We never had children. It just didn't happen for us. There was a time in my life I was distraught about that. Oh my goodness, I'd get so upset, I'd cry buckets, but when I look back, I wonder if that's what made our relationship so strong. We had nothing to distract us, you see, it was just the two of us, for so many years, growing up together, growing old. Falling more and more in love every day. I miss him so much!"

The last words came out as a sob and Caroline reached forward but Marilyn shrunk back. "It's alright, honey, I'm okay, I… I get like this sometimes. But it helps, you know, returning to places that were familiar to us, although of course it's painful too."

"I can imagine," murmured Caroline, but she could tell by the way that Marilyn looked at her that she didn't believe that. How could she, a single woman, identify with a widow? Caroline had to concede she didn't believe her own words either. She *couldn't* imagine. It was as simple as that. Would any man ever hold her in such sway?

Marilyn pushed her teacup away. She'd barely touched it. "It's our anniversary this week," she revealed, staring into the distance. "That's when we used to come here, for our anniversary." Again tears were falling from her eyes, a gentle stream, one that might never truly cease. Earlier, she'd thought she'd detected sadness in Marilyn, now she realised how trivial a summarisation that was.

Reaching up, Marilyn wiped at the tears and then continued to scratch at her neck. "This is our place," she said, her gaze still averted. "And it will *always* be our place."

Chapter Nine

When Caroline left Marilyn's room, she still couldn't face returning to her own – not to sit and mull over what she'd learnt about Marilyn and Leonard, it was too depressing. Originally, she was on her way to the lobby and she decided to reinstate that plan, taking her chances with the elevator again, which this time behaved itself well enough.

She'd just chosen her seat in the lobby; sitting directly beneath the chandelier, when the hotel doors were pushed open. Another arrival! She had to blink to believe it.

Standing in the exact spot that she and David had stood, was another man – tall, elegant, a cashmere overcoat adorning his angular frame, and a somewhat playful smile on his face. Unlike her and David, he didn't look ruffled at all, certainly not as though he'd stepped out of the arms of a storm. His blonde hair should be awry, his cheeks flushed, snow clinging to him, instead he looked…perfect, better than the airbrushed models in the magazine at her fingertips – the cut of his close-fitting suit expensive too.

As he made his way towards the lobby desk, Caroline was mesmerised.

"Raquel," he exclaimed. "Lovely to see you again."

The girl at reception smiled, a degree or two less bored

than before.

"Hello, Edward! You'll be wanting your usual room, I presume?"

"You presume right." The man almost purred before swinging abruptly around to survey the lobby. "We're busy then," he added.

Not particularly, Caroline thought, wondering what he could see that she couldn't. As his eyes rested on her, she seized her chance.

"Hello," she said, jumping to her feet. "You made it then?" Only belatedly did she realise she'd mimicked Raquel. She hadn't intended to this time, the words had just slipped out.

The man – his name, Edward, suited him, the regality of it – seemed as amused by her as David sometimes was.

"I did indeed," he answered, his voice like liquid gold.

With one hand she gestured towards the hotel doors. "The weather, it's so awful."

All he did was nod. *Dammit, he's making me work for this.*

"How did you get through?" she continued, desperate to know. "Did you drive?"

"Drive?" As he repeated the word, he raised an eyebrow. "You can't drive in this."

"But you got here somehow."

"That's right, I did."

Turning back, he took the key to his 'usual' room, leaving her by degrees irritated and fascinated. Making her way towards the elevator, his back straight, confidence in every stride, Caroline was left to wonder one more thing: was he on the eleventh floor too?

* * *

Back in her seat, flicking through the pages of a magazine, barely able to concentrate for thinking about Edward, the time passed quickly enough, despite Caroline fearing that it would drag. Dinner was in an hour and so she returned to her room to change her clothes, the elevator once again working perfectly. Reaching the eleventh floor, she walked past Elspeth's room, and past Marilyn's, Edward still on her mind: a mysterious man, who'd appeared just as mysteriously, who'd *materialised*. Perhaps he'd straightened himself out just inside the hotel doors, before climbing the handful of steps to where he could be seen properly. But why go to such trouble? And he said he hadn't driven to the Egress – she'd made a point of asking him. Well, he couldn't have bloody well walked! He was teasing her, having a little joke. Hence his playful smile. Mischievous, that's what he was. *And interesting.* She couldn't deny it. Perhaps he owned some incredible four by four, or he drove a snowplough. That idea tickled her – someone dressed like Edward did *not* drive a snowplough.

A burst of laughter matched her own and she turned to the side. Where had it come from? Elspeth's room again? She'd passed it, though. She was between 1104 and her room. She backtracked and lingered outside 1104. There was movement, or at least a sense of it. In fact, the entire floor seemed livelier than before. Just like Edward's arrival had woken Raquel up, the entire eleventh floor had followed suit. There were more sounds, not just from 1104 but also in the air, the low murmur of two people conversing, another burst of laughter, canned this time, from a radio show probably or the TV. Her eyes travelling

86

downwards, strips of light were evident beneath doors. Like Edward, where had everyone come from? Sitting in the lobby, she'd have noticed people arriving, and before that on the eleventh floor, *this* floor, in Marilyn's room – she'd have *heard* them. Surely.

But they can't get through, even Edward admitted that. You can't drive in this.

A pain shot across her forehead. She felt nauseous, dizzy even, had to lean against the wall for support. Just as quickly, the feelings subsided. In truth, she *forced* them to subside. Perhaps it was something to do with the bang she'd received when she'd crashed the car, some sort of delayed reaction. Whatever it was, she couldn't afford to get sick. She had to make the best of her time here; pray that the weather would change soon enough and that she'd be on the road again. As for where all the people had come from, they must have been here already, closed doors concealing them. Certainly, last night, there'd been more people at dinner than she'd anticipated. Dinner... She'd see David again, a whole host of characters, with tall, regal Edward amongst them no doubt.

* * *

As she entered the ballroom, dressed in slim-fitting black jeans, a red blouse and ankle boots, attire she felt more comfortable in, she spotted David. He was sitting at the table they'd occupied for both dinner and breakfast.

"That territorial streak of yours really is very well defined," she said upon reaching him.

He looked confused but only for a moment. "Honey, this is our table, where we first got to know each other.

That has value, you know, *sentimental* value."

If he noticed how she coloured at his words, he gave no sign. Once seated, a waiter took the order for their wine; white this time, at her request.

"Gotta ring the changes somehow," she jested.

"If you insist." His reply was equally as good-humoured.

Picking up her menu, she pulled a face. "This formality is all very nice, but you know what I'd kill for right now?"

"Tell me."

"Pizza."

"Pizza?" His eyes roamed over the menu. "Nope, not available. You can have Oysters Rockefeller, shrimp by the dozen, clams, salmon and catfish, steak done however you want it, and even a gourmet salad with cranberry vinaigrette, but it's no deal on the pizza."

"Damn! And no chance of getting a delivery?" After all, if Edward had got through…

"Sweetheart, if a delivery man can battle his way here in this, he's a better man than I."

"Just think, though, if he did manage it, we could hitch a ride back with him."

"Yep, straight into the heart of civilisation." He nudged her. "Hey, look, here come the troops."

Elspeth had entered the room – a *shrunken* Elspeth, no longer as giggly, or as frenetic as before, her face, without make-up, as pale as her milky eyes. Alongside her was Marilyn, one hand continually patting Elspeth's arm in a reassuring manner.

John Cole was next, the sight of his bowed head tugging at Caroline's heartstrings. She knew something of Marilyn's background; she would like to know something of his too, primarily what had caused that air of dejection that hung over him?

She leaned into David. "Should we invite John over?"

John, however, had already sat down, again at the table he'd chosen the night before, as much a creature of habit as any of them.

David looked concerned too. "Why don't we ask him to join us for coffee afterwards instead?"

"Good idea," Caroline agreed, catching David's intimation that he might be happy in his own company, as she sometimes was.

Althea was next, her assistant in tow, the order of people almost exactly the same as before. But where was Tallula and the mysterious teenager? And Edward. Where was he?

No sooner had she thought of Edward than once again he appeared – she half expected a puff of smoke to accompany him. He was standing at the entrance to the ballroom, dressed in another suit, charcoal grey this time as opposed to the navy of earlier, a white shirt left open at the collar. His hair was again immaculate, a boyish fringe swept to one side, that smile of his even more mischievous as he gazed ahead.

She found it so hard to take her eyes off him, to explain to David who he was. Not that he was asking – he was staring at Edward too. In fact, she wouldn't be surprised if all heads had turned his way. There was something about him…

Tallula entered, almost a match for Edward in height, certainly as slim, and came to a halt beside him. Caroline frowned. Did they know each other? How come? Immediately she checked herself. So what if they did? Why be surprised about it?

The pair lingered, as if realising that they were objects of scrutiny and revelling in it, standing perfectly still, like works of art in a museum, existing solely to be admired.

It was Althea who broke the silence with a simple cough, effectively snapping Caroline out of the reverie she'd fallen into.

"David, that's Edward. I met him in the lobby earlier, he's a new arrival."

She'd whispered the words as if the information was confidential somehow, causing David to whisper back. "A new arrival? How'd he get through?"

"I don't know. I did ask, but he wouldn't say. Oh my goodness, he's coming over!"

And he was, Tallula by now hanging onto his arm, every now and then glancing at him with nothing less than adoration on her face. Caroline gulped. Was he going to join them? Did she mind? Maybe not him, but Tallula she wasn't sure about.

It wasn't their table he stopped at first, it was Elspeth's and Marilyn's. He exchanged a few words and a smile with them, Marilyn more forthcoming than Elspeth. Elspeth kept her head lowered, as if overcome with shyness. After them, it was John's turn. He looked uncomfortable that they should approach him, reaching for his glass of water and gulping as if somehow it fortified him. Like Elspeth, he answered whatever it was they were asking but kept his head lowered the entire time, his eyes, for the most part, elsewhere. Leaving him to it, they stopped at several other tables before finally reaching Caroline and David.

"Ah," Edward drawled, focussing entirely on Caroline. "We meet again."

Stooping slightly, he held out his hand. Hesitating for only a second, she held out hers too and he took it. The touch of his skin was like an electrical bolt, almost stopping her from breathing. He noticed, his smile becoming less mischievous and more seductive.

Taking it one step further, he lifted her hand to his mouth, and pressed his lips against it. "Sweet Caroline," he murmured, caressing each word, in turn making her wonder what it would be like to be caressed by him. He hadn't done this to any other female guest, just her – singling her out, favouring her. Immediately guilt set in that she should be enjoying such attention and she glanced sideways at David. Although his expression was neutral, his nostrils flared ever so slightly.

Swiftly Caroline withdrew her hand. What Edward had said – those words, that term of endearment – it was so familiar to her. And then she realised. "You know my name!"

"I made it my business to find out."

Beside her David rose to his feet. "*My* name's David. David Mason."

Caroline flinched. Was she imagining it or was there a hint of a challenge in David's introduction? The fact that he'd stood up reinforced that notion.

"Good evening, David, I'm—"

"Edward, yes I know."

David's neutrality had slipped. He was definitely on the defence, but why? Was he the jealous type and, if so, what was he jealous of? That Edward had kissed her hand? Irritation flared. She was *not* David's date. They were merely two people thrown together by circumstance. She wouldn't deny he was attractive, certainly his smile was – so different to Edward's – and his easy-going manner. In his company she'd laughed – a lot. His territorial streak, though, which seemed to have extended to include her, and so soon, was something that jarred rather than flattered.

The two men were shaking hands but once again a frisson had marred the otherwise easy ambience. Glancing at Tallula, Caroline noticed her eyes darting between Edward and David, as if she was expecting something – the frisson to develop into an uproar?

Having had enough of the situation, Caroline stood too and gestured to the two empty chairs beside them. "Why don't you join us?" It wasn't strictly what she wanted, but it was the polite thing to do and it might put an end to any more presumptions from David.

"We'd be—" Edward begun but his words died out as overhead the lights began to flicker, not just once or twice but several times, at one point plunging them into complete darkness, albeit for only a moment or two. The lights regaining their composure, Edward turned from Caroline and David and looked straight at Althea, whose gaze was just as cool. "Oh dear," he said, raising an eyebrow, "that big old storm's playing havoc."

Again, darkness descended, and Caroline gasped at the suddenness of it. Her hand sought David's, grateful when his fingers folded around hers without the slightest hesitation. There'd be light again soon, all they had to was wait…

Laughter broke the silence. Not only that but clapping, a manic clapping.

"What the hell?"

It was David, trying to work out who was responsible as frantically as she was.

Able to see again, she spotted Elspeth sitting beside

Marilyn, laughing and clapping, just as a child might, one that was watching a spectacular firework display, or a thrilling circus show. Any minute now, Caroline expected her to whoop and cheer.

Edward and Tallula started laughing too but not with Elspeth, *at* her.

"Oh, this is priceless, absolutely priceless," said Edward, addressing Tallula.

"The woman's mad," replied Tallula, her voice nothing less than scathing.

Incensed, it was Caroline who jumped to her feet, "Now hang on a minute," she began, intending to rein in their behaviour, but Elspeth again drew their attention.

"More, more, I want more!" she was shouting.

What was wrong with her? Why was she acting in such a bizarre manner? Deciding to ignore Edward and Tallula, Caroline hurried forward, only briefly noticing that David was keeping up with her. The closer she drew, the more obvious it was. Elspeth was drunk – her eyes rolling in her head, unable to focus. Had she spent all day drinking? She must have done to get into this state. Her skin, not only pale, was haggard – her age more evident. She had to be in her forties, this woman who was acting like a child.

"Elspeth?" Caroline said, but Marilyn shook her head. She was the one who wanted to calm her down again, to act the surrogate mother. Caroline looked at David for confirmation of what to do, he shook his head slightly, the answer clear: let it be, and then John caught her attention – his head bent, he was chewing furiously at his nails, tearing at them almost, his body rocking to and fro, a slight movement, but no less disturbing because of it. Did he need comforting too?

"Enough!"

The word, when it rang out, silenced them all. Even Edward and Tallula.

Caroline spun around. Who had shouted, and in such an authoritative manner? Was it Althea, that frail old lady, that *ancient* lady? It was. She was standing upright, short in stature and having to hold onto the table in front of her for support, but nonetheless impressive, a core of strength running through her that was steel-like. Caroline was awe-struck, so was David. Glancing at Edward, his face looked pinched, but angry too. There was definitely anger bubbling away beneath that flawless surface of his.

"Dinner is a sacred ritual at the Egress," Althea continued, "and it will be observed."

Although bemused by her words, Caroline understood what she was saying. Dinner *was* important; it gave structure to the day, a chance for guests to socialise, to refuel.

"Those who wish only to make a nuisance of themselves, please leave."

She was not addressing Elspeth, only Edward, who in turn was struggling to keep his face passive, doing his utmost to prevent not a smile but a grimace from twisting his features. By his side, Tallula had grown sulky, glancing again at Edward, nudging him, as though daring him to contest her. Caroline held her breath. Would he?

In the moments that followed she had to admit to being fascinated again. Did Althea and Edward know each other too? Certainly there seemed to be some kind of tension between them, one that had a depth to it, a history. It was simply too deep to be something only recently spawned. She didn't know Edward's age. As with Elspeth, she found it hard to guess at – he could be anywhere in his thirties or forties. That made him unlikely to be her son, more like a grandson or great nephew. Whatever he was, there was a bond between them, a *connection*, shared qualities, that same air of regality in particular, of ownership. That was it! They *owned* this place, if not on paper, in attitude.

"Edward, what are you going to do?" There was acid in Althea's voice as she posed the question.

"I'm going to dine, of course," Edward took his time to reply, a smile on his face that had no hope of reaching his eyes. "You wouldn't believe how hungry I am."

Grabbing hold of Tallula, they made their way to the table farthest from the old woman.

Chapter Ten

Despite what had happened at the start of dinner, the rest of the evening continued without incident. As soon as Althea had eaten, she left the ballroom, Caroline noticing Edward's eyes trained on her as she did so, although she bestowed on him not another glance. Even Elspeth had simmered down, if not behaving normally, at least there were no more outbursts. Caroline and David continued to talk, Caroline keeping the conversation carefully neutral. She liked him, very much, but she was leaving this hotel, this country, as soon as she was able to. There was no point in giving him the impression she was up for anything other than friendship. Certainly she was not in the market for a one-night stand. That wasn't her style. She checked herself. Perhaps it wasn't his style either. His earlier aggression towards Edward may have surprised her, but she could have jumped to the wrong conclusion about the source of it. It might have nothing to do with her at all.

"What are you thinking?"

David had leaned closer, genuine curiosity on his face.

"Oh nothing," she answered, perhaps a tad too quickly. But what else could she say? Certainly not the truth: *Oh, David, I was just thinking that perhaps you fancied me, that you wanted a tumble between the sheets. That earlier, when Edward kissed my hand, you started to act strangely. I thought perhaps you might be jealous of what he'd done.*

If those words came tumbling out she'd sound as immature as Elspeth!

At his table, John started to rise.

"John," Caroline called out, not just grateful for the distraction but remembering the agreement she'd made with David earlier, "would you like to join us for a coffee?"

John looked startled at the prospect, like the proverbial rabbit caught in the headlights. Any minute, she fancied, she'd see large beads of sweat breaking out on his forehead as sheer terror engulfed him. "Oh…no thanks. I'm very tired."

"Me too." David's manner was casual, an attempt to put John at ease perhaps. "But we'd really like it if you could join us, just for a little while."

John simply stared at them and then, when he did speak; it was not to give them an answer. "It's not going to get any better, you know that, don't you?"

"The weather, you mean?" Caroline checked. "I did catch the news earlier, and yeah, it does look as if it's going to be grim for a while. I'm from England, and I've never seen so much snow. But there'll be a break soon; life will get back to normal. It can't last forever."

"Normal?" John seemed to ponder that concept, his lips compressing into a thin white line. Having lowered his head, he raised it. "I'm sorry, I need to go to my room. I'm sorry," he apologised again, backing away from them, from everyone.

"Hey, it's okay," David called. "No pressure. Maybe next time."

After his departure David and Caroline had coffee together, David ordering a whiskey as well, although Caroline declined on that score. Across the way, Edward and Tallula had their hands up by their mouths and were whispering to each other. Marilyn and Elspeth were long gone, Marilyn having shepherded her charge from the room.

Despite continuing to enjoy David's company, some of Caroline's earlier spark had diminished. She was worrying about John. He seemed such a lost soul. One that was kindling a maternal instinct in her as much as Elspeth had for Marilyn.

A giggle escaped Tallula and again Caroline glanced over.

"They're quite the pair, aren't they?" David remarked.

"Hmm? Oh, yeah, they are. They seem well suited."

"To each other maybe but not to this place. I'd have thought the Egress was a bit too…downbeat for them."

Maybe, always supposing they'd *chosen* to come here and not had to because of the weather. Edward having a 'usual' room, however, suggested the former. Even so, Caroline had to agree, they did look out of place. They were more the kind of couple you'd expect to find swanning around a luxury resort in the Bahamas – a *dazzling* couple.

"Hard to take your eyes off 'em, isn't it?"

Caroline turned to David. "Sorry? What do you mean?"

He shrugged, gave her one of his smiles. "They seem to have caught your attention, that's all."

"My attention…" Her voice trailed off. "I still don't understand what you mean."

David leaned back in his chair. "You've been staring at them pretty much all night."

"All night?"

Again David shrugged.

"I haven't."

"I don't blame you. Like I said, they're quite the pair."

"Maybe they are, but you're wrong, I haven't been staring, not all night."

"It doesn't matter—"

"No, it does matter," she protested. "It's like…it's like you're…insinuating something."

"Insinuating?" A frown darkened his features. "I'm just making conversation."

"It's not a conversation I particularly like," she declared, unsure why she was getting so het up but unable to stop herself. It was as though she were on a fairground ride, one gaining momentum. "Earlier, when Edward introduced himself, you weren't exactly friendly."

"I was."

"You weren't."

His sigh was one of exasperation. "Caroline, you're imagining things."

"Imagining?" How dare he patronise her?

She stood up, her chair scraping backwards and the noise reverberating around the room as it tended to do. Why wasn't there any music being played, a room as cavernous as this should be filled with music. Sweet Caroline… Those were the words Edward had said whilst he'd kissed her hands, words that had set David off. No way she was imagining anything. "Do you know what, I'm tired too," she announced. "I'm going to my room."

David stood as well. "Look, Caroline, I'm sorry, I didn't mean anything by what I said. I wasn't implying anything. The last thing I want to do is upset you."

He reached out a hand, but she reared slightly to avoid it. "Who I choose to stare at or not, as the case may be, is my business, not yours."

"Caroline," David continued to plead as she turned on her heel and walked away, knowing without having to look at them that Edward and Tallula were staring at her too, the latest person in the ballroom to make a show of themselves. Well, let them. She didn't care. Soon she'd be in her room. She could shut the world out. She might have dreaded its solitude during the day, but now she yearned for it; it was so much easier to be alone.

* * *

"Hold the elevator please."

Just before the doors could close a hand thrust between them, its talon-like nails perfectly manicured. Not David then. Clearly he knew better than to try and appease her.

'*Such a temper you've got,*' her mother would say, '*you should have been a redhead.*'

Like Elspeth? Mad as well?

Caroline, stop it!

Damn him for not being the one prising the doors open, for it being Tallula instead.

"Sorry," the younger woman said, sidling in, "but hopefully you're in no big hurry."

"It's fine," replied Caroline, biting down on her lip.

"He's finishing his whiskey," she continued, "he'll be up soon."

"Who?"

"Who'd ya think?"

"I have no idea." She could be referring to either

Edward or David; Caroline didn't bother pressing her as to which one.

Tallula's lips formed a smirk. "What floor are you on?"

"The eleventh."

"Of course."

"What floor are you on?" Caroline enquired, genuinely intrigued.

"I'm on eleven too."

"I haven't seen you there."

"Nonetheless, that's where I am."

Finally the elevator started to ascend – sluggishly.

In such close confines with Tallula, Caroline could smell the perfume she was wearing, a smell she was sure some might think intoxicating – musky, earthy, with overtones of patchouli perhaps? She, however, would say it was suffocating, making her head hurt again. Edward had been so close to her at the dining table, how could he have borne it?

"You like him, don't you?"

Again Caroline was caught off guard. "I'm sorry, I really don't know—"

"Edward, you like Edward."

"Edward?" Not just her cheeks, her whole body flamed. She checked the visual display and noted with dismay that they were only at the second floor. *Come on, hurry up.* Unfortunately, the elevator refused to comply. "I don't know him. I'm sure he's very nice."

"I saw you staring."

Shit! David had been right; she'd been too obvious. And yet she was sure she hadn't stared *that* much. It was as if she were being victimised.

"I'm sorry if you thought I was staring, I—"

"You like David too." This time it was a statement, not a question. "But you're scared."

"Scared?"

"Yeah, you're terrified. You're not used to liking someone so much. And so what does someone like you do in that situation? You sabotage it."

Someone like her? What on earth did she mean by that? The temper that had surfaced at dinner – that she was supposed to have back under control – started bubbling away. "Look, I don't know who you are, or why you think you know so much about me, but—"

Tallula's laughter was as cold as her whole demeanour, as the weather that raged outside, effectively cutting Caroline off in mid-flow.

I have to get out of here. Not only did her head hurt, her nausea had returned. Edward might have borne being so close to this woman, but there was no way she could.

Hurry! Hurry! Again she urged the elevator ever upwards.

"Don't panic," Tallula said, still amused.

This woman was cruel, Caroline realised. The worst kind of bully. The kind who'd assassinate you with a smile.

"We're almost there," she continued.

They'd just limped past five.

"Almost," Tallula repeated, just as there was a loud thud. "Oh no, would you believe it, we're not almost there, after all."

Stunned, Caroline stared at the visual display – they'd stopped at six. Immediately she was suspicious. Had Tallula planned this? When she'd entered the elevator, she hadn't seen her press any buttons, but that didn't mean she hadn't. The woman was as sneaky as hell.

The elevator doors started to open, slowly, slowly, as if they were in on the prank too, colluding with this strange woman who stood as straight as an arrow, displaying the same confidence as Edward had earlier, confidence that bordered on arrogance.

Caroline almost threw herself at the number pad and, with one finger, jabbed at eleven. The doors didn't close, as she'd hoped. On the contrary, they opened fully.

"Christ!" she swore under her breath.

"Oh dear." Tallula sighed long and low. "What do we do now?"

"Take the stairs, of course," Caroline said, brushing past her. As their arms touched, she experienced the same jolt that she had with Edward, but this time it left her feeling tainted, longing for her room again, and for the hottest of showers. She really wasn't prone to disliking people, especially not on first sight without knowing a thing about them, but she couldn't deny it, she disliked this woman – *Princess Perfect, Ice-Cold Tallula* – intensely. Disliked also that Tallula thought she knew her when she didn't. Those comments about David, about her being afraid, were ludicrous. She'd had relationships in the past, plenty of them, and sure they'd ended in various ways, but not because she'd *sabotaged* them. She wasn't always the one to blame.

"Honey," the woman's hand was on her arm. "You need to breathe, just breathe."

"I... What?" Her mind had gone off on such a wild tangent, she felt precisely that, unable to breathe, her chest heaving up and down really quite painfully. "Sorry... I..."

"I know what the elevator's like," Tallula continued. "How temperamental it is. Just give it a minute and it'll…reset itself."

Ice-Cold Tallula had morphed into Kind, Caring Tallula – a persona that didn't suit her, not when her concern didn't reach her eyes, the truest of blues, with no warmth in them at all. "I know," she whispered, in a sudden change of mind, "let's explore."

"Explore?" Why on earth would she want to do that at this time of evening and with her, of all people? "I just want to go to my room. I'll take the stairs—"

"I wonder who's on this floor? Anyone exciting do you think?"

Breathing hard again, Caroline answered, "I don't know. I don't care."

"It's busy, though, isn't it?"

Caroline peered along the corridor; it was even gloomier than the second floor, full of shadows. "Not particularly."

"Oh, it is," said Tallula, her heels sinking into the red patterned carpet as she started to walk forwards. "You know it is."

God, she wished she'd stopped presuming that she knew what was going on in her head. But she mustn't react; she couldn't, not with a total stranger. *You and David aren't exactly life-long buddies and yet you laid into him quick enough.*

She had and – removed from the situation – she felt ashamed.

Tallula was speaking again. "Don't all these closed doors make you curious about who lurks behind them? There are so many people, aren't there? So many lives. All of us together and yet only a few stand out, make an impact, for good reasons, and for plenty of bad reasons too. Sometimes the bad reasons are the ones that stand out the most."

What was this? Now Tallula was getting philosophical on her? And yet…she did wonder, often, about people, their stories; the comedy, and the tragedy that everyone experienced, the highs and the lows. People *mattered* to her, her family primarily, her friends, her lovers. But there'd never been any lover who mattered above all the rest.

Tallula continued walking, one finger trailing against the wall. "Who lives in a room like this?" she asked, tapping lightly at 601, trailing her finger again, tapping at 602, her touch feather-light so as not to disturb the residents within, *if* there were any residents. She couldn't hear any signs of life despite Tallula insisting it was busy. Tallula was at room 605 when Caroline asked the question, mainly of herself, if she were honest.

"I wonder if this is the floor where the teenager and her family are?"

Tallula spun around to face her. "What teenager?"

"The one that was in the elevator the day I arrived. She's got long black hair, was wearing a yellow blouse and a plaid skirt. I didn't catch a glimpse of her face, but I got the impression she was sulking. I haven't seen her since, that's all, and it's not a particularly big hotel…"

Tallula's mouth was open. "You've seen the architect's daughter?"

Caroline frowned. "I don't know whose daughter she is, and like I said, I haven't seen her since, not at dinner, or in the lobby, but she must be here still. She can't have left."

"Oh, she hasn't left," Tallula all but sneered.

"Do you know her?" Caroline asked.

"I know *of* her. Poor cow."

"Hey, I'm not sure you should be calling a kid names!"

"I feel sorry for her, that's all."

Caroline couldn't help but be intrigued. "Why? Because of her parents?"

"Her parents? No. It's got nothing to do with her parents." She shook her head, seemed impressed almost. "I'm surprised you've seen her. Usually it takes longer."

She should have expected it: more riddles, more teasing. The girl was trying so hard to be enigmatic. Before Caroline could reply, however, Tallula was on the move again.

"Now this room," she was saying, tapping at the door opposite 605, "has a *very* interesting occupant."

Before she could reply, a voice startled them both.

"Why are you here?" At the end of the corridor, beside the door that led to the stairwell, stood Althea, no assistant with her, she was all alone, the contours of her face rigid with age rather than soft. When neither of them answered, she spoke again. "This isn't your floor."

Immediately, Caroline scrabbled for a reason to justify their presence. Gesturing behind her, she said, "The elevator got stuck."

Althea eyed her, her gaze burrowing. "You should go."

"Relax." It was Tallula, trying to appear as casual as ever but not quite managing to pull it off. "We're exploring. There's no law against it, not the last time I looked."

"Always looking for an argument, aren't you?" Althea replied.

Tallula blanched. "I'm not arguing, I'm—"

"You think you'd have learnt by now who *not* to pick an argument with."

"Look…" Tallula began but words seemed to fail her, she simply couldn't carry on.

Althea addressed Caroline. "These rooms are in the process of being renovated."

"I... I don't see any sign of it," Caroline ventured.

"That doesn't mean it's not happening."

"But—"

Tallula interrupted Caroline, stopping her from arguing too. "Better not upset the big boss woman. Her heart might give out, *if* she's got one, that is. Let's just go."

"Back to the eleventh floor?" Althea checked, unfazed by the insult.

Tallula nodded, as sullen as any teenager.

"Then I'll accompany you."

"But the elevator," Caroline tried again, "it's—"

"There is nothing wrong with the elevator," Althea insisted, heading towards them, reaching them much sooner than Caroline anticipated. Again, she was struck by her agility; she was as light as a ballerina, and certainly as graceful.

Falling in behind her, Caroline looked at Tallula, wondering if she might be pulling a face behind Althea's back, the kind of thing a scolded child might do, but she wasn't. She followed too, but her breathing was heavy still. She was angry. More than that: incensed. Why? Because Althea had interrupted whatever stupid game she'd been playing?

In the elevator, it was Althea who leant towards the keypad, jabbing at eleven.

Immediately the doors closed, as if they dared not disobey this powerhouse of a woman either. Such a hold she had over everyone, *everything*. Only Edward and Tallula so far had shown resentment because of it. As they travelled there was silence – barely even the sound of breathing anymore. All stood perfectly still, staring ahead. Tallula was the first to exit. Once they'd reached their destination, she couldn't wait to get away. Caroline kept an eye on which door she disappeared through. It was 1107, opposite her.

Stepping aside to let Althea exit next, Caroline followed behind, keeping a respectful distance. At 1106, she paused. So did Althea.

"It's not late," the old woman announced.

Caroline checked her watch. It was after eleven. "I know, but—"

"Join me for a nightcap."

Casting a longing glance at her room, she continued to follow Althea, all the way to the corner suite.

Chapter Eleven

When Caroline entered Althea's room, she gasped. Classier than Marilyn's room – no chintz to it at all – it was as though she'd travelled back in time, all the way to when the hotel was first built: the early 1920s. Recalling an interior shot from one of the photos in the lobby, it resembled that exactly – with everything brand new instead of nearly a hundred years old. Surfaces were dust free, shiny; the carpet beneath her feet still had a spring to it. At the windows, curtains were the same colour as hers – burgundy – no sun damage at all. Double doors sealed the bedroom from view, but the living room housed an elegant sofa with a curved back and two deep-seated armchairs, all of which framed an oval two-tiered coffee table. Beneath the window, in a similar position to hers, was a writing bureau, the flap open, and with various papers scattered on top. Ornaments included a bronze of a girl in a short dress, her arms outstretched, and a globe balanced in her hands, from which a soft glow emitted. Various artworks on the walls caught her eye too, including one she'd like to get a closer look at if she had the chance. Very much lived in, it was definitely more a home than a room for hire.

"Please, take a seat."

It wasn't Althea instructing her this time, another woman had stepped forward – Althea's assistant.

Althea introduced them. "This is my maid, Jenna."

Maid? Caroline worked hard to conceal her surprise. Althea really was stuck in the past. Who called their assistants maids nowadays?

Once seated, Jenna, a young woman of similar age to Caroline, highly courteous in her manner with plain but somehow appealing features, offered them a glass of sherry each.

As Caroline took hers, she smiled. "I haven't drunk sherry in years."

Althea's lips curved but only slightly. "I find it pleasurable to begin a meal with sherry and to end the night with a glass too. Creatures of habit, aren't we, in so many ways."

That phrase had crossed her mind earlier too, in the ballroom, when David had chosen to sit at the same table as the night before; John Cole too. David… she winced to think of him. As soon as she could, she'd apologise, resurrect their friendship, and not play the saboteur.

"Are you enjoying your stay here?"

Jenna, ever discreet, had melted away, leaving Caroline to ponder Althea's question.

"I didn't intend to stay here," she answered at last. "And now I'm stuck for a day or two, or at least until the roads are cleared. But yes, it's a very pleasant hotel, as one of the other guests said, it's more personal, not as generic, as *bland*, as so many hotels tend to be nowadays. How long have you…" she hesitated, "lived here?"

"Since the beginning," Althea replied, sipping at her sherry.

"Since the..." Again, Caroline's voice trailed off. The hotel opened its doors to the public a long time ago – ninety-four years to be exact. Althea was old, but *that* old? If she'd been born here, it was nothing less than incredible. Glancing over the top of her glass, she noted the woman's face was heavily powdered, a glint of light in her eyes – dark brown originally perhaps, now more sepia in colour – her white hair carefully styled but wispy in places. If she were born here, perhaps it was to a maid, or a housekeeper, who'd lived in too.

"You seem curious," Althea remarked.

"Oh no, not at all, I'm just...taking in my surroundings. This room is wonderful. You must have seen a lot of people come and go during the years."

"I have."

"I can't imagine what it's like, to live in a hotel."

Her smile vanished. "Not as easy as you might think. But we make do."

We? Did she mean Jenna and her?

"Have you never wanted to move somewhere more private?" Despite fearing she was being too inquisitive, Caroline couldn't seem to stop asking questions. Althea fascinated her, perhaps as much as Edward had.

"I will, when the time is right."

At her age, the time might never be right, not anymore. Fearful her expression might convey her thoughts, Caroline turned her attention to the artwork, to the picture that had intrigued her earlier. Pointing to it, she said, "Can I take a closer look?"

"Go ahead."

Rising from her chair, she crossed over to it. It was chillier around the edges of the room, causing her to shiver a little as she leaned forward to get a good look at what was in front of her: an artist's rendition of the Egress, a pen and ink drawing that had been printed onto paper, another promotional piece. Accompanying it was what looked to be an extract from a newspaper article. Wishing the room was lighter, she began to read it: *A New Hotel for Williamsfield! Grand but accessible, formal but friendly, it is somewhere to celebrate every type of occasion; a social center, a gathering place. From diplomats to downtown workers, all are welcome!* Below that was another extract, perhaps from a different article. *Experience the sheer luxury of this new hotel spanning eleven floors. Every one of our 100 rooms is as unique and as special as you are.* A final piece of text read: *A place to rest, to relax, and to make memories. Every day is special at* the *Egress.*

Having digested all this information, one thing stood out – the pride that had been taken in the planning and construction of this building. There'd been a lot of love, a lot of hope behind it; the word 'special' repeated on the page and repeating in her mind also.

"It's such a special place."

Althea's voice made her jump – so did the realisation that the woman was standing behind her, not seated at all.

Caroline turned to face her. "My mother and father stayed here once," she explained. "They spent their honeymoon here. My mother's from Williamsfield originally, you see, although she moved to England to live there with my English father, and that's where I live, where I was brought up. She always talked about the Egress fondly; she insisted it was special too. They were caught in a snowstorm, just like I've been; they holed up here, on the second floor, in the corner suite, a room like yours. That's why I came here. I wanted to get a look at the hotel they'd talked about, to connect with them again, their memory. It may sound silly, but it's what I wanted. They're dead now, both my parents. My mother died only last year. Cancer. It was cancer that killed them both."

It was only when she stopped speaking, babbling even, that Caroline realised she was crying. Just like the words that had burst from her, so had the tears, as if she'd held onto them for too long and finally the dam had burst. "I'm sorry," she spluttered, horrified at her behaviour, for bringing her sorrow to this woman's door. "I'm really very sorry."

There was only concern on Althea's face. "That's it, let it out. It's not good to keep emotions trapped. Certain things must be faced."

Faced? Was she referring to her grief? But it was so hard to give it free reign. There was always the fear it might overwhelm her.

"Face up to your fears too. You might not find them as bad as you think."

Caroline started. Had the woman just read her mind? *Get a grip, Caroline!* Of course she hadn't, she was simply reacting to the state she was in – the *obvious* state. "Do you have a tissue?" Her voice was tremulous as she asked.

Jenna drifted forward as silently as Althea tended to do. In her hand was a lacy handkerchief – 'A' embroidered into the corner in a fancy gold script.

"Oh no, I don't want to ruin it. I meant a paper tissue. Toilet roll will do."

"Take it," Althea said, relieving Jenna of it and handing it to Caroline herself. "I insist."

Caroline obeyed; it was hard not to where Althea was

concerned. As she wiped at her tears and blew her nose, she studied Althea again. This was no daughter of a maid or a housekeeper, she realised. This was a woman born into a far more privileged family than that; a woman whose status was inbred, who carried her superiority in a genteel but thorough manner. Perhaps she was the daughter of the owner of the Egress and therefore instrumental in drafting that welcome note left on her pillow?

"Did you write it?" she asked.

"Write what?"

"The welcome letter."

"You like it?"

"Very much," Caroline replied, "and the idea that we're all on a journey."

"We are, even those like me who settle."

"Does it ever end?"

"The journey?"

Caroline nodded.

"Would you like it to?"

"No, I don't mean that, I'm just wondering, that's all."

"Caroline…"

"Sorry, I have to go back to my room. Do you mind? It's been another long day."

At once Althea stood aside.

Handing the sherry glass back to Jenna, Caroline thanked her. "It was lovely."

"The handkerchief," Jenna said.

"Oh, but—"

"Please."

Embarrassed, Caroline handed that over too. It wasn't until she was at the door that Althea spoke again.

"So your parents spent their honeymoon here?"

Caroline only half-turned. "They were supposed to go to the Pocono Mountains, but the weather…"

"Ah yes, the weather, of course. How old are you, Caroline?"

It was the second time she'd been asked that today. "Thirty-three."

"It was the 1983 storm that trapped them?"

Caroline nodded.

"When did you turn thirty-three?"

"Only just, at the beginning of this month."

"Which means you could have been conceived here?"

"My mother said something on her deathbed—"

"But you suspected it anyway."

"Yes, I've always suspected it."

"Interesting."

Caroline reached for the door handle.

"Goodnight," she said, leaving before another word could be exchanged.

Chapter Twelve

Who is it? Who's there?

There was someone in the room again, pushing against that invisible barrier, trying to reach out. Not just someone, a whole army of people, if they could be described as people. Mere shapes, no substance to them at all, but their emotions were real enough: raw and hard hitting, causing Caroline to turn her head away, to screw her eyes shut.

Hiding again, Caroline?

She drew a sharp breath. Who'd said that? One of the tormented? Because that's what they were, these strange, terrible invaders – every last one of them. Or was it her thought manifesting, just as those in the room were trying to do?

She had to see; she couldn't continue hiding. Face up to her fears, as Althea had said. Only then might they subside. When she opened her eyes, she gasped. She was no longer in her room, in bed, beneath the sheets. She was in the corridor and David was too, a few feet in front – not dressed in black this time, he was all in white. Staring at something to the left of him, he didn't seem to notice her. Should she speak, attract his attention, or seize her chance, and walk away? Hide again.

No, she mustn't.

David, it's me. I'm right in front of you.

He continued to stare, but at something other than her.

David!

Gradually, he turned his head, she braced herself, but he looked right through her, turned to the right instead, to stare at something there.

What is it? What can you see?

There was something about him that was so vulnerable, that easy grin of his wiped away, as though it had never existed.

What should she do, reach out, and comfort him?

Commit to him?

She shook her head.

This wasn't about commitment; it was about being a friend.

That's right, Caroline, kid yourself further.

I'm not, I'm—

You're so deluded, so afraid.

Who are you?

She was arguing, but she couldn't see who with.

What are you frightened of? That you'll get hurt? Of course you'll get hurt! Everyone does. It's part of the game. Might as well play it.

Rather than reach out, she copied David, turning her head from side to side, the walls of the corridor closing in on them, the tunnel ever narrowing.

And then further movement caught her eye.

Edward and Tallula were striding towards her, their legs so long, almost spiderlike, able to cover large distances, able to see her when David couldn't. Where was he?

Where had he gone? In the moment that the other two had captured her attention, he'd disappeared.

Having replaced David, Edward gave her no choice; he grabbed her hand and brought it up to his lips once more, the feel of them as soft as velvet, lingering there. As he did so, Tallula glanced from one to the other, adoration for him, and savage dislike for Caroline.

But he's kissing me. I'm not kissing him!

Which only made Tallula hate her more.

Where the hell was David? And Althea, where was she? Would she see what Edward was doing, Tallula too, and intervene? Would she save her?

Why don't you let me be the one to save you?

Something in Edward's words made her skin crawl. She didn't want him to save her, to touch her even, not again. Did she?

Mesmerising. There is something just so mesmerising…

The green of his eyes matched her own, his gaze as penetrating as Althea's, more so. Able to worm its way inside her, grow claws, digging deeper and deeper.

My, he said, as if he'd found something. *My, oh my, oh my.*

What is it, Edward? What's there?

His expression changed. He looked stricken all of a sudden, or at least he was pretending to be.

Interesting, he murmured, echoing Althea.

Hearing that, she started to back away.

But, Caroline, I thought you wanted to know?

No, no, I don't, not anymore.

Tallula grinned, or was it grimaced? *She knows already.*

Liar! Caroline shot back at her. *I don't know anything. I don't!*

118

Really, Caroline, you must stop hiding. Edward seemed so disapproving.

Hiding from what?

The truth. It seems you're diseased too.

Diseased? Her mouth fell open. *You bastard! You vicious, vicious bastard!*

From stricken to crestfallen, he almost pouted. *I can't help it if the truth hurts.*

She'll start crying in a minute, Tallula taunted. *Cry baby, cry baby, yeah, baby, cry!*

Who were these people? What were they?

This hotel, she had to get out. It wasn't special at all.

Which way should she go? Towards the elevator or the stairwell? Which was safest?

Opting for the stairwell, she broke into a run.

But David's the other way, Edward called.

David?

Forgotten about him already?

She shook her head. Of course she hadn't.

Some girlfriend you are.

I'm not his girlfriend.

Leave him to die then.

What was that? He was going to die as well?

Coming to a standstill, she sunk to her knees, the weight of grief so terrible.

No, she screamed, the tears that Tallula had predicted starting to fall.

She wouldn't – *couldn't* – bear such agony again.

No! No! No! No! No!

* * *

Sitting up in bed, the darkness surrounding her, Caroline

brought her hands up to her ears to drown out the screams that still reverberated around her head.

"Oh Christ, another bad dream."

She was awake now, though, definitely awake. So why wasn't it fading? She wanted it to fade!

Reaching out, she switched the bedside light on – shadows! Her room was filled with them. But that's all they were, no figures of any kind, with their hands up in front of them, their faces turned to the side, trying to break free. Even so, her nerves were still jangled.

There were other noises, she realised; the night not as quiet as it should be. A door opening and closing, footsteps too, their pace urgent.

The screaming – it wasn't just an overhang from her dream. Someone was actually screaming! Right here. Right now. On the eleventh floor.

Jumping out of bed, Caroline grabbed the clothes she'd discarded earlier, and tugged them on. Not bothering with her boots, she headed for the door, pulling it open to stand in the corridor. The commotion was coming from one of the rooms closest to the elevator, Marilyn, or Elspeth's? The door to 1107 was ajar too – Tallula's room. Further along, where the corner suite was, she thought she heard a click as if the door had been shut rather than opened. If Althea and Jenna had decided not to investigate on this occasion, she didn't blame them. They could be dialling down to reception for back up.

Having tried to understand the situation, she padded towards the elevator, whose doors remained open. Why was that? Had they got stuck or something? The screaming had stopped – thankfully – but she could hear the low murmur of voices, both male and female, sometimes urgent, sometimes soothing. They were coming from Elspeth's room.

She stopped and had to take a breath. This was as surreal as any dream.

The dream… Being in the corridor reminded her of it. *It seems you're diseased too.* Vividly she recalled Edward's face as he uttered such vile words, the glee that he hadn't tried too hard to hide. Was he referring to the illness that had killed both her parents? Why would saying that please him? And David, how vulnerable he'd been, he'd fallen, and so had she, onto her knees, screaming.

David?

His was the male voice, causing her to move again, to pick up pace. Within seconds she was at the entrance to Elspeth's room, staring in. She'd never seen such a mess. Food wrappers, cups, and saucers were strewn everywhere, as well as clothing, towels and make-up. A lamp had been knocked over, and lay on its side, the bulb spluttering. In the midst of such carnage was Elspeth, sitting on the floor hugging her knees, her hair wild, and her face dirty with tear tracks. In her hand she was holding something which looked like a photograph. In amongst the debris, Caroline spotted several other photographs, some of them torn, others whole but crumpled. What they depicted she didn't know; she wasn't close enough to see. Either side of Elspeth knelt David and Marilyn. As she was observing, so was Tallula, leaning against the far wall, a pinkish silk nightdress clinging to her slim frame in a manner entirely inappropriate to the situation. The expression on her face was also ill fitting, there seemed to be delight in it. Unable to believe that was the case, Caroline blinked and checked again. There was no delight. There was nothing. It was as if she'd realised she'd been caught and switched to neutral.

Caroline drew a little closer. "David, what's happening? Is she okay?"

At the sound of her voice, he lifted his head.

"Caroline, hi." His whole manner was subdued. "She's calmer now." Turning his attention swiftly back to Elspeth, he added, "How about we get you up, sit you on the sofa?"

Elspeth's hand immediately shot out and grabbed his arm. "Don't leave me!"

"I'm not leaving you, honey," David assured her. "I'm staying right by your side. Marilyn, should we try and lift her?"

Marilyn readily obliged, working with David to practically carry Elspeth to the sofa, that photo clutched in her hand all the while. Their actions, *his* actions, were so tender, so gentle, that for a moment Caroline felt like crying. *Cry baby, cry baby!* It was another echo from the dream, Tallula taunting her. It was a good job the younger woman didn't catch the look Caroline threw at her this time as there was such venom in it. What was she even doing here? It wasn't as if she was trying to help.

She came to see what the commotion was, just like you did, Caroline. And she did NOT call you a cry baby. It was a dream, only a dream.

Something she needed to get her head around.

"Shall I fetch a glass of water for Elspeth?" she asked.

It was Marilyn who answered. "Not yet, just. Give us a minute."

The three of them huddled on the sofa looked as intimate as lovers. Marilyn was clasping the woman close, whilst David ran a hand up and down her back, another soothing gesture she knew, but one that caused a pang within her. Both continued to talk to Elspeth, words that were incomprehensible unless you crept a little closer – *intruded.*

That's what she felt like, an intruder, as much a voyeur as Tallula.

If there was nothing she could do, if she wasn't wanted, she might as well return to her room, although a dream-filled sleep didn't exactly appeal to her right now.

"David, you know where I am if you need me."

This time there was no answer, causing that pang to sharpen. Would Tallula do the decent thing and leave with her? She showed no sign of doing so and, on a purely selfish note, Caroline was grateful. Hardly enamoured of her before, the dream had sealed that dislike, symbolising perhaps a deep-seated distrust, an instinct she wouldn't ignore.

Back in the corridor, she lingered, unsure of the reason why. Perhaps she wanted David to come after her, explain the situation, put her mind at rest regarding Elspeth.

You want his attention, don't you, all of it?

She shook her head. Thoughts could be so traitorous sometimes, revealing facets of your personality you didn't always like. But she needn't be at their mercy. She could quash them – God knows, she'd done that enough in the past. There was good and bad in everyone, you had to choose which side you gave dominance to.

Oh, Caroline, stop playing the analyst. Go back to bed!

David wasn't coming after her and nor did she want him too. If he did, if he put her wants above Elspeth's needs, he wouldn't be the man she thought him to be. That poor woman, whatever her problem was, needed both him and Marilyn by her side.

Turning in the direction of her room, she heard another noise, a more mechanical one. She turned back towards the elevator. No longer stuck, the doors were closing. Perhaps someone from another floor had called it, or perhaps not. It pleased itself that elevator. But before they closed fully, she caught a glimpse of movement, someone inside.

Squinting, she took a step forward so that she could see better, but it was too late. The doors shut her out. All that had registered was a tall figure, slim with a flash of blonde hair.

Edward.

Chapter Thirteen

"Sorry, this is a terrible line, I'm near Williamsfield, in the state of Pennsylvania. I don't know what it's like where you are, probably dreadful too, but we're in the grip of a severe snowstorm. It's been three days now…"

"Hello… Hello… Could you speak up a bit?"

Sighing, Caroline moved to another area of the lobby, hoping the signal might improve.

"I might need to change my flight home from Boston to London in a few days' time. I'm just checking that that's okay, how much it might cost, that sort of thing."

"The Internet… If you go to our site…"

The Internet. Yeah, right. A great idea if she could log onto it. Even when she'd checked at reception about Internet connection after her first night here, Raquel had just shrugged, said she was having the same problem and to persevere, that at the Egress it dipped in and out. Often Caroline had wondered what it would be like to live life without being plugged in 24/7. She was sure as hell gaining an insight now.

Ending the call, she said thank you, regardless of whether she could be heard or not.

Walking further, she stopped by one of the picture windows, and with her free hand, pushed the net aside. It wasn't snowing at the moment, but the skies were still threatening and outside it lay deeper than ever, no sign of road clearance. Maybe it was different in town and city centres, but this highway was clearly not a priority on anybody's list. On the TV that morning, the news had once again compared the storm to the one that occurred in the 1950s, which had killed a staggering 353 people, and injured 160 others as it swept across twenty-two states. Drawing on the gravity of that, there'd been warnings, yet again, to stay indoors, to stay safe, and for neighbours to look out for each other, to pull together. *There is still significant snowfall to come today but we expect to see a break in it during the days that follow. Emergency services are overwhelmed and so give them a helping hand. If you don't have to travel, don't. It really is as simple as that. Sit tight and stay warm. If you're in need of assistance there are emergency numbers you can call, you can find these at the bottom of the screen or go to www.national...'*

At that point, Caroline had switched the TV off, fed up of listening to people phoning in about how the snow was affecting them or hitching a virtual ride beside the pilot of a helicopter who was busy taking aerial shots of Pennsylvania, the state that seemed to have borne the brunt of such freakish weather. If only she'd stayed at Violet's instead of pressing on. Thinking of her, she checked again for a return message. Again, there was nothing. Violet wouldn't just ignore her, though, or her plight. As she'd resolved to do, she tried calling her. The line just rang and rang. She'd end up writing to her at this rate, once she was safely ensconced at home, telling her all about her 'adventure'.

David had entered the lobby. Not alone, he was talking

to someone, although who it was, she wasn't sure, David was partially blocking her view. As soon as their conversation was done, she hurried over, praying he'd accept the apology she intended to deliver.

"David," she called.

"Oh, Caroline, how you doing?" His voice was as weary as he looked, stubble on his chin where he hadn't had the time or the inclination to shave.

"I'm fine. How's Elspeth?" she asked.

"She's okay."

"And you?"

"I'm okay too."

"I'm sorry I didn't stay last night. I didn't get the impression I was…"

"Needed?" He finished her sentence when her voice trailed off. "It was difficult."

"Did Tallula stay?"

"Tallula? I don't know when she left. It was mainly just Marilyn and me, we sat with Elspeth until the early hours, waiting for the high to pass."

"The high? Oh." She glanced around to check no one was in the near vicinity, and then, keeping her voice low, she whispered, "Drugs?"

David nodded. "A whole heap of 'em."

"Poor Elspeth," Caroline commented.

"Poor Elspeth," David echoed.

"She had a photo in her hand…"

"That's right, she wouldn't let it go."

"Who was in it?"

"Just her," David informed her, "when she was a child. There were several photos actually, all from her childhood."

"What's the significance, do you know?"

"No. I did ask, so did Marilyn, but she really wasn't making any sense. She kept babbling, saying she'd changed her mind, that she didn't like it here, not anymore."

"So she's been to the Egress before?"

"Like I said, Caroline, I don't know."

"Where's she now?"

"She went with Marilyn to her room. She's still there probably. I'll go check later."

There was a period of silence between them – an awkwardness that hadn't been there before dinner last night, when he'd accused her of staring at Edward. Immediately, she corrected herself. He hadn't accused her; he'd simply mentioned it. She'd done the rest, letting her imagination get the better of her, which seemed to be par for the course lately.

"I'm sorry about last night."

"Last night?" For a moment he looked confused.

"At dinner."

"Oh, right, yeah. There's no need."

"But I am, I'm—"

"I'm sorry too. I really didn't mean—"

"I know you didn't."

"Hey," he declared, "our first row!"

"Our first…? Hopefully our last too."

A familiar grin developed. "That'll depend on how long we're here for."

"It can't be long now. They're forecasting a break in the weather soon. Um…talking of Edward—"

How quickly that grin faded. "We weren't."

Technically he was right, but they had been alluding to him. "It's just he was on the eleventh floor too last night."

"Was he?"

"When I came out of my room to investigate what was going on, the elevator doors were wide open, as if they'd got stuck or something. When I went back, they'd sprung into life again, but there was someone inside, and I think it was him."

"Visiting Tallula, perhaps?"

"Yeah, she's in 1107, so that must be why. Although he must have left later than Tallula, she'd already hitched up a ride with me."

"He did, about half an hour later. Like me, he ordered a whiskey nightcap."

"Did you drink it together?" she asked, surprised.

"No," David looked vaguely disgusted at the notion. "He wandered over to my table with his glass, but sideswerved at the last minute."

Teasing him, Caroline couldn't help thinking, just as she'd been teased in the dream.

Something else bugged her. "How come *you* were on the eleventh floor, David?"

"Because of the elevator," he said with no hesitation at all. "I got in, I was sure I pressed two, but it shot me all the way to eleven, and damn fast too. That elevator can sure fly when it wants to. The doors opened and I heard screaming. For a moment I thought it was…" His voice trailed off as he looked at her intently. "And then Marilyn appeared, said it was coming from Elspeth's room and to follow her. The door was locked but one good shove and it gave way, that's when we found her, sitting in the middle of her room, screaming and crying, that photo in her hands."

"If only there was a doctor in the house," Caroline

lamented.

"Or a psychiatrist."

Hope flared. "Perhaps there is!"

David shook his head. "Sorry, Caroline, I've already checked. There isn't."

"She must have a psychiatrist of her own, though, a contact number?"

"If she has, she's not saying. Look, don't worry too much. Marilyn's doing a pretty good job of looking after her."

"Sure, but what about afterwards, what happens to her then?"

"When we get out of here?"

Caroline nodded.

"We'll cross that bridge when we come to it."

He was right, under the circumstances they'd simply have to make do. Changing the subject, she asked David if he'd like to join her for coffee. She'd already had breakfast in a ballroom that was largely empty, only John in situ and he'd sat there alone too, staring at his bacon and eggs, barely touching them, but downing glass after glass of water.

To her surprise David declined. "Maybe later, I've got a few things to do."

"Oh?" She couldn't help but enquire. What was so urgent?

"Work," he answered. "Some calls to make."

"Oh, right. Good luck with that." She genuinely meant it. "I've just been onto the airport, enquiring about changing my flight if it comes to it. The line was terrible."

"What about going online?"

"The Wi-Fi's terrible too."

"Really? I've used it a couple times."

She was surprised. "Who's your provider?"

"AT&T."

"I'm with them too. My provider switches over automatically, but no joy."

"If you want to borrow my cell," he offered, "you're more than welcome."

"Thanks. I might take you up on that."

"Anytime."

"See you at dinner?" She couldn't disguise the hope in her voice.

"Yeah, why not? A man's gotta eat."

She smiled. "Look after yourself until then."

"You too, Caroline."

Neither of them made a move to turn, not initially, her feet rooted to the spot, as his seemed to be. His eyes, they held so much depth, she was sure she could drown in them. What would that be like, to totally submerge yourself in another person, to just let go?

"See you." He was the first to break the spell. She almost resented him for it.

"Sure," came her somewhat strangled reply.

As he made his way to the elevator, she retraced her footsteps, back into the lobby, staring somewhat aimlessly about her. Where could she go? What could she do? How could she pass so much time?

John emerged from the ballroom and entered the lobby too. Briefly hesitating, he walked over to the piano before coming to a standstill.

Figuring she had nothing to lose, Caroline headed over too.

"Do you play?" she asked, drawing closer.

John, who'd been staring at the piano, clearly hadn't noticed her approach if his reaction was anything to go by. "Oh," he said, his body jerking. "What do you mean?"

"The piano, do you play it?"

"No, no, of course not. Why would I?"

"You were staring at it, I just wondered…" For a moment Caroline regretted her decision. Was this going to be hard work, chatting to John? Maybe he wouldn't *allow* her to chat to him, he'd cut her dead at every opportunity. She'd give it one more try.

"I had piano lessons when I was young, I was hopeless, though. Don't think I've got a musical bone in my body; even the recorder was beyond me. My brother, Ethan, he's good. He was a guitarist in a band for a long time. He doesn't play anymore. Nowadays he lives in Canada, with his wife and two children. He loves it there, the great outdoors."

"Do you have children?" For once John was making eye contact.

"No. No, I don't." After a brief hesitation, she asked, "Do you?"

"Such gifts they are, a blessing. Everyone should have kids."

"John," Caroline's voice was gentle as she said his name, "would you like to have coffee with me? I can ask Raquel if one of the waiters might bring it here."

"Coffee?" Again, he appeared confused, not the drug-addled confusion of Elspeth, but by something much deeper, much bigger even. "I… I…"

"Let's face it, John, there's not much else to do around here. Why don't we sit for a while and have a cup of coffee together? At least it'll help to pass a bit of time."

Staring at the piano again, John contemplated her words. At least she hoped he was.

Once again silence hung in the air, his agitation wrapped up in it, and hers too – she wanted to know more about this enigma standing before her, but not in the same way she wanted to know about David, about Marilyn, Elspeth, even Edward and Tallula. There was something about John. He'd suffered – was suffering still. She wanted to reach out and hug him, tell him that it would be alright. Hard to do when she had no idea what was wrong.

Be careful not to patronise him, Caroline.

She heeded her own warning. If he started to talk, she'd listen. That's all some people wanted, someone to hear them out.

"John?" she prompted again.

"I'll take a drink with you," he conceded, "but no coffee, just a glass of water for me."

* * *

It turned out that John was from the Deep South, near Memphis in fact, a town called Millington; his accent not initially giving that away, it was gentle, rather than defined.

"You're a long way from home," Caroline said, in between thanking the waiter for bringing them a cafetière and a large jug of water and pouring for them both respectively.

"Home does seem a long way," he replied, so often staring into the distance or down at the glass he held in his hands. "I miss it."

It wasn't a case of simply listening to John as she'd previously resolved to do; it was a case of working hard to get him to say anything at all. Caroline persevered because of the feeling she had inside – that whatever he was hiding was causing him great distress.

"Never been to the South before, but it's on my list of places to see. My mum was an Elvis fan you see, so was Dad come to think of it, his records were played a lot in our house when we were growing up. I'd love to go to Memphis, visit Graceland, Sun Records, you know, places like that, but I'd also like to see Nashville, the Carolinas, and Tennessee too. You read about Southern hospitality, is it all it's cracked up to be?"

Her words teased a smile from John. "It sure is, ma'am, there's nothing else like it."

"You were talking about kids earlier, you got any?"

Even as he answered the smile left him. "Two. A boy and a girl."

A glance at his left hand also told her he was married.

"I miss 'em," he continued, this time unprompted.

"Are you travelling for work?"

He took a sip of water. "No."

If it was for leisure, he looked far from relaxed. She had to do something to get him properly conversing, this man who seemed beaten by life. "Tell me about the South."

"The South? It's…hot, for a start."

She laughed. "I'll bet it is."

"Even at this time of the year it's pleasant outside, no snow or nothing. Nothing like this. Maybe an inch or two on occasion, but it's rare."

"But in the summer, John?"

"In the summer it's sweltering. I don't mind, though, I love the heat, *Southern* heat that is – it's like a lover, wrapping its arms around you and holding you close. And if you need cooling down, frozen lemonade does the job real good. My wife makes sure to keep a batch in the fridge. We can never get enough of it." At the mention of his wife, he faltered slightly, but then continued. "Southern hospitality you know about, but what you might not know is that most people who are born and bred there don't have much, not by your standards, anyway, but they'd give you the shirt off their back if you needed it. They're a generous people, people with heart and soul. That's where America's soul is, you see, in the South. The further you travel from it, the less soul there is."

"You sure are selling it to me," Caroline replied, as wistful as him suddenly.

"The sound of the cicadas, the music in the air; there's a rhythm that runs right through the landscape. Anyone can pick up on it. You don't have to be a Southerner; you just have to listen hard enough. And the countryside, it shimmers, like a mirage or something. Of course, it's the heat that makes it do that, but it doesn't matter, it's still magical; stops you in your tracks wherever you are, takes your breath away. You know the best thing to do? Find a dirt track, a stretch of river, just your honey and you, take a radio with you, and turn it up full blast. That's what we used to do. And when the sun's gone, the stars come out instead. But believe me, that's no reason to get upset. They shine just as bright."

Caroline's coffee cup was empty, so was John's glass of water, but she didn't want to alert him to this fact in case it stopped him talking. She held onto it instead, grateful that he needed very little prompting now, loving the sheer poetry of his words, the passion for the place he'd grown up in, wishing she felt even a quarter of that for her hometown.

"I got married real young. I was nineteen, Ellie was eighteen, but we didn't have kids right away, we worked hard first, wanted to provide for them, give them the best."

"What did you work as?"

"I was in construction, Ellie was a schoolteacher, good jobs, good money coming in. And then the children came along, the greatest blessing of all."

"How old are your children now?"

"Ben is ten and Maddie is twelve. Both got a mop of shiny blonde curls, just like their mother, and the bluest eyes you ever did see, like a cloudless sky on a summer's day."

There he went again, getting poetic, it was clear he loved his family very much too.

She had to ask. "John, why are you here?"

"Here?" For a moment he didn't seem to know where 'here' was.

"At the Egress?"

He lowered his head, began shaking again.

Mentally Caroline kicked herself. *I shouldn't have asked.*

"John—"

"My daddy, I hated him."

Caroline stared, unsure as to whether she'd heard correctly. "You hated your father?"

"He was no good, a drunk, and a mean drunk at that. I was glad when he ran out on us."

All poetry, all wistfulness was gone.

"But my mamma, she cried. Oh how she cried when he left, despite what he used to do to her. She was scared you see, of something bigger: how she was going to make ends meet with three kids to look after. She did find work eventually, she had to, but it broke her heart to be out of the house for so long, from early morning 'til dusk, and my two younger brothers running wild because of it. I tried to help, but I was young too. One of my brothers, Arley, got into trouble with the law, bad trouble. And if her heart wasn't broken before, it was then. And all because my daddy left, because he got in his car one night and he kept on driving, all the way to hell, I hope."

"Oh, John, I'm so sorry." It wasn't just his words that had shocked her; it was the pain with which they were delivered. She winced as he lifted his hand and chewed at nails that were already stumps.

"Mamma didn't last long after Arley got sent away. She was a proud woman, you see, Southerners are, and the shame of all that had happened...it finished her. No matter that no one judged her, that the people who mattered understood, tried to help her even. But pride stopped her from accepting that help. With Mamma gone, I had to find a way to help myself. I found myself a girl, my Ellie, had a family, and I swore I'd look after them, that I would *always* look after them. That I'd be twice the man my daddy was."

"It sounds as if you are, Jo—"

Again John interrupted. "I'm not travelling for business or for leisure. I've left the South."

"You've left?" Caroline asked, stunned by this revelation. "But why?"

John's back straightened, almost in defiance, his hands lowered now but clasped together, his knuckles turning white. Eyeing Caroline once more, he opened his mouth to answer. "Because I'm not like my daddy, that's why. I'm a whole lot worse."

Chapter Fourteen

Even though Caroline asked him to stay, John refused.

"I'm going to my room," he said. "I have to."

Still he was shaking, and his tongue kept darting out of his mouth as if to lick at dry lips.

"I'll see you at dinner, perhaps," Caroline called after him, but he didn't turn, didn't reply.

She glanced at her watch. It was barely noon.

In the time remaining, she wondered if she should go outside again, breathe some fresh air. The snow was still deep, the sky still threatening, and the landscape more of a wasteland than ever, bleak as opposed to pretty, nothing enticing about it at all. She decided against it. Where was the fun of it, without David?

Rising to her feet, Caroline sighed. She could understand Raquel's boredom. If she worked full time in this place she was more trapped than any of them, having to report for duty in all weathers. Where were all the guests? The lobby was bereft again, of everyone but them, people opting to lock themselves in their rooms rather than linger in open spaces.

She had to do something to pass the time.

Explore. That's what she'd do. Avoiding the elevator, she headed towards the stairwell instead, which was located directly opposite it – hiding behind a set of double doors. Pushing them open, she encountered concrete treads edged with yellow safety stripes, its steel bannister plain rather than ornate. Purely functional, guests were clearly meant to avoid it, which wouldn't be a problem if the elevator worked like it should. Before ascending, she looked downwards. The stairs to the basement were shrouded in darkness, an abyss; home to nothing but storerooms, electrics, and cobwebs she'd bet. There was a 'Staff Only' sign attached to the concrete overhang. They were welcome to it, she decided.

Taking a deep breath, she started to climb, reaching the second floor and lingering outside 210. Should she ask Raquel if anyone was staying in it or if it was simply being renovated? If the latter, perhaps she could go inside and take a look. *Leave it, Caroline. Imagine how the room looks instead.* She pondered that advice, and in the end agreed with it. If it was occupied, she didn't want to see someone else's belongings in place of her parents', and if it had been renovated, then it would be a different room entirely. In the realms of imagination it was perennially warm and cosy, with her mother's dresses hanging in the wardrobe, her father's shoes neatly stowed there too, a packet of Lucky Strikes on the writing desk, and in the bathroom, so many of the lotions and potions that her mother loved. It was their room, their sanctuary, and although she might have been a part of it – *if* she'd been conceived there – she wanted it to remain that way.

Back in the stairwell, she decided to avoid the third floor; she didn't want to risk bumping into David, he might think she was stalking him. On the fourth, there were indeed signs that some updating was actually taking place – finally. In a storage area beside the stairwell, various decorating materials were neatly stowed, including a ladder, buckets and rags, and a few tins of paint, as yet unopened. By the time she reached five, she was bored. Perhaps, she'd return to her room and watch a little TV, or choose a book to read on her Kindle, even take a nap. There was nothing of interest. Just one more floor – for the purpose of exercise – and then she'd call it a day; skip the rest. On six, she started her trek down the corridor, slightly out of puff from the exertion of the stairs. So where were the decorating materials on this floor? When she'd visited briefly with Tallula, she hadn't seen any. And, if anything, it was shabbier than the rest, the lighting weaker than ever. It was as knackered as her, she decided, resolving to ride the elevator to eleven instead of walking further, the prospect of a long, lazy afternoon at last holding appeal.

Halfway along, she paused and turned towards the door Tallula had paused at too. It was slightly ajar. Curious, she crept closer, there was music being played, nothing modern, something very old-fashioned, a tinny quality to it. One foot on the threshold, she realised there was something wrong with the door number. Raising a hand, she ran her fingertips over it. In between two sixes was a zero, the top right hand curve of which was missing, the bottom part of the curve pushed in slightly.

She took a tiny step backwards, peered at it again.

Oh my God!

No sooner had she realised what was wrong than the elevator doors opened, grabbing her attention instead. Inside was the teenager – the architect's daughter.

Before Caroline had a chance to react, they closed just as another opened – the door with 666 on it.

"Caroline! To what do I owe this pleasure?"

It was Edward, dressed casually this time. He had on some kind of housecoat, the material a faded red paisley. A breast pocket, two side pockets, the collar, and a sash belt were all picked out in black, the entire ensemble covering a vest top and loose grey trousers. On his feet were black leather slip-ons and in one hand he held a cigarette, smoke coiling like serpents around his head. There were various *No Smoking* signs dotted about, but clearly, he held no regard for them.

Taking a deep drag of the cigarette, he turned his head to the side when he exhaled and then looked straight back at her, his eyes, the shape of them, were feline somehow.

Finally, she found her voice. "Sorry. I was just passing." Immediately, she blushed. What a stupid thing to say. You didn't *just* pass a hotel room that was on a separate floor to yours. She apologised again. "What I meant was, I'm exploring other floors, trying to waste a bit of time."

"You're not going downstairs for a spot of lunch, as you English might say?"

"A spot of…? No, I find breakfast and dinner plenty at the moment."

Edward adopted a woeful expression. "Naughty Caroline, skipping meals is bad for you. I tend to take lunch in my room. You want to join me?"

What could she say, how could she tactfully decline?

"Caroline, I insist."

There was something in the way he said it that made it impossible to refuse. Deciding it was a polite enough invitation, and that she only needed to stay half an hour or so, she accepted. She'd found out something about David, Marilyn and Elspeth, so it might be interesting to discover something about him too, primarily his relationship to Althea. She only hoped that Tallula wasn't in residence. If she were, she wouldn't linger for a minute.

Edward stood aside to let her pass and as she did, she couldn't help but glance at the door again, at the broken number. Edward noticed.

"Ah, my room number, 606, or is it 666? Hysterical, don't you think?"

"Hysterical?" That wasn't the first word that sprang to mind.

Shutting the door behind him, he continued, "To be honest, I'm impressed you noticed, there are plenty who don't. I admit, though, it is subtle. You have to stop and take a good look. Housekeeping keep offering to fix it. I always refuse. Why ruin a good joke?"

She remembered what Raquel had said when Edward first arrived. "Is this your usual room?"

"More often than not."

She shook her head – this man, he was determined to remain as enigmatic as possible.

Fully inside, she was once again amazed. The poster in Althea's room had declared all rooms unique and his certainly was. Another period room, it suited a decade or two later than Althea's – the 40s perhaps? Each item of furniture, from the brown leather armchairs placed opposite each other, the ornate gilt-framed mirror that hung on a far wall, the writing desk with its green leather inlay, the lamp that sat on top, resembling an oyster shell, and the hand-woven Persian rug beneath her feet, looked antique. Unlike Althea's room, the double doors to the bedroom were wide open, his bed perfectly visible – a lavish affair with carved mahogany posts, the silk sheets ruffled.

As in Althea's room, there was no TV, just a very simple looking record player, with a stack of vinyl records beside it. The singer she'd heard was still busy crooning.

"Let me fix you a drink," he purred, walking over to a drinks cabinet similar to Marilyn's, another highly polished piece, and extracting two tumblers from it. "Please, sit down."

It wasn't as warm in his room as it was in others. She shivered slightly and clasped her hands together, tried to focus on them rather than him. Her gaze kept being drawn back, however, as he poured an amber coloured spirit into their glasses – whiskey, it had to be.

He handed her glass over. "Not too early in the day for you, I hope?"

"I don't normally drink whiskey," she replied, but in this instance she was strangely glad of it, certainly for its warm afterglow. Pulling up one of the armchairs to sit beside her, he clinked his glass against hers.

"Cheers," he said.

"Cheers," she mumbled in reply.

He'd invited her in for lunch, but there was no sign of any food. *Perhaps he meant a liquid lunch.* She sipped again at her drink, his close proximity causing her to tremble as much as the chill air. This close to him she could see how perfect his skin was, no open pores, barely any lines, it was skin that most women would die for. His teeth too were enviable, white rather than yellow, perfectly straight and framed by full lips. He was a beautiful man; there was no denying it. The opposite to David, not as rugged, or as rough around the edges. Instead he was polished, everything about him neat and precise. He seemed to enjoy that she was staring at him, lapped it up and although she felt embarrassed that she was doing so, she had to fight to look away, regretting that she must – for the sake of decorum if nothing else.

Bringing the glass to her lips again, taking a gulp rather than a sip, she desperately tried to think of something to ask him. The obvious came to mind.

"How long have you been at the Egress?" Because like Althea, it was clear that he lived here.

"A long time."

"Your room is amazing. There are so many antiques."

"I like it well enough."

"I said to Althea—"

"You've been talking to Althea?" Was she mistaken or did he bristle at that?

"Yes, I'm on same floor as her."

He leaned forward slightly. "Which room?"

Should she tell him? Was it safe to? Almost immediately she berated herself. Of course it was safe, why wouldn't it be? And he could find out easily enough anyway. "I'm in 1106."

He leant back in his chair, relaxed. "Still a distance away then."

"From Althea? Yes, I suppose so, I'm sort of in the middle." Should she mention Tallula? She couldn't resist, curious as to what his relationship was with her as well as Althea. "Tallula's on my floor too, just opposite, but then you know that, don't you? Last night, when Elspeth was in such distress, I saw you in the elevator."

A smile played about his lips. "Are you sure it was me?"

Again, his attitude nonplussed her. "Who else might it be?"

"There's many that wander this hotel at night."

At his words, her hand reached up to clutch at the neck of the jumper she wore.

"Something troubling you, Caroline?"

"No." If he wasn't going to give away anything about himself, why should she?

"I'm not…unsettling you, am I?"

"Not at all," she denied, holding his gaze again, this time defiantly.

"You're beautiful."

"What…?" The compliment – unexpected – disarmed her.

"I thought that the moment I met you."

Was that really true? In the lobby he'd treated her with nothing less than indifference. At dinner, however, he'd come over and kissed her hand. He hadn't done that with any other female he'd greeted prior to her.

He also went to the trouble of finding out your name.

Yes, he'd done that too.

"Isn't Tallula your girlfriend?" she asked, surprised at her own daring.

"Tallula?" He laughed, a booming sound, but strangely containing very little humour. "I like her. In many ways she's my kind of gal, but…" – and here he paused, inclining his head a little – "I'm like you, Caroline, I'm not big on commitment."

"What?" Tallula had said something similar. Had together they discussed her? "You don't know that about me," she protested. "You don't know me at all."

"Caroline, Caroline." Immediately he was contrite. Placing his empty glass on a low table in front of them, he leant closer still. "Forgive me. Have I offended you?"

She swallowed, felt confused by his change of character. Had he offended her? She honestly didn't know.

"If I did," he continued, "it wasn't my intention. It's just... I can sense a kindred spirit. You're as intrigued with me as I am with you."

It was true – he did intrigue her. He was unlike anyone she'd ever met before, as unique as the hotel. And yet...he was calling her a kindred spirit. Effectively saying she was similar to him. Was she? Again, she didn't know whether to be flattered or quite the opposite.

"Is Althea your grandmother?"

Having asked the question, she couldn't believe it when he recoiled.

"Althea is no relation of mine."

"Oh, I—"

"She should admit defeat, move on."

Defeat? What was he talking about? She was desperate to know but she was also wary of antagonising him further. "Look, ignore me, I shouldn't have asked."

For a moment or two he seemed to unravel, the grimace he wore destroying his good looks, obliterating them like an ocean tide might destroy a sculpture in the sand. And then before she could blink, his smile was back. If anything more dazzling than before.

Reaching across he took her glass and placed it on the table too. Before she could react, ask him what he was doing, those lips she'd been admiring brushed against hers.

Her heart began to hammer furiously in her chest. He was kissing her. *Just* kissing her? Or was there more on his mind? Did he want to *seduce* her? She recalled his bed, the enormity of it, the silken sheets, waiting to be ruffled further.

"Sweet Caroline," he murmured, making her ache, for him, and for the grief that still raged inside her to be dampened down. Could he do that? Could he help?

"Edward," she found herself murmuring his name too. "I—"

"Don't say another word, Caroline. I *know* how deep your grief is."

He couldn't know. And yet how wonderful it would be to believe him.

She closed her eyes. *Let this be.* Those were the words spinning around in her head, as if someone other than herself were whispering them. *Don't be afraid.*

Her breath caught in her throat and butterflies danced in her stomach.

Don't be afraid.

She inhaled and as she did, she detected an odour, faint but repugnant. It was a sour smell, cloying, just as Tallula's perfume had been when she was with her in the elevator. Where was it coming from? Edward? And what was it? Some sort of aftershave? No, it couldn't be. No one would bottle a smell like that. She'd expected him to smell of whiskey and cigarettes, a masculine smell that would excite her even more – not this…not decay.

Now she was the one who recoiled. "Edward, please." She said the words gently, aware that she mustn't upset him, that he could turn again if upset, no longer be the suave gentleman he was, the cliché, sitting there in his silk dressing gown and his leather slippers – like something out of a film, someone who didn't exist at all; a figure that dwelt only in nightmares. "Edward!" she said again, urgency in her voice as, with one hand, she had to push hard at his chest before being able to rise from the chair he'd pressed her into.

She wasn't brave enough to look at him, to see what emotions were flitting across his face. *Don't be afraid.* This time such advice fell short. "I… I have to go."

Edward jumped up too, effectively blocking her exit. If she wanted to keep some distance between them, she had no option but to retreat further into the room.

"Caroline…"

At least he didn't preface her name with 'sweet' this time. Something she was grateful for. Those were her mother's words to her, her father's. From Edward's mouth they were a mockery, not healing the grief in her at all, but exacerbating it.

Why did she ever think it was cold in here? It really wasn't. The heat was unbearable, like being caught in an inferno.

"Caroline, perhaps I was a little presumptuous. Come on, sit down, let's start over."

Still she backed away. "No, I really do need to go."

"But, darling, that's the wrong way."

That term of endearment did not sit well with her either.

"Look, Edward, I'm not feeling very well, I feel quite sick, in fact. And the kiss," – she could hardly bear to think of it – "that was a mistake. Please, let me go."

"I'm not stopping you."

But he was, he was backing her into a corner. The stench that had assailed her when his lips were on hers had dissipated, but if he closed the gap, it'd be there again, not just on his skin, on his breath, but coming from somewhere deep inside him.

She touched the windowpane beside her – longing for

its coolness. "Look, it's snowing again," she muttered, attempting to divert his attention.

Abruptly she turned – a childish ploy, she knew – *if I can't see you, you can't see me* – and continued to babble about the weather, how awful it was, that hopefully this was the last big snowfall, that soon the thaw would begin and they could return to normal, whatever normal was – she was beginning to forget – when something below caught her attention. Someone who was out there that shouldn't be, in a dress of all things, a *summer* dress, kneeling down, her hands raking at the snow, clawing at it.

"Elspeth." Her voice was a whisper at first. "That's Elspeth!"

Edward reached her side. Despite her earlier apprehension, it was something that barely registered. Instead she was rapt, continuing to stare. Another figure joined Elspeth – David – a coat in his hands, which he threw over her. Immediately she shrugged it off, her hands clawing at her dress too, exposing more flesh. As David drew closer again, she lashed out, intent on doing damage. Much to Caroline's amazement, he didn't back away. He simply tried again.

"It must be the drugs," Caroline whispered, "messing with her mind." Her fear of Edward completely on the backburner, she turned to him. "We need to go and help, get Elspeth inside before she freezes to death."

"Elspeth?" His full lips curled. "Elspeth's a liability."

Caroline was stunned. "Elspeth's in turmoil!"

Concern lending her both strength and bravery, she pushed past him, and fled from the room, Edward doing nothing to stop her this time.

Chapter Fifteen

Deciding against the elevator, Caroline flew down the stairwell, almost stumbling on one occasion, having to hold onto the handrail so that she could steady herself.

By the time she reached David and Elspeth, just outside the hotel doors, the snowfall getting heavier and heavier, she was gasping for breath. Marilyn and John had joined David, who was still struggling with Elspeth, both of them aghast as she continued to kick out, not laughing or crying but yelping as if she was the one being wounded.

"Oh my, oh my," Marilyn kept muttering. She was crying too, tears running down her cheeks to fall like silver droplets into the snow below.

John had placed a tentative arm around Marilyn's shoulders in an effort to console her, one hand patting the side of her shoulder in what could only be described as an awkward manner. Nonetheless, Marilyn seemed grateful for his presence, leaning into him, crying some more, fingernails scratching at the irritation on her neck.

"What's happening? What's going on?"

As she said it, Caroline looked from side to side. She was half expecting Tallula to be waiting in the wings, as the voyeur, delighting once again in this woman's situation.

But she was nowhere to be seen and nor was anyone else, not even Raquel had ventured out from behind the lobby desk. And Althea might be an old, old woman, but she was the manager, wasn't she? Why was she leaving guests to deal with a situation such as this yet again? As for Edward – her eyes darted upwards, towards where she figured his room might be. Whatever impression he liked to give, he was no gentleman, far from it.

"David," she called, "shall I call someone, get an ambulance?"

David heard her, looked up. "In this?"

Damn it, he was right, they couldn't get out and no one could get in, but there must be something they could do. The woman needed professional help. She hated to admit it, but Edward was right – Elspeth *was* a liability, to herself as well as to others.

"Just help me get her inside," David instructed. "She's frozen."

Immediately darting forward, Caroline bent down to help. David's second instruction – 'Back up, Caroline, back up, she's going to lash out again' – came too late. Elspeth's fist, as cold as marble, and as hard, smashed into Caroline's jaw, sending her flying.

"Shit, are you okay?" David lurched towards her.

She held up a hand. "Stay with Elspeth, I'm fine." A blatant lie, her jaw was on fire.

David's torn expression spoke volumes. He knew Caroline was right in insisting he prioritise Elspeth, but his concern for her was apparent – very. Although now was not the time to think of it, Edward's kiss rushed to the forefront of her mind and she felt terrible all of a sudden, as though she'd committed a huge betrayal. *Don't be afraid.* She'd told herself that many times in his room and still the words were in her head.

From nowhere a wind whipped up, surprising her; a great gust, as if a giant had filled his lungs and was now busy exhaling. The top layer of snow got caught up in the gust and started to whirl.

"David!" She had to shout to make herself heard.

The powder rose higher and higher, like a wall surrounding them. She could barely see further than the five of them – no horizon, nothing. It had all disappeared. Perhaps this final snow dump was going to be the worst. They just had to ride it out.

Scrabbling to get to her feet, her eyes watering, not just because of the weather, but because of the pain of the blow she'd received, Caroline realised someone was singing.

"Amazing Grace! How sweet the sound, that saved a wretch like me."

The voice was sweet and melodic, a purity to it that matched the snow, but who did it belong to? She looked towards Elspeth. It wasn't her, but she'd calmed, incredibly, reacting almost straightaway to the much-loved hymn. It was Marilyn singing, leaving the sanctity of John's arms, and walking forward, her hands by her side, her head held high.

"I once was lost, but now am found. Was blind, but now I see."

Only briefly did Marilyn glance at Caroline, a look in her eyes that urged her to join in, which she duly did, John too, not stumbling over the words as she was, but reciting them as perfectly as Marilyn. The wildness in Elspeth tamed, David managed at last to drape his coat across her shoulders, covering up her near nakedness, warming her flesh.

As Caroline helped David pull Elspeth to her feet, she noticed the tears on her cheeks were frozen, as though they hadn't been freshly shed, as if they'd been there for all time. Despite not knowing what Elspeth's reaction might be, she reached out a hand to wipe at them, the woman standing perfectly still whilst she did. It was a pointless task, however, as more tears replaced them.

With both of them supporting Elspeth, they walked forwards, Marilyn following behind, continuing to sing, the lyrics causing tears to well in Caroline's eyes too. She could never understand why such a melancholy tune accompanied such joyful lyrics.

As they trooped towards the hotel doors, John fell into step behind Marilyn. It felt as if they were in a procession; one that was all too familiar to her, and she and David the pallbearers. Once inside, Raquel came hurrying forwards – at last.

"We need to call an ambulance," Caroline told her. "Immediately."

"They'll never get through in this weather," replied Raquel, echoing David.

Caroline's temper flared. "I still want you to call them, to do something, rather than just stand there behind that desk of yours, looking so bloody bored."

"Hey! I didn't want to crowd her."

"Oh, Raquel, there's no danger of you crowding anyone, I don't think." Caroline looked around her, at the complete lack of staff, the lack of anyone for that matter, people turning a blind eye, not wanting to get involved, dismissing Elspeth as a mad woman probably, fearing her. Even so, leaving her to freeze half-naked in the snow? It wasn't on. "As a guest of the Egress, Elspeth is your responsibility. Now get on the damned phone and ask for advice if nothing else. The poor woman's likely to be suffering from hypothermia."

For a moment Raquel stood firm, boredom replaced by a touch of defiance and then she slunk away, Caroline staring daggers at her.

"Nice work." It was David congratulating her.

"Let's hope she hurries," Caroline responded. They couldn't just stand there, in the lobby, waiting for advice from Raquel. Elspeth needed to warm up properly.

"Take her to my room," Marilyn said, clearly thinking the same thing.

Again David looked at Caroline. Why not take her there? It was as good a room as any. She was about to nod when the elevator doors opened and Althea came towards them, Jenna keeping apace.

"What's happened?" she asked.

Caroline wanted to berate her too for belatedly getting involved, but her courage failed her. Instead, as dutiful as Jenna, she explained all that had transpired.

"She needs dry clothes," Althea said, as soon as Caroline had finished, "warm blankets wrapped around her, and warm drinks too." Turning to Elspeth, she asked her to cough.

Caroline frowned. Why was she asking that?

As obedient as a child, Elspeth did indeed cough, not once but twice.

Althea appeared satisfied.

"Raquel is phoning the medics for advice," Caroline continued. "We're waiting—"

"No need to wait," Althea interrupted. "I've already

given you the advice you need."

"But—"

David backed Althea up. "She's right, Caroline, that is the correct advice."

Althea turned to David and looked him up and down as if seeing him for the first time. "You can take her to my suite," she said at last. Another command.

"Oh," Marilyn piped up, "we've already sorted it out. She's coming with me."

"You're on the eleventh floor too." It was a statement from Althea not a question.

Marilyn nodded.

To David, she said, "And you're on the third."

"That's correct," David replied. "Room—"

"310," Althea finished. "You have a corner suite."

"I sure do," was his wry reply. "Lucky me."

Althea's nostrils flared slightly. "I hope so, David, I truly do. Alright." She gave Marilyn a brief nod. "Take her to your room, she's safe with you."

Safe? What did she mean by that, this woman who was diminutive but no less enigmatic than Edward, who Edward couldn't bear the mention of? What was going on between them, with Elspeth too, with Marilyn, and John and Tallula? Out of all of them, David seemed to be the sanest by a country mile; she only hoped he thought the same of her. Then again, having got angry with him at dinner because he happened to mention she was staring at Edward might make him reconsider. That fiery streak in her might impress him when it came to Raquel, but not when turned against him. She'd apologised once, but at dinner tonight, she'd offer to foot the bill for a bottle of wine – God knows they'd earned it – and she'd be 'Sweet

Caroline', as her mother had always intended.

Raquel emerged from the office behind her desk waving a piece of paper in her hand, her manner as leisurely as ever, causing Caroline to bite down on her lip.

"I've got the details you wanted," she drawled.

"But no hope of them actually coming here?" Caroline checked.

"None at all."

"Damn," Caroline swore under her breath.

"Caroline," David said, "can you help me get Elspeth into the elevator?"

Marilyn jumped into action. "There's no need. *I'll* help."

"It's okay…" Caroline begun but Marilyn was determined.

"Elspeth knows me and, as has already been pointed out, she feels safe with me. We mustn't linger anymore. Look at her, poor darling, she's shivering so much!"

Practically pushing Caroline aside, Marilyn took Elspeth's arm. "Come on, David," she urged again. "Let's get going."

"Okay," David replied, "but, Caroline, get some ice on that jaw, will you?"

"I will."

"Promise?"

"I promise."

Althea stood aside, as did John and Caroline, John looking relieved that the drama was over. As for herself, she couldn't work out if she was annoyed at being ousted or not. Something else was bugging her too: Althea had said Elspeth would be safe with Marilyn, not *feels* safe, which is how Marilyn had interpreted it. To her mind there was a difference.

The elevator doors concealing the trio, she was left with John and Althea, Raquel too, whom Althea took by the arm and led to one side. Caroline couldn't hear what she was saying to her because she kept her voice low, but Raquel looked defiant again, displeased, although she held her tongue and didn't answer back. Instead, she took up her usual position behind the lobby desk, Althea continuing onwards to the ballroom. Lunch was being served and, although Caroline wasn't hungry, it might offer a chance to spend a bit more time with John, to learn why he considered himself a worse man than his father.

But John was already in retreat.

"John," she called, but he didn't seem to hear her. She raised her voice and tried a second time. "John!" He must have heard that time, but again he gave no response.

She sighed in defeat.

He wasn't ready to confide in her again, she realised.

Perhaps he'd already said too much.

Chapter Sixteen

This was the third night she'd be spending at the Egress – a hotel she hadn't meant to stay in at all – and Caroline had to admit: she was nervous. The thought of seeing Edward again – whom she was both angry with for his disinterest in Elspeth's plight as well as his interest in her...an interest she'd almost returned – concerned her, as did the prospect of another nightmare. She couldn't ever recall having two in a row; three would make it a hat-trick, a gruesome one.

Outside the storm was still in full force. Snow had been falling all day, the wind not letting up either, shunting it back and forth. Spending the majority of her afternoon in her room, alternately reading and napping, Caroline found the lights had started to flicker again. The TV, which she kept on for company as much as anything, joining in.

Several times she wondered whether David was okay, and if he was still with Elspeth in Marilyn's room or had gone back to 310. Certainly, she hadn't heard movement outside, but it was a long, long corridor, she reminded herself, and she was in what was akin to a bubble, separated by walls and doors. She'd considered going to check on them several times but couldn't get rid of the sense she'd be intruding again, that Raquel was right; the worst thing you could do was crowd Elspeth. She was as fragile as a butterfly, as easily damaged. Irrevocably, perhaps? She hoped not. But it was plain to see there was a world of hurt in her, drugs being the Band-Aid that couldn't prevent the pain from soaking through.

All she could do was while away the time until dinner, praying the electrics would hold firm, and that she wouldn't be plunged into darkness whilst alone and in her room. Another hour passed.

And another.

Bloody hell time dragged at the Egress on occasion. She was practically climbing the walls as her watch edged towards eight o' clock. Leaving the confines of her room, she headed towards the elevator, hoping David would be at dinner, that he wasn't otherwise detained. It might even be a full house, guests just as fed up as her of... *Of what, Caroline? Being alone?* She nodded, made light of it. *You can have too much of a good thing, you know!* One thing she'd readily admit to was being bored with the same old scenery. How she longed for vistas that were ever changing; for hills and mountains, for towns and villages, for air that was cool and crisp. Maybe she'd considered stuff like that a God-given right before, but now it seemed such a privilege.

The elevator was up to its usual tricks, the doors not immediately shutting when the button for the lobby was pressed. Once they'd slid into position, there was a bump and a grind, a sense of moving upwards before grinding again and going in the right direction. Exasperated, Caroline rolled her eyes. She'd appreciate a 'normal' elevator in future too.

In the lobby, she nodded politely to Raquel, who was still sulking. No longer peeved, Caroline felt sorry for her again. When did she ever get to eat, to drink, to enjoy a bit of time off? There must be someone she shared shifts with – that someone probably stuck at home in Williamsfield or thereabouts, just as she was stuck at the Egress, having not got out before the storm took hold. Caroline knew there was such a thing as protocol, but should she offer to fetch her a drink, a glass of wine even? Surely under these circumstances protocol could go to hell. Deciding to make the offer, she walked over.

"Wine?" Raquel queried, an eyebrow shooting up.

"I thought you might like a glass. I don't know when you get the time to eat or—"

"Althea might have something to say about that."

"I know, but—"

"Although Edward, he'd encourage it."

"Edward?" Caroline queried.

"The other manager."

She couldn't hide her surprise. "He's a manager too?"

"Surely you realised?"

She'd realised he was someone of note, swanning about the place, but not that he managed the Egress alongside Althea, certainly he hadn't mentioned anything about it to her whilst she'd been with him in his room. "I thought he and Althea might be related."

Raquel snorted. "Don't let either of them catch you say that. They're not exactly…" she paused, "fond of each other."

"I'm aware of that," Caroline replied, raising an eyebrow too. "And too late I'm afraid, I've already asked Edward if Althea was his grandmother."

"His grandmother?" Raquel's mouth fell open. "What did he say?"

"Well, he said…no."

"Just don't make the same mistake with Althea."

She certainly wouldn't. "Are there no other managers here?"

Raquel shook her head. "Two's enough, don't you think?"

For a hotel this size she supposed so, although managers in conflict wasn't exactly the healthiest of scenarios.

Her stomach growled, reminding her how hungry she was.

"So there's nothing I can bring you?" she asked again.

"I'll eat…and drink, later. But thanks anyway."

"You do go off duty at some stage, don't you?"

"I don't sleep at my desk, if that's what you're implying."

Caroline laughed. "I wasn't implying anything."

Picking up a pen, Raquel started scribbling in that register of hers. Taking the hint, Caroline dismissed herself, glancing at herself in one of the mirrors she passed on her way to the ballroom. She'd chosen to wear another pair of skinny jeans tonight, blue this time, and a blouse that was emerald green in colour. She'd also toyed with her hair, sweeping it up in a bun, a few tendrils hanging down either side, and applied make-up perhaps a little more thickly than usual. Her fringe covered the bruise on her forehead well enough, but she'd had to use foundation and concealer to cover the one that Elspeth had inflicted. Usually she didn't have so much time to spend on herself. If she went out in the evening it was often straight from work. Now, she had nothing but time.

Standing at the entrance to the ballroom, she could see that the same tables had been set, posies reinstated, and a variety of people sitting at them, including Marilyn and John, together on one table. She smiled; glad they'd struck up a tentative friendship. Tentative because each looked slightly awkward in the other's company, perusing the menu just a fraction too long, John pouring water for them both, splashing a little over the sides and onto the tablecloth, and looking abashed that he'd done so.

There was no Elspeth. And David... Where was he?

"Hello, stranger."

A voice at her side made her jump. "Oh, there you are," she exclaimed, sounding as breathy as Raquel had at one point during their conversation.

David smiled. "I've missed you too." He made a show of looking at his watch, slightly adjusting its tan strap. "It's been, ooh...all of six hours since we last met."

"Under onerous circumstances," Caroline pointed out. "How's Elspeth?"

"She wanted to return to her room after a while. She fell asleep almost immediately once she was back in her own bed. She was knocked out and little wonder. Marilyn and I wouldn't have left her but Jenna, the woman that's always with Althea—"

"Her assistant," Caroline interrupted. "Or her maid, as Althea insists."

"Does she?" David chuckled at that. "Well, she knocked on the door and offered to sit with her, to give us a break."

"And Marilyn was okay with that?"

"Yeah, she was. Jenna's very nice, very...wholesome. I don't think she'd have let anyone else take her place, though."

"Including me."

"Don't take offence, Marilyn's a bit of a mother hen,

that's all."

This woman who'd never had children.

"I haven't taken offence, honestly. I think Marilyn's great. I don't know what we'd do without her. Hey," she continued, "did you know Edward's a manager as well as Althea?"

"I had put two and two together. Not exactly the dream team, are they?"

Caroline laughed. "Far from it. Althea's been here from the beginning, that's what she said. She was either born here or moved in with her parents when she was a baby."

"Really?" David seemed impressed. "So you've spoken to her?"

"Yeah, she invited me in last night for a nightcap, after our…our…"

"Spat?" David finished when she hesitated.

"You know I really am sorry about that."

"You've already said."

"I know but—"

"But nothing. There's no need. Let's forget it, make up for it tonight instead, and enjoy ourselves. As for Althea, good job getting an invite. I kept trying to talk to her yesterday, but Jenna – her *maid* – kept putting me off: she was tired, she was working, she was having a nap – the usual excuses. I even tried when Jenna was with Elspeth. With her out of the way I thought it might be easier."

"And was it?"

"Nope, she didn't bother answering the door."

"So, what did you want to talk to her about?" Caroline asked.

"Well…nothing. Nothing important anyway. Just a few issues with the hotel."

"What issues? To do with the electrics or something?"

"Something like that, also my coffee maker isn't working. I need to have it replaced."

Caroline was incredulous. "All this fuss over a coffee maker?"

"Hey! I'm an American. I run on coffee!"

"So try Edward. He's a manager too."

David sighed. "Or, like John, I could learn to love tap water."

"I can't see that somehow."

"Nope, you're right, that's taking it way too far. Whatever, we can't hang around here, we're blocking the entrance. We'd better go in and grab a table before they all fill up."

"Our usual?"

"If no one else has snagged it."

"They haven't, I've got my eye on it."

The minute they were seated Edward entered the room, back to being suited and booted, his eyes searching for and finding hers, holding her gaze, forcing her to be the one to look away. Tallula was on his arm. She looked breathtaking, even more so than before. Her hair spiked up in a punk style, and a black rose, probably made of chiffon, clipped to one side. The dress she had on was as white as her hair and once again clung to her hips and waist, nude high heels giving an endless quality to beautifully shaped legs. An ice-queen if ever there was one, although the way she clutched at Edward's arm spoke of desperation, to Caroline at least. She must know her man was a player and yet she clearly longed for him. Before she could contemplate it further, more guests entered the room. Not the black-haired teenager – she'd still not put in an appearance – but Elspeth, accompanied by both Jenna and Althea, the pair of them flanking her, on guard. Edward whipped his head around to look at them enter – the two managers, still at loggerheads with each other if his expression was anything to go by.

"Are we having wine again this evening?" David asked.

"With all this going on? Are you kidding me?"

Jokingly, he palmed his forehead. "You're right, what was I thinking? This is no time for abstinence." Lifting one hand, he summoned the waiter to place their order.

Another night was underway at the Egress, with the same guests, the same situation, the same animosities, the same madness, and the same agitations. But amidst it all was David. Once her glass was filled, Caroline raised it, and drank to that at least.

Chapter Seventeen

"You're kidding me. Surely you're kidding me!"

"I'm not, I promise."

"You are, you're teasing me, getting all... *American* on me."

David looked aghast. "American? Caroline, what's so American about what I've just told you?"

"That you're the son of a preacher man?"

"That's right, I am."

"And yet you're not religious, in fact you don't believe in God at all?"

"No, I don't."

"Because you're a rebel?"

"Because I've got a mind of my own, thanks."

"But you're still close to your dad?"

"Sort of. I mean he's not thrilled about it, but he's respectful. As I am of him."

"You tolerate each other's point of view?"

He sighed. "That's about the sum of it."

"And your mother?"

"What about my mom?"

"Do you get on with her?"

"She's very supportive of my father."

"I see." Caroline leant back in her chair. "David, how old are you? I haven't actually asked."

"Thirty-two."

"Oh! You're younger than me, I'm thirty-three."

"When's your birthday?"

"I've just had it, beginning of November."

"Mine's at the end of November, so you see, we're closer than you think."

She couldn't argue with that. "One more question."

"Fire away."

"Have you got any brothers or sisters?"

"Nope."

"So, you're the *only* son of a preacher man."

"Caroline, I fail to see what's so funny."

"Why are you laughing then?"

"Because… Because…" Desperately, he tried to suppress that trademark grin of his. "I'll have you know the singer of that particular song was English, not American."

"Dusty Springfield?"

"Correct."

"What's the name of the man in it?"

"No clue."

"Oh come on, you've got Internet, haven't you? Look up the lyrics."

"Sorry, I didn't bring my cell to dinner with me."

She screwed up her nose. "Don't worry, I think I can remember. It's Billy something."

"Billy Ray."

"So you *do* know, after all."

Swaying in her chair, she began to hum, causing David to adopt a look of horror.

"Don't do it," he pleaded. "Don't start singing the

damn song."

"Oh please. You have to let me. The chorus at least."

"Caroline…"

She proceeded to sing how the only man who could ever reach her was the son of a preacher man.

"Caroline, please!"

The only boy who could ever teach me—"

"I doubt I could teach you anything."

"Don't be so sure of that!" The wine had gone to her head; loosening her up, causing her to flirt again, shamelessly flirt. She'd even caught herself batting her eyelashes, for God's sake, another realisation that made her giggle.

"You know, everyone's looking at us," David pointed out.

She leaned closer. "I'm not being *that* loud. Am I?"

"You might be," he replied, and then he sighed. "Ah, to hell with it, we're having fun. You gotta have fun in a place like this."

"We are," she agreed, "we're making the best of it."

"Having the time of our lives."

"Woah! Steady on. You'll be wanting the storm to continue at this rate."

"Maybe," he said, holding her gaze.

Caroline stared just as intently and then, when several moments had passed, started singing a few more lines from the Dusty Springfield song, causing David to rest his head woefully in his hands. Deciding that she'd tortured the poor man enough, she lifted her glass and drank some more wine. They'd finished one bottle already and were steadily working their way through another. Around the room, the conversation was in full flow, even Marilyn and

John seemed to be getting along, Marilyn still scratching at her neck every now and then, and John staring more at the jug of water in front of him than at his dinner partner, but there were smiles between them every so often. Elspeth remained subdued, but considering what had happened, it was a miracle she'd made it to dinner at all. At Edward and Tallula's table several waiters were milling, making a fuss of the manager and the woman he couldn't commit to. They might have done the same with Althea, but Caroline caught her dismissing any hovering waiters on several occasions, albeit politely. Edward, on the other hand, encouraged their attention, sending them to and fro with various demands, no doubt all of them frivolous, Tallula enjoying by proxy the power he wielded.

Damn it. Tallula had caught her staring again, a challenge in her frosty eyes, Caroline was certain of it, her smile widening as she pushed back her chair and jumped to her feet. Caroline flinched. What was she up to?

"Is everyone done with dinner?" the ice queen shouted.

David looked as surprised as Caroline. As for the others, rather than anyone rushing to answer her, a hush descended, knives, forks, and glasses held aloft.

The lack of response didn't deter Tallula. "I spy with my little eye…we have indeed finished. But the night's still young. *We're* still young." Not quite daring to meet Althea's eyes but clearly aiming her next words at her, she added, "Some of us, anyway."

With one finger she beckoned a waiter. "We want music," she announced, "and lower the lights, it's too damn stark in here." Re-addressing the room, she asked for everyone's help in pushing back the tables. "Come on, this is a ballroom, let's use it for what it was intended for. Let's dance!"

Around Caroline, people started to move, reluctantly at first but then with more conviction. By her side, letting others do all the work, Edward continued to sit with his legs crossed. From the look on his face, Caroline could see he approved of Tallula's antics.

"David?" she asked. "What do you think?"

He shrugged, picked up his glass of wine, and drained the last of it. "We were saying something similar, weren't we? About making the best of the situation. As for dancing, I've got two left feet, but that doesn't stop me from wanting to dance with you."

His words caused her to drain her wine too, which rather than slake her thirst, ignited one that was greater. "Okay, let's do it," she said. She could do with letting her hair down, having fun – even if it was at the behest of Tallula.

It was wonderful to see such life in the room, to witness the dance floor being revealed for the first time in who knew how long; to hear the first strains of music bursting through the speakers. She'd been expecting something old-fashioned, something more suited to Althea's generation, old classics to suit a classical room, but that wasn't the case. This was a modern tune, one she was familiar with, but was struggling to place.

David noticed her confusion. "It's Lady Antebellum, *Need You Now*."

"Oh yeah, of course." It was a song she loved. "I'm really going to enjoy tonight."

"Because it's been so terrible up until now?"

"No, not terrible… Interesting."

"You can say that again," he replied.

"One person in particular."

"And who might that be?"

"The answer might surprise you."

"Only if it's me. Is it?"

She flashed him another coy smile. "That'd be telling."

As Lady Antebellum rushed headlong into another chorus, she had to admit, she might not like Tallula, but her enthusiasm to party was admirable. Even Althea, whom she expected to be furious at such proceedings, seemed resigned to it. Her table, already on the outskirts of the dance floor, remained where it was. She was sitting at it still, but she wasn't glowering, she was merely...observing. On Jenna's face, there was even a hint of a smile, going a long way to combat her plainness. Elspeth too was more enlivened – although whether that was a good thing or not, she didn't know. She was a simmering volcano and therefore unpredictable.

As the lights were lowered, Caroline spotted Tom. She hadn't seen him since he'd showed David to his room on their first night here. He was looking relaxed, still in uniform, but not as buttoned up somehow. Raquel hadn't joined them yet, but would she? Take up that offer of a glass of wine? Surely Althea wouldn't protest, the girl must be allowed to have some fun too. As for the teen, what a shame if she was still locked in her room, she might have enjoyed this. Then again, if her parents were amongst several people who'd already taken to the dance floor, perhaps she'd find it more excruciating than ever!

A hand came around her waist – David's. "Come on," he said, steering her towards the dance floor. "A dance and then another drink perhaps?"

There was no perhaps about it, she wanted to dance, to

drink, to be as close to him as possible. She'd have to watch it, though, she was lightheaded already, staggering slightly as they joined the dancing couples, David having to steady her, both of them giggling about it.

Lady Antebellum gave way to Dolly Parton and *Jolene* – another favourite of hers. There was definitely a country edge to the music being played tonight.

Edward and Tallula were smooching on the dance floor as opposed to dancing, Tallula grinding her hips against his, her lips nuzzling at his neck. Commitment-phobe or not, he was clearly enjoying her efforts. They looked exquisite together, making her wonder what she and David looked like. Did they suit each other half as much?

The smell of him close up was nothing like the one she'd experienced with Edward. Certainly he had a scent that was unique to him, but it was intoxicating rather than repellent – soap and water, and a hint of musk that stirred something deep within.

"Sorry, so sorry!"

It was Marilyn and John, bumping into them slightly. They'd also started dancing – not the dirty dancing of Edward and Tallula, or the slightly more restrained dancing that she and David were indulging in, but sweet and old-fashioned, John holding her at arm's length in a sort of waltzing stance. There was nothing romantic about it, but neither did either of them intend there to be, Caroline guessed. They were simply two lonely people reaching out to each other during a time of need. Seeing that Marilyn had managed to coax shy John into enjoying himself, choked her slightly. She barely knew them, barely knew David, but there was something in each of them that struck a chord.

Something in Althea too, and Elspeth…

"Hey, what's that tear doing on your cheek?" David whispered into her ear.

She was surprised. "Is there? Oh, I didn't realise. I'm not sad, not at all. I'm happy." A realisation that oddly made her feel like crying more.

"Good, because I want you to be happy, Caroline." David's eyes were every bit as penetrating as Edward's, but with one difference, they didn't frighten her. "But there's something that's upsetting you, I know there is, despite how you try and hide it."

"My parents," she whispered, not bothering to hide it anymore.

"They're dead, aren't they? What happened? Was it recent?"

"Recent enough."

"I'm sorry. What can I do, Caroline? How can I help?"

"Just do what you're doing, continue to hold me."

David was only too happy to oblige, his grip becoming tighter.

Another song came on – *Hotel California* by The Eagles – she couldn't believe it; it was another firm favourite. Out of the corner of her eye she could see that Elspeth had risen to her feet upon hearing the first familiar beats of such an iconic song, swaying some more as the drumbeat kicked in, as much as Caroline was swaying in David's arms.

If wine was a drug, then the song was too. Everything about the evening was intoxicating. She let her head fall back upon her shoulders, losing herself in the haunting lyrics, comparing herself to the hapless traveller in the song, both of them strangers in a strange place, but she was getting used to her surroundings at least, and to the people.

No longer feeling isolated, but a part of something.

Bringing her head forward, she laid it against his chest.

"Oh, David." Her words were barely audible, but he must have heard, as he responded by brushing his lips against her hair. A travelling salesman, the son of a preacher man. Like Edward, he was every cliché in the book, but he was also strong and kind-hearted, refusing to judge anyone, doing what he could to make things better.

"Caroline." He was murmuring her name too, and still she kept her eyes closed, whilst The Eagles played on, wanting to prolong this moment, to make it last forever. Perhaps her mother had felt the same in her father's arms. Perhaps they'd even danced on this very spot. She wanted to remember them, but she also wanted to forget. That was their time, and this was hers. It was happening at last.

"Sorry."

The second apology when it came, forced her to open her eyes. It was not as genuine as Marilyn's had been. If anything there was cold amusement in it.

It was Edward. She should have guessed. "We were dancing with our eyes closed too."

"It doesn't matt—" David began but Edward cut him short.

"You look gorgeous tonight." His focus was entirely on Caroline. "What do they say? The belle of the ball." His tongue flicking out, he ran it across his lips, slowly, pointedly.

Inhaling, Caroline cast a quick glance at Tallula. Did she know that Edward had kissed her? David certainly didn't. And that's how she wanted it to stay. Tallula, however, was a blank canvass, deliberately concealing any emotions.

"As I said," David reiterated, "it doesn't matter. We'll just…move away."

"Move away?" Edward repeated, and it was clear from his attitude that he didn't like David either, the animosity between them real not imagined and growing in strength. "On the contrary… David, is it? I think you've been hogging Caroline too long. Shall we swap?"

There was a slight reaction from Tallula this time: the tiniest of jerks. As for Caroline, she was dumbfounded. The way he'd suggested they swapped partners made them sound like chattels rather than human beings. David clearly thought the same.

"I think it's best we carry on as we are," he answered.

"Or we could ask the lady?" Edward suggested slyly.

Sighing, David turned to Caroline. "Do you…?" His voice tailed off.

'I…" She was at a loss for words too. So easily her happiness had been spiked.

David's gaze was gentle. "Caroline, it's fine. If you don't want—"

"Go ahead." It was Tallula, her voice tight as she stepped aside. The song had changed again, a song she didn't recognise this time, something much slower, much lazier, that would give Edward a chance to pull her into his arms too. Almost as if he'd planned it.

People were beginning to look at them; she could sense it, all eyes on the four people standing on the dance floor, wondering if there was a problem. Even she didn't know the answer to that. It felt like Edward was being very obvious but then she was drunker than she realised.

"Just the one dance," she said to both David and Edward. Was she really slurring? She was beginning to feel dizzy too, a feeling that only intensified as Edward wasted no time in getting their dance underway. He whisked her away from David, from Tallula, leaving the pair of them standing, staring after them perhaps.

She sniffed, curious to see if there was that stench again but the only scent she could detect was aftershave, a spicy smell that reminded her of the interior of a church. It was another mockery. There was nothing sacred about Edward.

The beat picking up, he started to whirl her around. He was a good mover, agile, but the spinning she could do without, it was scrambling her brain further.

"Edward, stop."

Because he didn't respond, she questioned if she'd said the words or simply thought them. Perhaps the latter, hence why he was ignoring her.

"Edward, please, can you stop?"

She'd definitely said that and loudly too, but still he didn't take any notice.

The room – it was like it had no axis. It was spinning with her, faster and faster, a merry-go round, the furniture, the people blurring, becoming mere shapes, like the shapes in her dream, the ones with no faces, no features at all. All of them caught on the ride, unable to step off.

"Edward!"

What the hell was wrong with him?

"Edward!" It wasn't as if the music was that loud. "For fuck's sake, Edward!" He was going to be sorry if he continued, very sorry. She'd be sick, all over him and his fancy, close-fitting suit. And he'd deserve it. Oh God, why wasn't he listening to her? "Edward, please." This time her words were punctuated with a sob. She couldn't take anymore. She tried to push against him, but his grasp was too tight, nonetheless she made fists with her hands, ready to beat at his chest.

"Edward!" It wasn't her who was pleading with him this time it was someone else. And no, he wasn't pleading, he was demanding. "Let go of her. Now!"

Afterwards, she wasn't sure who was at fault – Edward's for being lost in the music, just as she'd been minutes before, or her own? Perhaps she should have tried harder to push him away, made him see what he was doing, how ill he was making her feel. Whoever's fault it was, the fun was over. As David grabbed Edward, tore him off Caroline, the music came to an abrupt halt, their animosity finally bearing fruit.

Chapter Eighteen

Caroline had to retreat in order to avoid being caught in the crossfire. In place of the music was a collective gasp as onlookers were left in no doubt that there was indeed a problem.

David must have noticed she was in trouble and decided to take matters into his own hands. If Edward was not going to let her go, he'd make him. Retaliating, Edward had lunged at David, causing him to lose his footing and tumble to the ground.

"Leave him!" Caroline was horrified at what was unfolding, her nausea forgotten as she screamed at them, terrified that Edward would do David some serious damage. Again, Edward ignored her, and threw himself on top of David instead, the look in his eyes – one of pure hatred – nothing less than spine-chilling.

How could this have happened? How could the night have turned so sour?

The lights, on full now instead of dimmed, flickered in time with their movements, briefly capturing Caroline's attention. That's all they needed: a power cut.

Whilst on his back, David raised his arms to protect his face. She looked wildly around; someone had to do something, anyone. Thankfully, David managed to reverse his fortunes. He pushed Edward off, and clambered to his feet, the shirt he was wearing pulled slightly to one side, a button torn open.

"You bastard," he growled. "Come on, get up. If you want a fight, I'll give it to you."

"David, no," Caroline begged, returning to his side.

Tallula sauntered over to Edward. "You're not going to let him get away with that, are you?" she said, lending him a hand to get up.

Caroline's jaw dropped. "Get away with what? Your boyfriend started this!"

"Caroline," warned David, one hand reaching out to her, the other wiping at the sweat on his face. "Just let me deal with this madman."

She shook her head. "No, David, I'm the reason this has happened." Turning to face Edward again, he was back on his feet, his blonde hair not so coiffured, having fallen into a middle parting, revealing a slight bald patch, a sight she found almost as shocking as what was unfolding, that he wasn't so perfect, after all. "Back the hell off."

Edward snarled; a feral gesture. "Get out of my way," he said. "No one lays their hands on me."

"You're supposed to be the manager of this hotel!" she bellowed. "Act like one!"

"The manager?" he repeated, as if this was news to him. "I said get out of my way."

"Caroline," David was urging her too. "You really do need to move."

"There's no way. Edward, if you want to get to David again, you'll have to come through me."

Tallula sniggered, gave a little shrug, causing hatred to

surge in Caroline too. She was enjoying this spectacle, the little bitch! She wanted them to hurt each other.

"You're despicable." Caroline spat the words at her.

"And you're a fool," Tallula retorted. "A blind fool. Have you told your boyfriend about Edward, by the way, about being together in his room, about *kissing* him?"

"What?" Caroline didn't realise how much she'd been dreading this being revealed, until now. "He's not my boyfriend…" Damn! Why had she kick-started her denial with that? What was wrong with her? She turned to face David. "I didn't kiss him. Well, I did, but it wasn't like that, I didn't want him to kiss me." It was a blatant lie; she *had* wanted Edward, initially. For a brief moment he'd seemed like the answer to everything. "David…?"

Before he had a chance to respond, Tallula jumped in again.

"You're so confused, aren't you, Caroline? Who should you pick? Which one excites you more? It must be fun having two men fighting over you. Does it happen very often?"

At boiling point, Caroline took a step forward. Never having been violent before, she felt an urge to be. Striking this woman – this hard-hearted, troublemaking, arrogant excuse for a woman – would give her the greatest of pleasures.

"Caroline…" David stepped forward too. "Caroline, no!"

She hadn't realised she'd raised her arm, but she had, because David had hold of it, preventing her from raising it further.

"But, David, what she's saying—"

"It doesn't matter about that."

But it did, she knew it did. He'd hate her for kissing Edward. Wouldn't he? She'd hate it if he'd been messing with Tallula, this man who was just a friend.

"David…" she tried again.

"Leave it."

Tallula was clearly finding Caroline's discomfort – her anger – oh so hysterical. Edward too. She half expected them to start whooping with delight, as mad as Elspeth. Gradually she registered that someone was making a noise, but it wasn't either of them, and it wasn't whooping. It was a strange sort of noise, eerie and high-pitched, a *keening*.

All heads turned towards Elspeth. She was still swaying, but not to the beat, in an abject state of distress.

"Oh, Christ," Caroline whispered, guilt seizing her. She was responsible for this too.

By Elspeth's side, Althea rose, leaving her in Jenna's care once again as she made her way towards the group at war. No one dared move a muscle as she approached, not even Edward or Tallula. The woman wore her authority like armour.

Reaching them all too quickly, she glared at Edward. "I want you to stop this."

"Or what?"

"Or leave."

He threw his hands up in the air. "Leave? As if I can leave!"

"No one's keeping you here," Althea returned, not flinching at all.

Once again, he looked feral as he bared his teeth. "I'm here because of you."

Caroline glanced at David; he seemed confused too by

this exchange, sensing perhaps, as she did, this wasn't solely about recent events. It ran deeper.

"I'm warning you, Edward, I will not have you running riot in *my* hotel."

"This is not your hotel."

"I've been here since the beginning." Something she'd told Caroline too. "You haven't."

"That doesn't give—"

"You're not irreplaceable. Remember that."

"Oh come on now, better the devil you know, surely?"

"Not always."

Was Edward trembling slightly? Caroline couldn't be sure.

"And keep in mind something else," Althea continued. "There are rules. Adhere to them and teach that acolyte of yours to do the same."

He was either trembling or shaking with fury. "You've had your day, mark my words, mine is yet to come."

"You don't frighten me, Edward. Your kind never has."

"I'm one of a kind, Althea, perhaps *you* should remember that."

Beside her, Caroline felt David bristle too. Was he going to get involved again? Rescue another damsel in distress? But Althea wasn't in distress, far from it; she was the epitome of calm and composure, an affront to Edward's eyes as he turned his head away, unable to keep staring at her, despite having issued such curious threats.

"It's different here!" Elspeth had stopped keening and was shouting instead. "I don't like it. I want to leave. Shoo, shoo, get away, all of you! I *can't* stay."

Tallula was the first to respond, shaking her head in a wry manner. "All this talk of leaving. Haven't you been listening, Elspeth *honey*? It's impossible."

Marilyn reacted immediately to Tallula's sarcasm. "Don't you speak to her like that, don't you dare." Leaving a baffled John behind, she hurried over to Elspeth and Jenna.

"What are you going to do?" Tallula called after her. "Fawn over her again? Feed her more of your sugarcoated lies? Where's she going to go anyway? Who in hell would want someone like her? What did you call her, Edward? Oh, that's it; a liability."

"Edward!" Althea's nostrils flared. "I told you to keep her under control."

"Of course we'll be able to leave." Marilyn was almost as agitated as Elspeth. "There's no more snow forecast, the storm's passing, they said so on the TV. A couple of days and we'll be gone. Thank goodness." Fawning over Elspeth, as Tallula had described it, she added, "Don't worry about a thing. I'll look after you, after the Egress, I mean. If you want me to, if you need me to. I miss having someone to look after, ever since…ever since…"

Her technique may have been effective before, but Elspeth was having none of it now. She slapped Marilyn's hand away and backed off from Jenna too. "She's right, you're a liar, a big fat dirty liar. We can't leave. We're trapped. Ohhhh!" The word was like an explosion, containing so much dread. "I don't want this. Not anymore. I want it to go away."

She was sobbing loudly and, for the first time, even Althea looked rattled. "We have to take her somewhere," she said. "Encourage her to rest."

David objected. "We deal with her problem out in the open, we don't keep hiding her."

Althea was insistent. "All she needs is rest." Finally taking her leave of Edward, she returned to her table. David followed, as did Caroline.

"Elspeth, dear," Althea said, as she drew closer, "listen to me. There really is nothing to fear."

Spittle flew from Elspeth's mouth as she shook her head. "You don't know what I've seen. Other things. Bad things. They're here too, in this hotel. They're everywhere."

"*I* will keep you safe."

"You? You can't. You're… You're old."

"Elspeth—"

David interrupted Althea. "We have to find some way of getting her professional help. This situation, the state she's in, it's potentially dangerous."

"*We* help her," Althea declared. "There's no one else."

David was just as determined. "We call 911, if only to report the situation. Just in case she—"

"Work with me, David," Althea hissed, "not against me."

"Lady, I'm not—"

"Are we sure there's no doctor in the house?" Caroline interrupted, as desperate as David. "Because if there is—"

"Doctor? There's no one useful in this batch," Edward said with his usual derision.

"Batch?" Caroline repeated. What the heck did he mean by that?

"If I'm the manager, surely I'd know," he continued, daring her to challenge him again.

"Oh, honey, honey," Marilyn was not just appealing; she was *begging* Elspeth to listen to her. "Move into my room, it's next door to yours anyway, so there's no difference, not really. It'd be so lovely to have you. Think of it. We won't be lonely anymore, either of us." Tears started to pour down her face too, causing an anguished John to hover close by.

"We have to do something," Caroline whispered to David. She didn't mean rescue the evening as such, but certainly try and stop it from deteriorating further.

David nodded in agreement. "Althea, I'm going to reception to dial 911. If I insist it's an emergency, they'll do something; there must be a snowplough they can press into action."

"Don't you think there are enough emergencies in and around the state?" No longer mute, John had started speaking.

David looked at him. "Well, yeah, but…"

"So many are trapped or in danger."

"I know."

"So does anyone care about us?"

"John, you have to understand—"

"Do we even *deserve* to be cared about?"

There was silence for a moment, no one quite knowing how to respond and then Caroline spoke once again. "David," she instructed. "Just make the call."

Althea's eyes followed David as he hurried from the room. With her attention captured, Edward took the opportunity to stride forward, that terrible smile back on his face. Tallula was smiling too, although her eyes remained as cold as ever. What were they up to?

Althea, Caroline wanted to warn her, *keep your eyes on Edward not David.*

Instead, she was the one staring as he reached out a hand to Elspeth. Why the sudden concern? Certainly, he hadn't bothered to assist – to manage – when she'd been outside, half-naked in the snow, trying to tunnel her way out of here. The bad things she told Althea she'd seen, were they what she was trying to get away from? Perhaps the drugs she was using were causing her to hallucinate. *They're here in this hotel. They're everywhere.* She'd said that too. But what had she seen exactly? The same things that had haunted Caroline's dreams, souls in torment. And was it true? Were they really everywhere, not confined to 1106? That thought caused her to shake almost as much as John, when he'd poured from the jug of water, when he'd spilt it on the tablecloth. As much as Edward too, when he and Althea were arguing – afraid, enraged, maybe he'd been both.

A scream ripped through her.

It was Elspeth again, a single solitary sound.

Again, they all stared at her, some mouths hanging open.

She'd fallen, collapsed in a heap on the floor, a tangle of limbs clad in vivid shades of green, her red hair wilder than ever, like rusted coils. Marilyn dropped to her knees first, followed by Jenna, others rushing forward and crowding her, blocking her from view, from Althea's too – whose expression was indescribable, although shock was a part of it.

Caroline could understand that shock; she felt it too, along with dismay and confusion – *especially* confusion. Had what she'd just seen had any relevance, or was it mere coincidence? The moment Elspeth had collapsed had been the same moment Edward's hand had touched her flesh.

Chapter Nineteen

It was worse than she'd realised. Elspeth had stopped breathing.

No matter how much effort John and David put into trying to revive her, they couldn't. She was gone, no more than an empty vessel.

From feeling happy, Caroline was back to being numb inside, afraid of feeling anything, of the pain it would cause.

What is it that you're so afraid of?

This. Death. The great destroyer. And how quickly it could strike.

Marilyn's sobbing shattered the stunned silence. "How is this possible? How?" Turning his attention from the dead to the living, John tended to Marilyn instead. She clung to him, the carer needing care, solace in it for him perhaps that he was able to fulfil such a role. "I'm sick of death," she continued. "Sick of it. Poor Elspeth, that poor little girl."

It was Edward who suggested they should lay her body out in one of the rooms being renovated, confusing Caroline further. If he'd had anything to do with her death – and he couldn't have done, a simple touch wasn't enough to kill someone – would he really be volunteering to help right now? She blamed the alcohol, as well as the aggression of earlier – both were fuelling her imagination. She had to keep a grip on reality, not lose it.

David agreed with Edward's suggestion. Putting their differences to one side, the pair had lifted her body, David at the top end, Edward holding the woman's legs.

"The fourth floor," Althea directed. "Take her there. Room 409 is undergoing renovation."

Those in the ballroom who had witnessed the incident parted like a biblical wave to let David and Edward through. Caroline could hardly bear to watch as they retreated.

The crowd gradually dispersing, she lingered still, her eyes returning to where Elspeth had fallen, her teeth gnawing at her lower lip. Finally, she made her way to reception.

The emergency services had been called again and given an update of what had happened to Elspeth, not by David this time, by Raquel. When David had tried calling, he'd had trouble getting through, the line cutting out. Raquel had had no such trouble.

"It's done," she informed Caroline. "They know what's happened to Elspeth."

"What *has* happened, do you think?"

"A heart attack. That seems most likely."

"And what are they going to do about it?"

Raquel shrugged. "It's as they said, as soon as they can get here they will. They'll confirm the death and then take her away, to the morgue probably."

"The morgue? Is that in the centre of Williamsfield?"

"It is now, yes."

With little else to say, Caroline set her sights on the elevator, daring it to play up as she approached, as if it were somehow sentient. It didn't; no stutter, no splutter, no chugging, or grinding. In her room, she lay down on her bed and closed her eyes. She couldn't sleep. Not after what had happened. She simply lay there for what seemed like forever, staring at the ceiling; a crack in it that she hadn't noticed before, and in the far corner cobwebs that needed dusting. Sighing with frustration, she screwed her eyes tighter, tried to force sleep to play ball – oblivion would be very welcome right now – but it was no use, the cogs in her mind kept whirring. Was there nothing to be salvaged from the wreck?

That thought developing, she sat up.

What time was it? Not late. Not really. Was David back in his room? If so, would he be able to sleep after all that had happened, or was he just as restless as her? What would he think if she went and knocked at his door? Should she chance it?

Her heart began to gallop.

She'd met many men in her life, had a relationship that had lasted for over three years, fizzling out eventually and leaving her slightly mystified as to why either one hadn't tried harder to stick with it. *Better the devil you know*, as Edward had said, but like Althea, she didn't agree. There'd been another longish relationship – by her standards anyway – eighteen months plus. That had ended too, her feelings waning this time, not his. He'd professed to be heartbroken, had stalked her for several months after their split, begging her to reconsider. But she wouldn't settle for anything less than a two-way street. Her parents had set the standard – a good thing on the whole, she was certain of it. What they had she wanted too. She'd hold out for it. But no one had come close.

Until now perhaps.

Her body moving as though it had a will of its own, she swung her legs over the side of the bed, and, allowing only a brief pit stop to tug on a pair of jeans and a jumper, she made her way to the door. Grabbing her room key, she moved quickly, afraid that her mind would catch up with her – would start to throw obstacles in her way: *doubts*.

Reaching the door, she was about to press down on the brass handle, when a short sharp knock on the other side almost caused her to cry out.

Who could it be? Surely not…

Again, refusing to think too much, she yanked the door open.

It was. It was him! David.

Framed by the doorway, he was a welcome but wretched sight. Gaunt was how she'd describe him. His face thinner somehow, his skin even paler than Althea's if such a thing was possible. There was a bruise developing on his jaw, probably from the tussle with Edward, matching his bruised forehead, and in his eyes, there was such weariness.

"Caroline," he said. Not just a mere utterance of her name, there was a question in it.

"David," she replied, answering him.

He closed the gap between them in less than a second, wrapping his arms around her.

* * *

For once she could identify with the drowning man, with everybody who'd ever felt the need to hold on. Right now, in the bedroom of 1106, she was clinging to David as if her life depended on it. Every touch of his hand seemed to brand her, to mark her as his. She *was* his, she belonged to him entirely, and he to her, only happiness about that, no fear.

The memory of how they'd got to the bed was now a blur – perhaps she'd be able to recall it at a later date, when she thought about it, when she replayed it over and over again, as she knew she would, reliving it when the miles eventually separated them.

But there was nothing separating them now. They were as close as two people could be. That they should have found each other, been forced together by circumstance, by fate perhaps, was nothing less than a miracle. She'd fallen for an American man as her father had fallen for an American woman, falling deeper with every second that passed.

"Caroline," he was murmuring her name again. No question in it this time, just joy and wonder, his lips having left hers and tracing their way downwards.

She arched slightly; her head pressed back into the pillow. Every second was ecstasy, her breath becoming more and more ragged as he worked his way lower still.

Nothing else mattered, not Elspeth, the argument with Edward, Marilyn's grief, the mysterious teen, imperious Althea, or the storm that had imprisoned them. She was *glad* it had done so, sweeping her straight into this man's arms. It could rage forever, as far as she was concerned, because she didn't want this to end. Such joy shouldn't be tainted by what had happened earlier – the brawl, the revelation, the death. Perhaps it was wrong given the circumstances, but it felt so right.

Briefly he stopped and stared into her eyes.

Everything she was feeling was mirrored in his gaze.

Bittersweet – that's what this was.

He was hers and she was his, but for how long?

"*This* is all that matters." He could read her mind as well as her body.

She didn't dispute him. The here and now was all they had, all anyone ever had.

His lips sought hers again as he started to move against her, their hips grinding, gently at first but gaining in momentum, fingers dug into shoulders, into each other's backs; riding a storm of another kind, not a silent one this time, their cries, their gasps, were as loud as thunder, dredged up from the very depths, given release at last.

Live. Love.

Finally, she was doing both.

* * *

"Hey." Half-closed, David's eyes were almost as feline as Edward's.

"Hey, yourself," she answered.

Morning had come too quickly. The hours in between spent exploring each other as much as possible and dozing rather than sleeping – there was no way she could sleep.

With one hand, he reached out to push some hair behind her ears, his fingers lingering, brushing against her cheek too.

"You're beautiful, d'ya know that?"

She knew how he meant it, not just physically, but inside too, as he was to her.

As on the dance floor, tears filled her eyes, catching her

by surprise.

He pushed himself upwards to rest on one arm, surprise on his face too. "What is it? What's the matter?"

She rushed to reassure him. There was nothing she regretted, nothing at all. "I just don't want this to end."

"Why does it have to?"

"Reality. It'll kick in soon enough."

His lips curved into a wry smile. "This feels pretty real to me."

She tried to laugh too. "Some holiday romance, huh?"

"Holiday romance? Caroline! You sure know how to demean a situation."

She winced. "Sorry, but over-enthusiasm can scare a guy off."

"Not this guy. You be as enthusiastic as the mood takes you."

He settled back down beside her and drew her into his arms, into a protective circle, in which no harm could ever come to her. If only she could stay there. If only the world really would fade. The Egress was a special place, she'd been told that over and over again, she'd read it in the welcome note, and it was true. Certainly she'd found something special here, something that had previously eluded her. A thousand love songs suddenly made sense, classic works of fiction, poetry too. She got it, every last word; it was no longer foreign. But there was a world out there and, despite her efforts, it kept encroaching on her thoughts.

"You asked me if I was worried about work. Are you?"

He hesitated before answering. "Work? Why would I be?"

"You know, missing out on goals, targets, I suppose.

Getting into trouble with your boss?"

"My boss? No. I'm my own boss in many ways."

"Are you commission based?"

He pulled his head away to look at her, amusement on his face. "Hey, Ms. Daynes, you wouldn't be after my money, would you?"

She smiled too. "I earn enough to keep myself, thanks."

"That's alright then. Yes, I'm commission based, in a way, but it's not a problem, really. Don't worry about it."

A few moments passed, and then worry crept in again. "What about Elspeth? What happened to her, do you think? How can a person just die like that?"

Again he didn't answer straight away. When he did his voice was solemn. "We don't know how long she's been a user – it may have been years, plenty of 'em. The strain that puts on the heart is enormous. I'm no expert but I have to say, her behaviour was very erratic, her mind almost certainly fried. Even when lucid she tripped over her words, made very little sense. You can tell she's been in trouble for a long time."

Caroline felt like crying again. "That's awful."

"Yeah, I know. Drugs, they're a scourge. Once they get their hooks into you…"

She was the one to sit now, so that she could stare down into his eyes. "You know, you were so lovely with her, you and Marilyn, you did everything you could to help her. I think that's when I first…" Her words tailed off as her cheeks started to burn.

He wasn't going to let her get away with it. "First what, Caroline?"

She swallowed. Could she say it, was it too soon? "I… David, you know that thing with Edward—"

"Caroline, don't spoil this."

"I want to explain – I *have* to. It was nothing, just a kiss, unexpected and, in the end, unwanted. There was never a chance of anything more happening between us."

He nodded, sombre again. "Thanks. I think I did need to hear that, after all."

She took a deep breath. "David, what we have, what we've discovered, can we make it work? I know we're on opposite sides of the pond, but we're both free agents, at least." Expecting him to reply straightaway, she was surprised when he didn't. "David?"

He sat up too, causing her insides to turn to jelly. Had she read this wrong?

He took her hands in his and held them. "You've been truthful with me; I need to return the favour. I've already told you I'm not in a relationship, the first night we met, and that's correct, up to a point. There is a woman. Nothing's happened; we've not long met either. I like her and she seems keen on me, but…" He had to stop to take a breath. "She's not like you. I don't feel this way about her. I've *never* felt this way. Caroline, you're asking me if this could work. Here's my answer: it *has* to."

There was desperation in his words that she could identify with – that only intensified as his lips met hers again, lending an almost frenzied quality to their next bout of lovemaking. At the point of climax the tears started again. She couldn't prevent them. Bittersweet. Yet again she thought that – couldn't push the word aside – it *defined* them somehow. This should be the happiest time of her life. It was the happiest time. And yet…

Caroline, you have to stop fretting.

She was trying, she really was. Later, as they finally left

the sanctuary of her bed and padded over to the window to see what the day was like, worry caught hold of her again, its grip as powerful as any drug that might have ensnared Elspeth. David gazed outwards whilst she gazed at him, noting again the paleness of his skin, how the bruises stood out against it. And then she turned away; saw not just the grey, leaden sky that she'd grown used to, but also a tiny patch of shimmering blue. She should have been thrilled to see it, ecstatic, as it meant change really was on its way. But all it triggered was dismay. *It's the beginning of the end,* was all she could think, immediately trying to dismiss yet another rogue thought. *This is all going to end.*

Chapter Twenty

On the fourth night there was hardly anyone in attendance at dinner, as if people were in hiding. *Perhaps we should hide too*, thought Caroline, standing where she had so often recently: at the entrance to the ballroom. *Hole up in 1106 until the thaw really does set in.* But it wasn't feasible. Besides the pair of them having worked up a considerable appetite, David wanted to check on Elspeth's body, he felt a responsibility for her, a reluctance to leave her completely alone in the dark, something Caroline appreciated, even if Elspeth couldn't. It turned out Raquel wasn't averse to the idea. On the contrary, it was as if she half expected it, and handed over the key without further question. Caroline offered to accompany him to 409, but he'd been adamant there was no need. Despite declaring dinner a sacred ritual, she could see there was no Althea, events having taken their toll on her too, most likely. Edward was there, however, doing his utmost to look composed. David had said that the two men had indeed reached a truce, albeit an uneasy one, but she was furious with him still for attacking David.

"Don't be," David had advised, prior to dinner. "Ignore him, and ignore Tallula too, we'll be rid of them soon enough."

Hallelujah to that. Tallula was with Edward. She seemed completely unfazed by anything that had gone before. Rather, she behaved like the cat that had got the cream, leaning into him, one hand always on him, fawning as much as Marilyn ever had towards Elspeth.

Before taking a seat, Caroline stopped at Marilyn's table. She'd been sitting alone initially, John coming in to join her a few minutes later, and her eyes flickering towards the doorway until he did. Their mutual dependency seemed to have evolved naturally enough, loss being the glue that united them, although what type of loss it was for John, she still didn't know. Perhaps she never would – there was every chance she'd leave the Egress before an opportunity arose to speak to him alone again. Whatever it was, she was glad they had each other; their relationship might last after they'd left here too.

She and Marilyn talked about Elspeth, of course, Marilyn struggling for composure as her eyes started watering, one hand, perhaps inevitably, creeping up towards her neck – a nervous habit Caroline was beginning to think, certainly there was no evidence of a rash. On seeing her upset again, John had offered Marilyn water and she'd taken it, bestowing on him a grateful smile. When she'd finished drinking, she reached across, and patted John's arm, and then she'd let her hand linger, clearly deriving comfort from such nearness. The other topic of conversation between them had been the weather. It might be imagination at work again, but she detected disappointment in them that it was on the turn too.

After a while, Caroline felt like she was intruding on the couple, although she knew that would never be their intention. These weren't people who'd ever want to make anyone feel uncomfortable. They were good people, she decided, even John, despite his low opinion of himself. Making her excuses, she returned to her usual table.

When David arrived, he looked more haunted than ever. His eyes only briefly engaging with Edward's, and Caroline was surprised to note it was the latter who chose to avert his gaze first. Tallula, though, was another matter. She glared at David and continued to do so long after he'd sat down. Caroline wouldn't give her the satisfaction of glaring back. He was right – the most effective thing to do was not give them the attention they craved.

Dinner was eaten; catfish this time, for both of them. There was a very real likelihood the roads would be passable again from tomorrow, or if not, the next day. She hadn't listened to the news for a long time, couldn't summon up the interest if she were honest, but she'd gleaned that the snowploughs were now out in force. The world was opening up again, becoming theirs. She still had three days left before her scheduled flight home. Days that she and David had resolved to spend together, perhaps not here, at the Egress, but somewhere. And then… Well then, who knew?

Coffee finished too, David looked at her. "Your room or mine?"

"You fancy christening that too, do you?"

He shrugged. "Why not? I'll tell you something: my room has one thing going for it. One thing that's quite handy, considering."

"Considering what?"

His eyes led her downwards. "It's a hell of a lot closer. I'm raring to go."

She opened her mouth. "Mr Mason, I'm shocked!"

"Bullcrap, you're delighted."

"But… But…"

"Seriously, honey, modesty doesn't suit you."

About to protest, she decided against it. "Damn it, you're right. I'll race you."

They'd actually left the ballroom in a sedate manner rather than frenzied, their pace picking up in the lobby and then increasing further on the stairwell, often taking steps two at a time. Reaching 310, she was excited to see the interior too – another unique room.

Whilst he busied himself opening the door, a thought occurred. *'Not superstitious, are you?'* That's what Raquel had said when she'd given David this room. What had she meant by that? Just as the door swung open, she realised.

"Of course! Three plus ten equals thirteen."

David turned to her, a frown on his face. "What's that you said?"

"When Raquel gave you the key to your room, she asked if you were superstitious, do you remember?" It was clear he didn't, so she elaborated. "I was puzzled too. In this hotel there's no number 13, rooms start with the floor number, so on the second floor it's 201 to 210, then 301 to 310, 401 and so on and so on. Well…three plus ten equals thirteen, that's what she must have meant. Lucky for some, and it is, it's the corner suite."

David was still perplexed. "That's a bit of a stretch. I mean, 310 isn't the only room in the hotel that adds up to 13, there's 508—"

"607," she added, "706, 805, 904—"

"What are you, a math genius?"

"I do work in finance," she reminded him.

"Of course. I guess that explains the way your mind works." Reaching out, he grabbed her by the waist and pulled her over the threshold. Immediately a bolt of pain threatened to blind her, similar to the one she'd experienced on the night Edward had arrived at the hotel. It caused her to screw her eyes shut and turn her head to the side.

"Are you okay?"

"Yeah, I... It's nothing. I just need a glass of water, I think."

"It's not that side of garlic bread I had at dinner?" he quipped.

She tried to smile even though it hurt. "I had it too, remember? You insisted, so that we cancel each other out."

"Did it work?"

"Uh-huh."

"Phew, that's a relief. One glass of water coming right up."

He released her and she continued inwards, the pain only increasing. A large room with several windows, it had a solid feel to it, with sturdy pieces of furniture reinforcing that fact. The leather sofas, abstract artwork on the wall, and his coffee cup perched on the writing desk gave it a masculine energy. It suited him perfectly, this room. It was exactly as she'd imagined it to be. Reaching out a hand to steady herself against the desk, she couldn't help but think about the room below – 210 – the corner suite her parents had once occupied. It was close. Perhaps a little too close, surreal even. That's what everything at the Egress felt like – surreal – including her feelings about David, erupting out of nowhere to consume her. And yet, in *her* room, on the eleventh floor, it was as real as it got.

A noise. Laughter. She was sure of it. *Tinkling* laughter.

"Here you go." David had returned with the water. "Take a sip."

She did but it failed to revive her.

Concern caused him to frown. "Caroline, you really don't look well—"

"I'm fine, honestly." She had to be; she didn't want anything to mar their time together. "It's just... I don't know. Do you mind if we go back to my room?"

"Your room? Well, if you'd rather—"

"I really think I would. I'm sorry."

Back in 1106, she did indeed feel better – the pain gradually subsiding. But she was shaken by her feeling of weirdness in 310; couldn't quite forget it. And the laughter she'd heard – her mother's laughter – that had upset her too. Imagination was such a powerful thing, able to manifest something that wasn't there. Longing probably at the root of it.

If only her mother knew about her being here at the Egress. In some ways, she'd been born again. And yet...

God, she was tired. In bed, she'd asked David just to hold her first of all.

"Honey, I'll hold you all night long, if that's what you want."

She had no idea that she'd fallen asleep. Not until she woke up. A slight movement had disturbed her. Lying on her side, she forced herself to open her eyes, fearful of what she might see. It was dark, and in the darkness, there was indeed a shape, but one that was dear to her: David. He had left her bed and was pulling on his clothes, clearly trying to be as quiet as possible. She was about to call out, to ask him what he was doing, but confusion stopped her.

Fear again that she was the fool Tallula said she was. That he'd had a change of heart and wanted to escape too.

No, it couldn't be. Despite only knowing him for such a short length of time, she trusted him. You could fake many things in life, but not love. Although neither of them had said as such, that's what they'd shared. She knew the difference. Or at least she did now. She'd come to the Egress seeking connection, and she'd found it, in more ways than one.

Having dressed, he was leaving. She should call out, she really should.

Fear: it was such a terrible thing.

It was only as he left the room, that she found the courage to call his name, but too late. All she heard in reply was the door as it closed.

"Shit!" What should she do, go after him? Or maybe she should give him a little while, not be so damned suspicious. He might have wanted to fetch something from his room. In fact, that was most likely to be it. She'd settle back down and wait. Be patient.

Mere minutes passed before that patience ran out.

She'd go to the third floor, knock on his door, and ask if everything was alright. Maybe he'd come over all headachy too. Or maybe...maybe guilt was overpowering him. That woman he'd met, maybe she wasn't so insignificant.

Caroline!

Okay, okay, but she wasn't going to be too hard on herself. There was a downside to feeling this way about a person – something she'd always suspected. It left you wide open.

Go and find out what's happening. He's either in his room, or the lobby. Where else is he going to go? And remember, you

203

ran out of coffee earlier. He loves coffee. He could have gone on a mission to replenish stocks.

In the middle of the night?

Caroline, you're never going to sleep until you know.

It was so quiet in the corridor, everyone in rooms either side of it slumbering – everyone except Elspeth. It seemed to take an age to reach her room, but as she passed it, she could hardly bear to look. Room 409, that was where she was now – another room whose numbers added up to thirteen. Not so lucky, after all. At the elevator, waiting for the doors to open, the doubts she'd managed to suppress had a ball rearing their ugly heads.

What if he's changed his mind about you?

What if he's had his fun?

What if this is the kind of thing he does all the time?

What if the only people who were ever going to love you are dead?

At last the doors opened and she all but stumbled in.

"Don't play up, please don't play up," she pleaded, pressing the button for three.

It cranked into life, descending swiftly enough. The doors opening, she faced another long walk up a badly lit corridor, all the way to the corner suite. The silence, although expected due to the hour, was unsettling, the thoughts louder in her head because of it.

Outside his door, she tapped gently before whispering his name. There was no reply. Again, as quietly as she could, she pushed down on the handle, but it refused to budge.

Frustrated, she laid her head against the door. *Where are you, David? Where the hell are you?* She felt sick again, cold and shivery, an ache in her heart as well as her chest. She'd go to the lobby. If he wasn't there, then…well, then she'd return to 1106. She couldn't continue to haunt the corridors like some desperate wraith.

Back in the elevator, she pressed the button for the lobby. It refused to move. Sighing, she jabbed at it a second time, a third, and a fourth.

"Oh, for God's sake!" This wasn't funny, not at this hour. It wasn't funny at any hour, come to think of it. If there was only one elevator – and that was a travesty in itself – management should make sure it bloody worked!

Suddenly the doors closed and her temper, having flared, died down. She'd be in the lobby in a few seconds. Strange if Raquel was still there, a perennial fixture, sighing under her breath, rolling her eyes, as bored as ever. Imagining that caused a smile rather than a frown, although it was short-lived. The doors might have closed, but that was it – there was no more progress than that.

"Oh, come on," she urged, jabbing at the button again.

The doors re-opened. As they did, she had to stifle a scream, one of frustration *and* surprise. Standing before her was the teen; the girl Tallula had called the architect's daughter. Her head low, her features still very much obscured by her thick black hair, she entered, Caroline stepping aside to make room for her. Like last time, she turned her back on Caroline without any acknowledgement whatsoever and faced outwards. Also like last time, she made no move to select the floor she wanted, causing Caroline annoyance as well as alarm. What was wrong with her? And what was she doing roaming about at this hour? Surely her parents wouldn't condone such behaviour.

Realising it wasn't fair to take her upset out on an

innocent young girl, Caroline stepped closer to the keypad. "What floor would you like?" There was no answer. "I'm going to the lobby. Is that okay?" Still she got no answer. "Look, I just need to go to the lobby, have a quick look around, and then I can take you back to your floor. You know, I'm surprised you're wandering about at this hour. I am, but, well, I am an adult."

The girl continued to ignore her, causing Caroline to roll her eyes in a Raquel-like fashion. Pressing the button, there was relief again when the elevator started to move, albeit groaning, finding the whole thing as much of an ordeal as she was. She'd better try again with the girl. She couldn't just pretend she wasn't there. "Hey, are you okay? Seriously, I really think that at this time of night you should be in your room…"

Her voice trailed away as she realised something. The girl was wearing the exact same clothes as when she'd first seen her. Slightly old-fashioned when she thought about it – the A-line plaid skirt that ended just above her knees, the lemon blouse, the long white socks, the black slip-ons. And there was a smell too, one with a familiar tinge to it.

She swallowed. They were almost at the lobby. She could just get out and forget about the architect's daughter, leave her to her own devices. Or she could try harder.

Once again, she reached out a hand, not to touch the keypad this time, but the girl's shoulder. "Sweetheart, I'm a little bit worried…"

Her voice stuck in her throat; as if she were mute too, shock having rendered her speechless. The girl was frozen, absolutely frozen, and Caroline's hand froze too upon contact. It stuck to the girl, making it impossible to pull away.

What's going on?

Almost immediately images started to flash in her mind. The child – *this* child, smiling, laughing, and…teasing. Is that what she was doing, teasing? If so, whom? She couldn't see anyone but the girl, walking down a corridor, one that had concrete on the floor instead of carpet, whose walls were concrete too, wires hanging where lights should be – a building site basically, barely formed – the Egress in its infancy. She had her back to Caroline, and was wearing exactly what she had on now, tossing her luxuriant hair over her shoulder, turning her face to the side to reveal a tantalising glimpse of red lips and marble white skin. She was pretty, Caroline guessed. Coquettish.

Suddenly the girl laughed – not a particularly pleasant sound – it had too much Tallula in it. And as she did, the smell of decay grew more pungent.

The girl had stopped laughing now and was shaking her head, hair swishing from side to side. Caroline got the vivid impression she was pouting. The impression intensified as the girl stamped her foot – a display of petulance, anger even. Immature, but then so was the girl. She was young, a teenager trying to be a woman, running before she could walk.

The girl swung around. Frustratingly, so did Caroline's vision, the girl still had her back to her, but there was another person, there had to be, the one that she was arguing with. Not just arguing, they were screaming at each other, the atmosphere changing, becoming far more tense. The girl stiffened. Was she frightened? Caroline wondered. Had she lost control?

The girl took a step back, and then another. Caroline tensed too.

Be careful, she wanted to shout. *Watch where you're going.*

The place was a building site. And building sites were dangerous.

There was a scream – the horror in it more than a match for Elspeth's. No longer upright, petulant, or even defiant, the teenager was falling, hands grabbing frantically at thin air, her legs cycling madly as black hair formed a swirling mass around her. Falling and falling, when would it end? Her horror was Caroline's horror – both of them caught in the grip of terror. How was this happening? How? Neither one could understand it. Impact – a sound to make you sick to your stomach. Young bones smashed, blood quickly pooling, brighter than her lipstick. And her face…such a pretty face, destroyed.

As the girl turned, Caroline's hand was released, and she snatched it back. Bringing it upwards, she covered her eyes.

I don't want to see. Don't show me, please. I don't want to.

But the teen hadn't listened to her before, so why should she this time?

As the elevator ground to a halt, having to force herself to do it, Caroline lowered her hand and slowly, slowly opened her eyes. *Face up to your fears*, Althea instructed. Well, this was one of them. In response, the girl lifted her head – finally – parting that thick, thick hair of hers as though it were a theatre curtain, preparing for the great reveal.

It wasn't a face, not anymore, but a congealed mass of blood and bone. One eye was dangling from its socket, on a silken thread, the other pushed far into her skull, the pupil turned upwards, searching for something that was way beyond.

A travesty. An abomination. She wasn't real! Surely.

If she'd fallen, if she'd hit the ground, exactly where they were standing now, in the lobby of the Egress before the elevator was fitted, then she was dead, stone cold dead – not able to stand in front of Caroline, to show her a sight she'd never forget, one that would curdle every dream, haunt her even during waking hours.

If she'd fallen…

"Oh God, it wasn't an accident, was it?"

As the screams erupted from deep within her, as the elevator doors finally released their quarry, as she started to back away from the thing she was entombed with – an apparition, a ghost, the architect's daughter – as she stumbled and fell, was caught in someone's arms, someone with the strength that had deserted her, she realised the truth.

The girl had been pushed!

Chapter Twenty-One

How David managed to get her back to her room, Caroline didn't know. Her mind, her entire body, was rigid, as though she were dead too and rigor mortis had set in. They hadn't taken the elevator. There was no way she'd set foot in it again. She would have continued screaming blue murder if he'd insisted. He must have half-carried her, half dragged her up the stairwell, not taking her to his room – she wouldn't go there either, he seemed to instinctively know that – but all the way to the eleventh floor, to her room, 1106.

She wasn't screaming any longer, or gibbering. Instead her breath was coming in short sharp gasps that were rendering it impossible to speak. The miracle was that she was breathing at all. That her heart hadn't given out after what she'd witnessed.

"But what did you see?" David had bundled her into her room, closed the door, and sat her on the sofa, kneeling in front of her with both hands on her shoulders.

"I… I…" Words kept failing her. How could she describe what she'd seen? Who would believe her? She looked into his eyes. *He'd* believe her. David would know she wasn't capable of making such a diabolical thing up.

She had to try again. But first the tears came, her body needing to purge itself.

"It's okay, I'm here now," he said, pulling her to him. "I've got you. You're safe."

She wanted with all her heart to believe him. She *did* believe him, but once the floodgates had opened the torrent wouldn't cease. Tears shed not only because of what had just happened, but also for her parents; for their love and their life together coming to such a painful and undignified end; and for her own loneliness. Because she now realised that's what she'd been before meeting David – lonely, despite how hard she tried to deny it. Eventually, the river ran dry, leaving in its wake, not terror, not anymore, but peace, acceptance even – the last thing she'd expected after what had happened.

"David, that teen I met in the elevator on my first day here, she's who I saw. The architect's daughter."

"The girl who fell."

"What?" She hadn't mentioned that part to him, so how come he knew? "David?"

"She fell down the elevator shaft when the hotel was being built, in the early 1920s. She was, as you say, the architect's daughter. He never got over it according to what I've read. Never returned to finish the job. Another architect was appointed instead, but he died here too – but it wasn't an accident this time. He was found beaten to death."

"Beaten? By who?"

"It was never confirmed but he was a betting man, allegedly. There was a dispute about what he owed and that someone must have snuck on site while he was here alone one day and…well…"

"So there were two murders when the Egress was being built?"

"Two? What do you mean?"

"David, the girl didn't fall by accident, she was pushed."

"Pushed? But—"

"How do you know so much about her, and about the replacement architect?"

Even in such a dim light, she could see his skin flush. "It's… It's all there, in the public domain, although I have to say, you gotta dig hard for it. Two tragic deaths before completion didn't bode well for the hotel. You know how superstitious people are. The rumour was that the building was cursed even before it was finished. Because of that, the opening day was a failure, people avoiding the place rather than turning up in their droves, as hoped." He inclined his head slightly in that way he did when he was contemplating. "That could account for all those photos downstairs, the ones without any people – they'd gotten everything ready for the big day and it was a disaster. That reputation dogged the hotel. It still does, I think, to this very day. I bet it barely scrapes by. As you already know, there were plans for other buildings in this area of Williamsfield, lining the road all the way into downtown, the Egress at its helm. It was supposed to breathe new life into the area, put it on the map as a commercial business hub, and a special place to come and stay, but of course that never happened. Investors lost faith, put their money elsewhere, diverted roads even, leaving it to…" He paused again, frowned slightly. "Well, to its own devices, I guess. What's all this about the architect's daughter being pushed?"

Caroline swallowed. She had to tell the truth. "I saw

what happened to her, David. She showed me." Without embellishing it in the slightest, she explained. "She was flirting with someone, teasing them. Whoever it was, I don't think he appreciated it. I never saw his face, never got a glimpse, but I began to sense anger on his part, because this kid, she was making a fool of him. He was hurt. I got that too. Perhaps he didn't mean to push her, but she was threatening him...something about his wife and child, about getting Daddy to fire him. He lost his temper and lashed out. She fell backwards into the empty elevator shaft, into nothing..." Her heart beginning to race again, she had to take a deep breath to calm herself. "I felt her panic, David. Her terror, her sheer *disbelief.* Those feelings, they're so strong in her still, time hasn't diluted them."

"Poor kid," David lamented, and for a moment Caroline was stunned – but in a way that impressed rather than horrified her further. Here they were, the pair of them, feeling sorry for the abomination in the elevator, actually *sorry* for her. Because ultimately, she was a teenage girl, she'd been pretty once, a tease as so many teenage girls are, seeing what she could get away with, pushing the boundaries, playing with fire and getting burnt.

"Did anyone hear me screaming?" Caroline asked. She was stunned too that people hadn't come running from all corners of the hotel, considering the racket she'd made.

David smiled for the first time since he'd found her. "You were terrified, understandably, but you didn't scream the house down, you pulled yourself together quicker than most."

"I've seen a ghost, David. I've actually seen a ghost! What's she doing here? Why isn't she at rest?"

"I don't know. There's a lot I'm trying to find out."

"Find out? What do you mean? What else is there to discover?" For a moment he avoided her gaze. "David?"

He'd been squatting, but now he rose to sit by her, sighing heavily. "I'm sorry, I… I really did want to be truthful with you."

Her whole body seized. What was he going to say? What else was there to tell? And when he did, would all that had happened before pale into insignificance because of it, even the teen in the elevator? *This* was what being frightened truly felt like, she realised; the prospect of a tattered heart being stamped on all over again. "Is this about her again?"

"Who? Melissa?"

"If that's her name."

He shook his head. "No, no, this has nothing to do with her. I meant what I said: *you're* the one. As soon as we're out of here, I'll tell her what's happened. I'll end it."

Relief started to filter through. "So what is it then?"

"I'm not a travelling salesman."

"Oh." She tried to process what he was saying. "So what are you?"

"A private investigator."

"A private… Like in the movies?"

"The movies?" he queried.

"Yeah, I've seen so many American movies with private investigators in them. I… God, you're a cop!"

"I *used* to be a cop. I left the force a few years ago to go it alone."

"Okay, so you're a private investigator. Why lie about it?"

He hung his head. "It was just easier, I guess, and to an extent, confidential. I'm here because I think this hotel might be linked to a missing person's case."

"Who?"

"A woman called Helen Ansell. She went missing in this area just over a year ago."

"Have you interviewed the staff?" She remembered hovering nearby whilst he was speaking to someone, also saying he was busy when she'd asked him to join her for coffee. She'd wondered at the time what was so pressing. Now she knew, partly, anyway.

In answer to her question he nodded. "Not that I've gotten very far. No one remembers seeing her."

"Have you got a photo of her?"

"Yeah, here, it's in my wallet."

Retrieving his wallet from the back pocket of his jeans, he took the picture of Helen out and handed it to her. She was another pretty girl with a wide smile, her hair not quite the red of Elspeth's, paler in colour, strawberry blonde. "How old was she?"

"Twenty-one," David replied. "Barely twenty-one."

"What's her connection with the Egress?"

"She was drinking in a bar in Williamsfield – The Cocked Hat – and, according to the bartender, she was getting cosy with a man, someone who was quite a bit older than her, in his late thirties or so with blonde hair. It looked like they'd just met; certainly they'd arrived separately, Helen a good couple of hours earlier. She came up to the bar, he bought her a drink, and they went off to sit together. A little later they left. She sent her mother a text, just after ten, to say she was checking into a local hotel, that she'd be there for the next day or two, and she'd call her soon. We know the text was sent while she was at The Cocked Hat, or very close to it. That's the last trace

215

from her cell and also the place of her last credit transaction."

"No mention of this man to her mother, then?"

"No, we got the description of him from the bartender."

"Was she from around here?"

"No, again. She was from California, studying in San Francisco. She was taking a year off, travelling, exploring the country she lived in. Her father had insisted on it, apparently. She wanted to be a writer and he thought it would help her with that, give her the edge she needed. She'd done quite a bit of travelling before ending up in Williamsfield."

"And it was this hotel she checked into?"

"That's the thing, we don't actually know. There are several in the town itself. Nothing like this, though, they're more basic, but no luck so far. What makes it harder is there's been no credit card activity since the bar and no other hotels in the area have any record of her, which finally led me to here. This hotel's the last on my list before I spread the net wider. Of course it could be that she never made it to any hotel."

"You think she was murdered on the way?"

"She was on good terms with her parents, she'd kept in touch with them all through her travels, so to disappear like she did, it's out of character. She'd always been a good kid according to her folks, no trouble at all. Her mother... God, it's awful to see how broken she is. Her father too. They can't move forward. Because there's no body, because it's just a missing persons case, and the police can't spend any more time on it, they've got too much else to deal with. But Helen's parents need closure, they need answers, and that's what I'm trying to achieve."

"Oh, David." Caroline hung her head, trying to imagine what it was like to lose a child, grateful that she couldn't. "You're such a good man."

"I'm only doing my job."

"I know, but you care, it's obvious you do, and that's the difference. Not everyone who does your sort of work does. So…what were you doing in the lobby?"

"Like I said, no one's been particularly helpful at the Egress, and for the simplest of reasons maybe, because no one *does* remember her. The staff, they see a lot of people come and go – faces become a blur as faces often do. It's amazing how many people we don't remember in life."

Tallula had once said a similar thing. You come into contact with so many – hundreds upon hundreds – and yet only a few make an impact, for the best reasons *and* the worst.

"It could also be, of course," he added, "that she *didn't* stay here, but…I don't know. When I've questioned people, there's something about them. They don't quite look me in the eye when they answer. As a cop you're kinda sensitive to these things. I get the impression somebody does know something, but no one wants to say."

"Surely there are electronic records you could access?"

"It's a grey area in the USA. Hotels don't like to share guest information with the police, unless a warrant is shown. Even then, it's difficult to enforce. The argument is that it violates a person's right to privacy, and, in some ways, I agree. Basically, hotels don't have to keep electronic records for more than twelve months, and guess what?"

"You've already said it. Helen disappeared over a year ago."

"That's right. There's every chance that any record of

her staying here has been erased. There's a room behind Raquel – an office. She mainly keeps the door closed but I figured that's where the computer is, the phone, even the register from the lobby desk, in there at night, locked up."

Caroline's eyes widened. "And so what did you do, break in?"

"'Fraid so."

"I'm taking it you've already questioned Raquel about Helen?"

"In a roundabout way, and it was the same old same old: no knowledge of her at all."

"Have you actually told her you're a private investigator?"

He shook his head. "At the moment I'm playing the part of a concerned uncle. You're the first person I've told."

"Okay, I'm confused again. I get why you kept it from me, I'm not part of the investigation, but technically the others are, so surely you have a duty to inform them?"

"Caroline, just like people aren't too fond of the cops, they're not overly enamoured of PIs either. Like I said, initially it's just easier to pretend you're someone else, especially if we're stuck here. If firm evidence comes to light, well…that's when I up the ante."

She looked at him. "You're a fine actor."

"So, you bought that I was a travelling salesman?"

"Actually no I didn't, you don't fit the mould."

"Is that a good thing?"

"I like you as a PI better."

He smiled.

"So, you broke into the office, Raquel finally having left the desk unmanned. Then what?"

He answered her question with one of his own. "Caroline, what happened when you checked in? Did you see what was in that register that Raquel's always busy with?"

"No, it was under the shelf of the desk. I handed over my credit card and filled in a sheet of paper with my name and address and car registration. Raquel took it all to the back office, then came back with my credit card and handed me my room key."

"Yep, me too."

She was as baffled as him. "What are you getting at?"

"What I'm getting at is this: I found something odd in that back room, or rather I didn't find anything much at all. There was no computer in there, not even a phone. Sure Raquel could have used her cell to call 911, but to not have a landline, in a hotel? It's impossible."

"But there's a phone number for the Egress, have you tried it?"

"Yes, I have."

"And?"

"It's disconnected."

She searched for a reason. "The phone lines could be down due to the storm."

"Again, that's what I figured. But none of this is adding up."

"What about the register?"

"Oh, that was there alright."

"David?" Caroline prompted when he faltered again.

"It was laid open on the desk – in plain sight – and it was empty, nothing written in it at all. Every damn page was blank."

"Blank? But we've seen her scribble in it!"

"We *think* we've seen her scribble in it. What's in the office could be a dummy register, some strange kind of security measure, but again, why? What are they trying to hide?" He shook his head. "I don't know, it was almost as if someone knew I was going to break in, got there before me and removed anything of use. This place, it's not what it seems."

Which is why he hadn't dismissed what had happened to her in the elevator or put it down to hysteria.

"There have to be bona fide records," David continued, "and I need to see them, but I can't *demand* to see them, unless I get a warrant. And I can't get a warrant because of—"

"The weather."

"Yep, and the fact that I'm not a cop. I have to work with the cops to get one."

An idea formed. "What about Althea?"

"I've told you, I've tried to speak to her, several times. The timing's never right, according to Jenna anyway. She's tired, she's having a nap, or she doesn't feel well. Come back later, Jenna says, and I do, only to get the same response, over and over."

"Will you tell her you're a PI?"

"If I get the opportunity."

"Then let me try for you," Caroline responded. "I'll pave the way."

Chapter Twenty-Two

Morning arrived and with it would come change. Whether for better or for worse, Caroline had yet to discover.

The first thing she did on leaving her bed was to pad over to the window and look out of it; something of a ritual now. Whilst she stared outwards at a sky with even more blue in it than before, David turned on the TV. The signal was weaker than ever, despite the worst of the storm being over. The picture kept rolling and the presenter's voice cut out, but on CNN the warning was still clear: don't travel unless you have to, not yet.

Taking the stairs down to breakfast, at which Althea, Edward, and Tallula were absent, she and David hatched a plan. Caroline would go to Althea's room later that morning and try to speak with her, taking with her the photo of Helen Ansell.

"What about the architect's daughter?" Caroline mused. "Surely she'd know about her?"

"She might not know the truth," David pointed out, "just the legend. I know she said she's been here from the beginning, but her death and the death of the second architect happened while the Egress was still a building site. No one would have lived here during that time.

Besides, Helen is our priority and finding out the truth surrounding her."

Although Caroline agreed, her mind couldn't help but return to the teen. In the cold light of day it was tempting to think she'd imagined what she'd seen in the elevator. The result of stress, perhaps. But as much as she'd like to think that, she knew it wasn't true. The architect's daughter had truly existed. What was her name? She must have one – this ghost of a girl, as trapped as any of them.

After breakfast, they'd convened with John and Marilyn on their way out to the lobby, John complaining about the TV signal. "My radio's not working either, there's too much static. And have you noticed the lights? They're working but they're dimmer somehow."

He was right – the shadows around them, even in the lobby, were on the increase.

"When do you think the roads will be clear?" asked Marilyn, concern on her face but also something else – the beginnings of fear. John's agitation was worsening too, those shakes of his really quite persistent. Neither of them had ever mentioned anything to Caroline about the teen in the elevator, only Tallula seemed to know of her existence. She decided not to add to their apprehension by even hinting at what she'd experienced. The last thing she wanted was to plant the girl in their minds too, lest she start to take root.

In answer to Marilyn's question, Caroline replied, "Not long now, in a day or two."

"That's what I thought. It'll be strange, won't it, leaving here? Some things you can never get used to, but other things, you get used to them quite quickly really, don't you? What about Edward? Has anyone seen him this morning?"

Both David and Caroline shook their heads.

"I wonder where he is?" she mused. "And Althea too. I'd like to clear a few things up."

"Like what?" Caroline asked.

"Like payment for my room. I only intended on being here a couple of days, not five. I... I don't have much money to spare, you see. Not since..."

It was John who challenged this notion. "They won't charge, I'm sure of it. It wasn't our fault we got stranded. If they're decent folk they won't charge."

Strangely, this didn't seem to appease Marilyn. "But we have to pay something, don't you see? That's what I'm worried about. We don't just...get away with it."

Again Caroline glanced at David, confused by her insistence. John, however, hung his head, but not before she saw his eyes glisten. Had Marilyn's words upset him?

"John," Caroline ventured. When he didn't answer, she touched his arm. "John."

He flinched, as though her fingertips were red-hot pokers. "I'm sorry," he said, "I... I need to go to my room. I'm so very sorry."

As he turned towards the elevator, all three stared. Turning to Marilyn, Caroline thought she looked slightly glazed. "Are you okay?"

"Okay?" she repeated, the word clearly not registering. One hand came up to scratch almost viciously at her neck. "I'm going to my room too. I'm happier there."

Following in John's wake, she also left.

David ran a hand through his hair. "Huh? What just happened?"

"You tell me."

"I wish I could." Nodding towards the lobby desk, where Raquel was once more standing like a sentinel, he added, "Look, she's writing something in the register."

"We *think* she is. She could be doing a crossword."

David was having none of it. "There's no crossword, there's no magazine, and there's no novel of any kind. The only thing in front of her is an old-fashioned hotel register."

One replaced at night with a dummy in case of prying eyes.

"I suppose we'd better press on," David said, sighing. "Try our luck with Althea."

"Yeah," she replied, "but please, can we do one thing first? I'm desperate."

He raised an eyebrow. "Oh? Breakfast given you an appetite, has it?"

"What?" Confused at first, she then burst out laughing. "Oh, David, no, I don't mean that! I just want some fresh air, that's all. It feels like it's been so long." As she said it she realised it *had* been a long time – this was their fifth day, during which time they'd been out only twice. She was craving the fresh air, wanted to fill her lungs with the stuff.

Reaching the hotel doors, the snow had banked higher, making opening them trickier than ever.

"Geez, you think the maintenance men would have seen to this," David complained.

"*What* maintenance men?"

"Yeah, good point. This place operates with a skeleton crew."

"And yet there are two managers."

David looked at her. "It does seem like overkill, doesn't

it?"

As he resumed his effort with the doors, Caroline asked him how long he'd originally intended to stay at the Egress.

"A day or two, just to gather information."

"And if you had reasonable grounds for suspicion, you'd ask for a warrant to be issued?"

"Uh-huh. And if nothing comes of that, well…that's where Helen could be." He took a break to stare outwards. "Out there somewhere, buried deep."

He could be right, but the point is, she was *intending* to go to a hotel, now looking likely to be here, accompanied by a man; someone older than her, someone with blonde hair. Her spine tingled remembering that.

At last the doors opened.

"We don't have our coats with us," David noted as cold air swept in.

"We won't be long," she assured him.

It wasn't as reviving as she thought it would be, the air neither fresh nor crisp, but bitter. The snow was as solid as ever, the thaw that was promised less than evident. Wrapping her arms around herself, she shook her head and stamped her feet to keep the circulation flowing.

"Hard to imagine it ever being clear again, isn't it?"

David was right. It was. Harder still to imagine a world in colour; it had been white for so long. She had no idea what this place ordinarily looked like. Although they could see further than when they'd been out here with Elspeth, the horizon was still a blur, the white sky with its intermittent patches of blue melding only too readily with the landscape. She found the lack of contrast disorientating; the world having shrunk around them, she,

David, and the Egress, figures in a giant snow globe, with what lay beyond uncharted.

Instead of adjusting to the conditions, her breathing became more laboured. Turning to check on David, she saw his chest was heaving too.

"We'd better go in," she said, admitting defeat.

"Sure."

"And I'll head upstairs to see Althea."

He nodded. "While you do that, I'll wander over to Raquel's desk, lean in as close as I dare, see if I can work out what she's written in that book before she slams it shut on me."

"Good luck with that."

"Thanks, I think I'm gonna need it. Good luck to you too."

Exchanging a quick smile, they faced the hotel doors, Caroline actually looking *forward* to getting back inside. Outside it was just too damned hostile.

You have to leave at some point, Caroline.

She knew that, of course she did, but not today, not this morning.

This morning she had other things to do.

* * *

Leaving David, Caroline tackled the stairs again, not quite as out of puff when she reached the top, as she'd been the first time she'd tackled them. Her stamina might be improving, but that was the only positive. Her headache had returned, not a sharp pain like before, more a dull ache that had started the minute they'd closed the hotel doors behind them, and her jaw throbbed too where Elspeth had hit her. As for the cold she'd just experienced, it clung to her bones, her hands so stiff she could barely make a fist.

Outside Althea's suite she paused to look down the corridor – the elevator that she'd grown so afraid of was idling behind closed doors. Turning to face 1110, she took a deep breath and knocked, waiting patiently for Jenna to answer. The seconds ticked by with no sign of movement from within. Repeating the process, she waited again, frustration beginning to kick in. Where could she be? Boldly, her hand reached out to grasp the handle instead. She pushed it downwards, but it remained firm. Just as well really, she wasn't a sneak. There was nothing for it but to return to her room and try again later. Perhaps Althea was taking an early lunch in the ballroom, having travelled in the elevator while she'd climbed the stairs. They'd probably missed each other by minutes.

Turning towards her room, she caught movement just up ahead and froze all over again. There was not one person but two and it was as if she was seeing them through a gauze curtain. They had their backs towards her and were drifting, Althea-style, towards the elevator. Something familiar about them made her wish she could see them more clearly. Who were they, and where had they come from? There were ten rooms on this floor. Elspeth had occupied one, Marilyn another, Tallula the room opposite her. As for John, she'd neither seen nor heard him on this floor but that didn't mean he wasn't on it. After herself and Althea, that left four rooms with occupants unaccounted for. Had this couple silently emerged from one of them? And where was this haze coming from? It put her in mind of John again, when he'd talked about the Southern heat and how it had shimmered. That's what the figures ahead of her seemed to be doing – shimmering.

Forcing life into her legs, she drew closer.

The haze didn't lift and neither did she manage to close the gap between them, the corridor stretching as if it were a rubber band being pulled at both ends. Determined, she picked up her pace. She had to identify these people. The woman's hair was chestnut brown, such a rich shade, and the man looked tall and strong. Both were smartly dressed, as if for a day out, another thing that didn't make sense. Did they really think they could leave here? The man turned his head slightly as if addressing the woman by his side. Caroline squinted. That profile…there was something about it. The woman laughed and that's when her blood ran cold. It was a tinkling laugh.

Mum, Dad, is that you?

Abandoning all reason, she broke into a run. It was them! Her mother and father, as young as they were when they first came here, in their early twenties, on honeymoon. They were on the eleventh floor, not the second, drifting towards… Towards what?

"Mum! Dad!"

Neither of them acknowledged their daughter.

"Mum, can you hear me? Dad!"

They were so happy, their hands entwined as her mother laughed again.

"Mum, please!"

Why couldn't she close the gap between them?

"Dad!"

She longed to speak to them, to see their faces as she'd never seen them before, with no hint of the illness that was waiting to consume them. They were bursting with vitality, and their love – a love that she'd always admired, envied if she were truthful – was tangible, something she could reach out and touch. If she could only get close enough.

"Mum!" Her voice cracked as realisation set in. They weren't aware of her, they couldn't hear her, and she was never going to reach them. They had substance but they were still shadows and around them other shadows materialised, not as substantial, and not as far away either.

She screamed in frustration. It wasn't them she wanted to be close to.

Grabbing at her hair, she had to wonder, was she going mad? She felt as if she was. This hotel, with its strange inhabitants both real and unreal, was *driving* her to madness.

The shadows that circulated weren't like her mother and father at all – young and carefree, love oozing from them – they were entirely different.

One brushed against her causing her to inhale. The touch of it revealed its suffering, just as the teenager had revealed hers. A snapshot, but it was enough. In it there was confusion, bewilderment and a dreadful sense of loss. To the right of her, another shadow brushed past – she experienced guilt this time, sorrow at ever having been the instrument of pain, and fear too, in case there was a price to be paid for it.

Rather than continue forward, she started to back up. The shadows were accumulating, blocking her mother and father entirely. Where were they? Did they linger still, or had they gone? She couldn't hear laughter anymore, just a low hum, slow, steady, and hypnotic. Another shadow crept closer, there were plenty of them now, filling the void, and she flinched, almost vomited. The loneliness of whatever it was – *whoever* had touched her this time – was simply too much to bear. It was angry too: *you set the bar too high!*

If these were the same creatures that were in her dreams, then the barrier was no longer in place. She flapped her hands, as if to ward the shadow off, to ward them all off. She didn't want these entities breaking through, forcing her to face them, to validate them – they were simply too stark, rising up from a cold, cold place.

"No! No! No!" she started to utter, her voice getting louder with each protestation. "I'm not one of you. I'm nothing to do with you. Leave me alone."

Like her parents, they weren't listening either. Instead they multiplied, getting deeper and darker; a swarm of them, more terrifying even than the teen in the elevator. Some of them raised their arms, as though beseeching her, as though she had all the answers.

"I can't save you. Do you hear? I can't! I wish someone would save me!"

She hadn't realised how far she'd backed up. She was at the end of the corridor again, and there was nowhere else to go. Nowhere except Althea's room. The exit door was crowded, but Althea's room was clear, as if she was being steered there, directed.

But what' the use? The door's locked!

Except it wasn't. Not any longer. It was wide open.

Again, Caroline had to squint. Was it true what she was seeing? She'd tested the door handle. She knew it was locked. Althea wasn't there.

Was she?

There was a whisper in her ear. She had to strain to hear it, a voice that seemed to *glide* towards her.

You may come in now.

Looking ahead again and then to the left, she hurled herself inside 1110.

Chapter Twenty-Three

Slamming the door shut, Caroline lent against it, prayers tumbling from her mouth that it would prove effective, that oak, cement, and plaster would keep the phantoms out, if that's what those things in the corridor were? Half of her didn't believe it possible, but the other half felt safe in this corner suite, on the uppermost floor, as if the barrier were not just physical but spiritual.

Turning, she expected to see Althea standing in front of her, Jenna by her side – a formidable pairing – but there was no one. It was an empty room although one that was slightly different to before. Surfaces weren't as polished and a thin layer of dust seemed to have settled over everything, as if time had caught up with it and wreaked havoc, as time often does. Beneath her feet the carpet was worn, just like everywhere else in the hotel, fraying even, threadbare patches obvious at various intervals. The rhythm that had assaulted her ears earlier was now drowned out by the banging of her heart. It was still holding out despite everything. What a strange, strange place this was. She'd found both heaven and hell in it, but what if there was more hell to come? Right now, it seemed likely.

"Althea," she called out. "Are you here? Answer me if

you are."

When there was no answer, she walked to the double doors and pulled them open. The bedroom was as empty as the living room. So who could have unlocked the door?

Back in the living room, she stood for a while, trying to gather her thoughts, to rationalise the irrational. *You're safe*, she reminded herself. *In here, you're safe.*

The gloom, she realised, was in part due to the day fading. She crossed over to the window, her intention to open the curtains wider to let in what light she could, pausing only briefly at the picture she'd looked at before, the one celebrating the opening of the hotel. The picture was slightly askew, so she straightened it. *A place to rest, to relax, and to make memories*, she read again. It was true. To an extent.

Moving swiftly past it, she almost tore the curtains apart. The contrast in light – although slight – caused her eyes to sting and she shut them briefly, waiting for them to adjust. Once again, she tried to blame her imagination for what had just happened – unusual circumstances conjuring the unusual. More than that…the downright terrifying. Even as she tried to reason she knew it was no good. There was no explanation, none that she could find. There was something wrong at the Egress, and still she was trapped here, her and David, no release in sight for at least another day, not unless they started walking, enduring miles and miles of wasteland. *Wasteland?* What was here before?

A ledger on the writing bureau near the window caught her attention. It was laid out neatly, a slim pen positioned beside it. Grabbing the chair she sat down, tracing her fingers over the cover – once fancy, the brown leather was now cracked in places. Before she could persuade herself to do otherwise, she opened it. It was a list of names, a date beside each one, starting in 1922, when the hotel had first opened. Beside quite a few of the dates were ticks, but not all of them, for some that column remained blank.

Martha Bergstein, April 1922 (no tick), Ronald Greaves (tick), June 1922, Cory Howard, July 1922 (tick), Michael Adams, December 1922 (tick)… The list ran on and on. Caroline turned the pages, read more names, a whole litany of them, and then flicked through to a more modern era – her era – this exact month and year. There was Marilyn Hollick (no tick), John Cole (no tick), Elspeth Borchardt (no tick), Tallula May (no tick), her own name – Caroline Daynes (no tick), and David's, but it was just his forename scribed there.

It was a guest list, it had to be – the register David had been searching for – but there was no way it was complete. A complete guest list would fill several such books. What was it doing in Althea's room?

It's here because she's the manager.

Even so, it still seemed odd to Caroline.

She couldn't have started this ledger. She must have inherited it.

And yet the handwriting was the same throughout, something she double- and triple-checked.

So many questions filled her head that she feared it might burst. *What if Helen's name is in here too?* Helen Ansell, who may or may not have stayed at the hotel a year ago, a young woman who had disappeared, whose body was never found?

She flicked back to the beginning of 2015.

"Helen, Helen, Helen," she repeated the girl's name as her finger traced downwards. "Where are you?"

Her finger stopped. There *was* a Helen. Quickly her eyes flicked to the surname –Ansell. There was a date also, October 2015. And there was no tick.

"What the hell?"

Someone moved behind her.

"Caroline."

With no hesitation at all, Caroline twisted around. "Althea!"

At last she'd put in an appearance, Jenna in place behind her. Althea remained mute; giving Caroline time to note that the old woman looked neither furious nor surprised at her intrusion. And why should she? She'd been invited in…

"I… I wanted to see you. The door—"

"Was open, yes I know."

"But not at first, it was locked. There were things in the corridor, shadows, shapes. It sounds crazy, I know, but…" Her parents, were they in this ledger too? Seized by a sudden desire to know, she stopped talking and turned back to the book, flicking to nine months before her birth date. But there was no mention of Tony and Dee Daynes. Disappointment and relief flooded through her. Taking a deep breath, she pushed the chair aside and stood up to face Althea this time. "And then as you say the door was wide open, as if by some kind of magic. I thought I heard you whisper to come in. I *did* hear you whisper, but you weren't here."

"I'm always here," replied Althea, her manner as calm as ever, but there was something different about her, something Caroline had to work hard to make sense of. It wasn't her clothes, always a little old fashioned, they were nonetheless unremarkable: a long pleated navy skirt, a pale blouse and a cardigan, also in navy; nor the fact that her make-up was so heavy – the powder settling into the cracks on her face, her lipstick, a reddish colour, bleeding slightly. It was her shoulders that were different; they weren't as straight as before. They were more rounded, slumped almost. That was the thing that had always impressed Caroline about Althea: for a woman of her age, she carried herself with such grace, such aplomb, but now she seemed…tired.

Caroline pointed at the ledger. There was no point in beating about the bush, not anymore. She may as well come straight to the point. "A girl went missing last year, her name was Helen Ansell. It was thought she was making her way to the Egress, but whether she made it or not, nobody seemed to know. Until now. Her name's in that ledger. She *was* here, in October 2015."

There was a slight nod from Althea. "Do you know what the ledger's for?"

"It's a guest list, some guests anyway. My name's in it, so is Marilyn's, John's, Tallula's, David—"

"David?"

"Yes, he's the one investigating Helen's case, but it's only his forename. Did you write it?"

"The ledger is mine, yes."

"But it's…" How could she phrase it? "So old." Fishing in her pocket, she retrieved the photo David had given her and held it up. "Do you remember Helen?"

Again she nodded.

"Then what happened to her? What happened to all those people in the corridor? The girl in the elevator – the architect's daughter – the one who was pushed? There are so many people in this hotel, besides the guests, I mean, but they're not real. They're like tendrils of smoke. I'm not going mad, I'm really not. I've seen things. The architect's daughter showed herself to me. Her face it was so… It was awful. But I don't understand any of it. It's like a dream, a nightmare. It's like nothing I've ever experienced before, both the good and the bad. I've even seen the ghosts of my parents. Althea, my name is in that register too, but you know that. What's going to happen to me? To David? Are we in danger?"

Jenna moved forward, a frown on her face, causing Caroline to acknowledge that her voice had risen, that she'd been shouting.

Before she could apologise, Althea turned her head slightly in Jenna's direction and held up a hand – the message was clear: there was no need to get involved.

"Althea," Caroline continued, striving to keep her voice steady, "I'm sorry, but what is going on, with everyone? Tell me." Because if both she and David were in danger of any sort, they'd take their chances with the snow, they'd walk out of here.

It was as though Althea read her mind. "You can't leave, not yet."

"Tomorrow we can."

"Tomorrow, maybe."

"I'm scared." There was relief in admitting it.

"But you feel safe with me?"

"Safe? Yes. Yes I do." This room, Althea herself, they were as much a haven as David.

"Just be patient," Althea implored.

Hadn't she been patient enough?

"You can go back to your room now," Althea continued. "But—"

"There's no congestion, it's clear. And dinner tonight, be there."

"Dinner?" questioned Caroline. It was the last thing on her mind.

"Rituals are important at the Egress."

"You weren't at dinner last night," Caroline all but accused.

"Even so," replied Althea, offering no explanation at all. "I'd like you to be there."

"I just want to go home." Her voice sounded small, as childlike as Elspeth's.

"But where is home?" Althea asked, surprising her.

"I…" She found she couldn't answer. England without David didn't seem like home at all. Oh, David. How she longed for him, for his support. She needed him, she realised, having never needed a man before. "Althea, please, what is this place?"

Althea winced.

"Althea?" Caroline prompted.

"I can't tell you, I'm sorry."

"Why ever not?"

"Because you have to find out for yourself."

Chapter Twenty-Four

Althea was right, the corridor was clear – no shapes, no shadows lurking, no dead parents laughing and flirting with each other in the foreground; no *congestion* as she called it.

She was exhausted, as tired as Althea looked; every bone in her body leaden. Should she go to David's room or wait for him at hers? She wanted to see him so badly and yet she had no energy to contemplate tackling a flight of stairs right now. Her mind and body were in free fall, the dull ache in her head debilitating, clouding her mind, making it impossible to think. Everything was a blur.

You have to find out for yourself.

That's another thing Althea had said, but she felt more confused than ever, more upset than ever. In a world of bewilderment, the only thing that made sense was David.

She had to rest. She simply couldn't take any more. In her room, she sank onto the sofa, her head falling against the backrest. The girl in the elevator; Elspeth's body in a room below; Edward leaning in to kiss her, and being so tempted by him; betraying David... No, no, she was getting confused again. She hadn't betrayed anyone. She'd been a free agent, able to kiss Edward as much as she wanted to, and for a brief moment that's what she'd intended, but there'd been a smell…a terrible smell, emanating from his breath, from his skin, from deep within him, something rotten that festered. 666. What sort of a sick joke was that? And David in a room whose numbers added up to 13 – *you're not superstitious, are you?* That was twisted too. So much was twisted and yet so much was right: she and David; Marilyn's tentative friendship with John, which somehow eased their obvious pain. '*Because I'm not like my daddy, I'm a whole lot worse.*' What had John meant by that?

There were no more answers, only more questions, all of them stacking up one after the other. What was wrong with Marilyn's neck? Why was it a constant source of irritation to her? Was Tallula really as cold as she liked to make out? Just once she'd seen a crack in her façade, a less-confident Tallula, as lost as those in the corridor. Were they *all* lost, in some way? And Helen, there was no tick beside her name either, what did that mean?

She had closed her eyes but now she opened them and looked around. Just as she'd perceived a change in Althea, she realised that the room was different too, not the arrangement of furniture as such, although certainly one or two items seemed to be at a different angle. It was more the light that the room was bathed in. A bluish light rather than yellow, no warmth to it at all, as if all warmth had been drained…

Frowning, Caroline sat up. The lights were on, just as she'd left them, and the curtains open, even though it was dark outside. There'd definitely been a shift – the change she'd feared coming.

She wanted David, but Althea was closer. Should she

return to 1110 and knock on her door, to seek sanctuary again? The old woman's room was so much safer.

Rising to her feet, she ventured forwards, but, as had happened in the corridor, she couldn't reach her goal, the space between her and the door lengthening not shortening.

No, no, no. Vehemently, she shook her head. *Not this again.*

She'd reach the damned door; shatter this illusion, refuse to be at the mercy of it, of anyone. Taking a deep breath, she lunged forward, putting all her might behind that action, crying out with relief when her hand clasped the cold brass handle, when she pressed down on it, when it complied.

It felt like such a triumph, like breaking a curse!

And then her euphoria faded.

There was nothing on the other side, just more darkness.

Or was there something, after all?

As she continued to peer into the corridor, she started to make out more shapes, as black as their surrounds but writhing – that's what it looked like – as though the darkness was alive. And there was music too, the faintest trace of it. Not a pleasant lullaby, a heart-felt hymn, nor a favourite tune but an assault on the ears, despite how low in volume it was. The notes kept wavering, missing a few, running too fast, slowing down, but at last she recognised it: *Sweet Caroline.* It was her song, being massacred.

She slammed the door shut and turned around to find more horror awaiting her: Edward and his sidekick, Tallula, wide grins splitting their faces.

"Caroline," Edward said, the first of the pair to step forward. "Sweet Caroline."

His voice was liquid gold again, his eyes twinkling more than David's ever had. She tried to look away, but she couldn't. It was as though he held her in a vice.

He lifted his hand, and her own rose in response, mirroring him. She was powerless to stop it. All the while Tallula – *Ice-cold Tallula* – continued to grin, delighted by proceedings, not possessive at all of the man she idolised, almost willing him to go further.

With just the slightest tug, Edward pulled Caroline closer, the smell so peculiar to him evident again, burning her eyes, her throat, her insides. His grin became wolfish; his teeth – his perfect teeth – too big for his mouth suddenly, and yet still she couldn't resist him. Finally, their lips met, more than that, they *fused*; a gesture as intimate as any she'd ever shared with David, his tongue searching for her tongue, thrusting it deep, like a snake's head, searching – but for what?

Your soul, Caroline, he wants your soul!

Finally, she tried to push him away, but it was no use, he held her fast. And that smell. It was as fierce as he was, coating skin, blood, and sinew, drenching her.

She couldn't do this. She didn't *want* to. It was a violation, a betrayal. Tallula might be rejoicing in what was happening, but David would not forgive her again.

His memory gave her the strength she needed. She pushed harder, managed to dislodge him. "NO!" she shouted. "Get off me!"

"Sweet Caroline," he murmured, his eyes still half closed. "*Diseased* Caroline."

She inhaled. She didn't want this again either. "Just…fuck off will you. Fuck off."

Her protestations caused both of them to laugh louder,

to *howl* with laughter.

"Oh, Caroline, first your father, then your mother, and now you…" His eyes widening with fake sympathy, he added, "Oh, I'm sorry. You didn't know, did you? You had no idea."

"How? How can you say such things? You didn't know my parents, or what happened to them!"

"Caroline, I know everything. I know about you and David too. Are you really going to inflict yourself upon him now that I've made you aware of what a burden you'd be?"

Not laughing anymore, Tallula was sneering instead. "Selfish bitch."

Caroline took a step back towards the door. "You're evil, the pair of you."

"Hey, where ya going, baby girl?" Tallula's voice had changed, no longer the polished accent of a college girl, it had a Southern tinge to it, similar to John's. "Out into the void? Dontcha think you're safer with us? Edward's the one to keep us safe. Althea can't, she's too old. She's good for nothing. She should admit defeat. We're in control now. Edward will take you under his wing – even you, Caroline – poor, diseased you. *Especially* you."

Against the door, Caroline opened her mouth to scream, but there was no sound, just that song playing on a loop in her head, the distorted version – a song she used to love but which she now hated, that used to be so special to her, but had since been corrupted, with their laughter, their *crowing*, accompanying it. If anyone was diseased, it was these two. Their minds beyond help.

She closed her eyes, trying to hide in that way at least. She simply couldn't stare at them any longer – endure such cruelty.

"Caroline, Caroline…"

Which one of them was calling her now?

"Caroline, Caroline."

She wouldn't answer. She wouldn't!

"Caroline, wake up."

Why? To listen to more of their lies?

"Caroline, please, you have to wake up."

But if she did, if this was another nightmare, would it make them disappear?

She took a chance and opened her eyes.

"David?"

"Caroline."

"Oh, thank God!" Leaning forward, she grabbed him, checking that he was solid, that he was made of flesh and bone. "You're here, you're really here!"

"You fell asleep."

"Asleep?" Relief surged through her. "Edward and Tallula aren't with you, are they?"

"Edward and…? No, no, of course not."

"Why's it so dark? I can barely make you out."

"The electricity has gone out, nothing's working." He swallowed, clearly unnerved by it. "I came here as soon as I could. I took the stairs, raced up them."

"Where were you while I was with Althea?" At the mention of her name, a memory stirred: the point of her visit to 1110 earlier. "Helen *did* come to the Egress, David, your hunch was right! Her name is in a ledger that Althea keeps. Our names are too. Some have ticks beside them, and some don't. What does it mean? What does it all mean?"

He shook his head. "I don't know, Caroline, I'm

sorry...not yet. But there's something else. A more immediate problem."

"More immediate?" Christ, didn't they have enough to deal with?

"I went to check on Elspeth, that's where I was."

"Why?"

"I was worried about her. I had another hunch."

Still she was confused. "About what?"

His grip as hard as hers, he moved his face even closer. "She's gone, Caroline."

"What?"

"Her body's gone. Somebody went in there and moved her."

Chapter Twenty-Five

It took a few moments for David's words to sink in. Elspeth's body had been moved. Why? For what purpose?

David was so uneasy. "I don't understand," he kept muttering. "I just don't understand."

"Tell me again, exactly what happened. Don't miss anything out."

"I *have* told you, Caroline. I went to the room we laid Elspeth in, as I approached, I could see that the door was open – wide open. I've still got the key Raquel gave me, she never asked for it back, and obviously there's a master, although who has that I don't know. Anyway, I went in, straight to the bed, and there was no body. There wasn't even an indentation where her body had been. The sheets and the bedspread were perfectly smooth. Almost as if she'd never been there."

"Could the emergency services have got through? Did they remove her?"

"If that was the case, I would have seen something. We were in the lobby before, both of us. You went upstairs to go and see Althea and I went to check on Elspeth. As soon as I found out she was missing, I went back to the lobby to ask Raquel about it. I searched everywhere, but no one was around, and I mean no one, not a living soul. There are no tire tracks in the snow either. I then went to several other floors, and knocked on doors, trying to find someone I could speak to. Still nothing. That's when the electricity failed."

Caroline could feel the colour draining from her cheeks. "Elspeth was in room 409, wasn't she?"

"Yeah... So?" And then her meaning dawned. "Caroline, we have to stay rational."

"Rational? Something's going on here, something macabre. I don't pretend to understand what, not yet, but we *need* to make sense of this. The first thing we do is go to Althea's and demand that she tells us the truth. We refuse to take no for an answer. I'm sick of this game, if that's what it is. It feels like everyone's toying with us."

David's voice was uncharacteristically low. "What if we're better off not knowing?"

"There's no bliss in ignorance, David. Not anymore."

Standing up, she took her phone from her pocket and scrutinised it. Surprise, surprise, there was no return message from Violet, no Wi-Fi, nothing. If she made a call, she'd bet it would prove fruitless too. "David, have you got your phone with you?" He nodded that he had. "Can you get Wi-Fi?"

"Wi-Fi?"

"Please, just humour me."

Withdrawing his phone too, he did as she asked. "Yeah, there you go. Damn! There's no juice left in it, sorry. What did you want me to look up?"

"No... I... It doesn't matter. There's battery left in mine; we can use it as a torch at least. You know, a flashlight."

"Good thinking."

Shining it in front of them, they made their way to the door. As imperative as it might be to find out what was going on, it was a struggle to leave 1106, and the memories – the *good* memories – it had spawned. Several times she was tempted to rush back, close the door, and stay put, but she forced herself onwards.

The corridor wasn't completely dark, emergency lights were operating at least, their red glow making her think of devils. Glancing fearfully around, she was relieved to see no shadows of substance, that the way ahead was clear. Hand in hand, they walked to the corner suite and knocked on the door. Like the first time she'd tried, there was no reply.

"Try the handle," she urged, but it was no use. "She's gone again," Caroline muttered, even though in her head she could hear Althea, *I'm always here.*

"Let's try the other rooms," David suggested.

Standing outside 1109, David knocked first. When there was no response, he tried that handle too. The door swung open and he glanced briefly at Caroline before entering.

"Hello, hello," he called out. "Is there anyone here? Are you okay?"

The light from Caroline's mobile revealed there was no one lurking, but the room was an unholy mess. Furniture had been upturned, as if in upset or temper, and so much paper littered the floor, covering whatever carpeting there was. Empty bottles too – there were dozens of them, whiskey, bourbon, and vodka, all cheap brands with garish labels. She trod on one and nearly lost her footing. David reached out a hand to steady her.

"What's happened here?" Caroline's eyes were wide as

she stared.

David bent down, retrieved a piece of paper, read it, and then discarded it, repeating the process several times.

"What is it?" Caroline asked. "What do they say?"

"They're just…ramblings. I can't make out much of it, not without proper lighting, but the word 'sorry', that's easy enough to read, it's been written over and over again."

Caroline bent too. He was right, it was written in big letters, small letters, capitals, plus heavy-handed scrawls that had ripped the paper beneath.

David took the phone from Caroline and shone it at the sideboard. "Look," he said.

Turning her head, she gasped. Into the wood of the sideboard 'sorry' had also been written, each letter that was gouged the product of a tortured mind.

"Whose room is this?" she asked.

"No idea. Have you ever seen anyone using it?"

She shook her head.

David stood up. "Let's check the others."

All further doors yielded, and all rooms were empty of inhabitants. In Tallula's room, there was barely any furniture; it was stark, just like the woman herself, no personal touches, no warmth. In the bedroom, heavily starched sheets covered the mattress, crisp to the touch, and on the dressing table not a single cosmetic or perfume bottle resided, only the welcome letter, ripped to shreds and scattered like confetti.

Marilyn's room was next; a room with floral wallpaper and a patterned carpet. A special room, unique, reflective of the homely type of woman Marilyn was. However, it was none of that now. It was in as much chaos as 1109. Letters, photos, and clothes had been seemingly tossed in the air and left to lie wherever they fell. At the window, one curtain was hanging off its track, at another the curtains had been torn down completely. A teapot – it had to be the same one that Marilyn had poured from – was lying in pieces on the floor, broken cups and saucers beside it. The most ghoulish find of all was in the bedroom – a sheet ripped from the bed, knotted in several places, and then slung over the light fitting; the end looped to resemble a hangman's noose.

All too keenly Caroline could feel the pain, the anguish that still lingered, in here and in 1109. Still in Marilyn's bedroom, she felt compelled to lay one hand against a pillow. It was wet, as if a thousand tears had rained down upon it. They probably had.

"It's Elspeth's room next," David said, from his position elsewhere in the room. With no emergency lighting in the rooms, only in the corridors, she couldn't make out the expression on his face, but his voice was bleak enough.

She walked over to join him. "We know what it's like in there. It's chaos too."

"Even so, we should check, just in case."

"She's not in there, David."

"Caroline…"

She nodded, finally agreeing.

If only it had been in chaos, that would have been more fitting. Instead, there was nothing in it, no carpet on the floor, no curtains at the window, and not one stick of furniture. It had all been spirited away as Elspeth herself had been. Erased.

David was as aghast as she was, but he was something more: distraught.

"What was it about Elspeth? Tell me," she whispered,

her hands going around his waist.

He was clearly finding it difficult to speak. "It was... She reminded me of someone – a kid I used to know at school, one that...well, one that was as vulnerable as she was, who might have ended up the same way, as damaged, as drug-dependent, if she'd lived."

"Elspeth wasn't a kid, though."

"But she was, deep down. You remember all those photos that she tore up, the one that she was holding in her hand the first night she went wild? Those were all of Elspeth as a kid, a *happy* kid, with the sassiest of grins. But then something happened; I don't know what it was, I could never get her to say. It could be she had a tough time during adolescence. Whatever it was, it caused her to shut down, in mind at least, if not in body."

"Oh, David." His words, his *understanding*, reinforced what she already knew. "I love you."

He hugged her, as tightly – as desperately – as she was hugging him. "I love you too, Caroline."

In amidst the carnage it wasn't a perfect moment, but it should have been.

"Caroline—"

"David, you're shivering." He was, violently.

"I was going to say, I don't feel so good."

He was damp too, a fever burning right through him.

"Hey," he said, noticing the worry in her eyes as she reared back to look at him. "It's okay, I'll be okay if you just hold me."

She'd said something similar to him once – was it really just a day or two ago?

Returning to the circle of his arm, she breathed, "I never want to let you go."

"Fine with me."

Tears formed, threatening to blind her.

"Let's just...keep in mind what we've found," she continued. "The good stuff I mean, none of the bad. It was at the Egress that we met each other."

And whatever happened next, she'd always be grateful for that.

Chapter Twenty-Six

They had to return to the lobby.

"That's where everyone will be," Caroline said, remembering Althea's words earlier, her insistence that she come to dinner. "They'll be waiting for us in the ballroom."

As she extricated herself from him, he staggered slightly, his breathing laboured too.

"Can you manage the stairs?" she asked.

"Yeah, it'll be fine."

"It's just the elevator…"

"I don't think it's working anyway. There seems to be no back-up generator."

Negotiating the corridor yet again, Caroline kept her head low rather than look ahead, focussing on their progress step by step. Soon enough they reached the stairwell. A few times she was sure she heard the sound of shuffling, or a chair being dragged along the floor. She furrowed her eyebrows. Was that laughter again, tinkling laughter? Whatever the sounds were – and David seemed oblivious to them – she refused to let them distract her. Being on the eleventh floor was sapping David's energy, and, with only the light from her mobile to guide them, progress was slow on the stairs. Nonetheless, the more distance they put between them and the uppermost level, the more David rallied. He wasn't leaning on her as much, his breathing was better, and he didn't feel so hot to the touch.

"That's it, you're doing well, really well. Not far to go now."

Methodically she counted down the floors. The only thing that waited for them as they rounded each corner was silence.

"We'll be there soon," she murmured.

At the bottom, they pushed through the doors and into the lobby. It was dark and it certainly felt empty. But they must be here, the others. Where else was there to go?

Feeling David hesitate, she urged him onwards. "We have to, don't you see?"

"Caroline." He was a strong man but there was a tremor in his voice. "Just wait."

"But—"

"Please."

Once again, he drew her into his arms, his lips in the darkness seeking hers. She was surprised at first, but then relaxed into it. It was so different to Edward's kiss, infinitely sweeter, provoking not a rush of fear but tenderness, once an alien emotion, but now wonderfully familiar. But there was something that wasn't so sweet about it – an air of finality. As much as she wanted the kiss to last forever, she had to reassure him.

"David—"

"SURPRISE!"

Before Caroline could say another word, both of them turned their heads in the direction of the person who had yelled out – a female, with such delight in her voice, cruel delight. It was Tallula, of course. Having pulled the ballroom doors open, she was standing in between them, still clutching at the handles, staring at them as they were staring at her.

"We've been waiting," she declared. "What took you so long?"

Behind Tallula, other figures began to congregate, not shadows or shapes, although there were plenty of those too, hovering in the background. The people were figures she recognised: Edward, Althea, Jenna, Marilyn, John, Raquel, and Tom – they were all there. Not shrouded in darkness, there was a soft glow that made each of them perfectly distinguishable, the result of dozens of candles that had been lit and placed around the ballroom, romanticising the scene when truly there was nothing romantic about it.

"Come in," Tallula urged. "It's rude to keep us waiting." She bellowed with laughter, a sound that made Caroline wince. "You two can't smooch out there all night, you know."

"Edward." Althea's voice was tight. "This infernal teasing achieves nothing."

Edward sauntered forward, wearing that smile of his, the one that Caroline had come to detest, that she'd like to wipe from his face; to erase it as Elspeth had been erased. He cupped a hand to his ear. "Sorry, Caroline, did I hear right? You're thinking of Elspeth?"

Surprise rendered her speechless, giving David a chance to speak instead. "Where is she? What have you done with her body?"

"Oh, Elspeth, Elspeth," Edward mocked. "You always felt so sorry for her, didn't you, David? Poor little Elspeth, tragic little Elspeth. If the terrible thing that had happened to her hadn't happened – and you're right, it was in her teens, boys of that age can be really quite merciless – if the drugs hadn't messed her up further, do you think she'd have been a contender for your affections? Not much of a looker was she, but her legs were nice."

"You're a bastard!" David declared, darting forward.

Having to rush to catch up with him, Caroline laid a restraining hand on his arm. "Don't, he's not worth it."

"*I'm* not worth it?" Edward spluttered. "You should think about your own worth, Caroline, before you pick on me. Considering what's wrong with you, you're hardly a catch."

"Edward!" Again it was Althea, her raised voice as sharp as razors. "Behave!"

Immediately he turned on her. "Behave? What am I, an errant child? I'm more than that, and you know it. I'm *better* than that."

"You are no more than I," Althea spat.

Whilst Edward and Althea glared at each other, Caroline's eyes flitted towards the entrance. All she wanted was a world with David in it, not one populated by these…these… Her mind struggled to think of how to describe any of them. *Crazies.*

"We're leaving," she announced, desperate to put that plan into action. "There's something wrong with this hotel, with all of you, and we want nothing more to do with it. We're going to walk out of that door and find somewhere safe, somewhere far, far away."

Marilyn started sobbing, her hand reaching up to tear at her neck.

"It's alright, it's alright." John attempted to move closer

to her, but Tallula moved forwards several paces, effectively blocking him.

Seeing this, Caroline relented. "Marilyn, John, you can always come with us. I know it's cold outside, but we'll manage somehow. Elspeth's body has been moved. Did you know that? And your room, Marilyn, it's not the same as before. I'm not saying that you're responsible...but someone is. The whole of the eleventh floor, it's..." How could she explain the unexplainable? "We need to leave. And we need to get help for Elspeth."

Edward roared with laughter. So did Tallula. "Show them, go on," he ordered, gesturing to those standing to the left of him. "Show them what's happened to poor Elspeth."

David's entire jaw was clenched. "What has happened?"

"Show them!" Edward roared again.

Tom and Raquel, who'd been standing together, briefly glanced at Althea – she was shaking her head, but not at them, more at the situation as a whole. Finally, she looked their way, muttered something, and they moved away from each other. Behind them, slumped on a chair was Elspeth.

David's gasp was as loud as Caroline's. "Christ! Is she...?"

His words petered out as Tallula almost skipped over to Elspeth, reached out a hand and dragged her to her feet. Caroline had to blink several times to believe what she was seeing. "No, it's not possible." She turned to David. "I thought she was dead."

He kept his gaze straight, transfixed. "She was dead. She *is*."

"But... But..."

Elspeth stood there, beside Tallula, subdued rather than

gleeful, her head bowed as though she were ashamed, not staring at them – as Tallula was – defiantly.

Althea was muttering again. Jenna fetched her a chair and she held onto the back of it, clearly glad of its support. "Such a battle," she was saying. "It's always such a battle." The despair in her voice was reflected on Jenna's face as she stared at her mistress.

"Marilyn…" Caroline tried to provoke an explanation from her.

She looked up, not just scratching at her neck but gnawing viciously at her lip too. "I can't find him," she said, looking all around her. "I thought if I came here to the Egress, and on our anniversary too, I'd find him, he'd be waiting for me."

"Find who?"

"My husband of course! Where is he? Why isn't he here? I made my way back, after… After… This is our place you see, our special place. I've told you that before, haven't I? He felt that as strongly as I did. That's why I did it – to be with him again."

Half of her didn't want to ask; the other half knew she had to. "Did what?"

Marilyn bit down harder, drawing blood, Caroline was sure of it.

Beside her, David tugged at her arm. He was right they needed to get going, but what about John? Could he explain this latest terrible twist? "John?" As always, he needed prompting. "John!"

Eventually he responded. "I'm sorry. I'm so, so sorry."

Her heart lurched. The paper on the floor in 1109, the scraps with 'sorry' scrawled all over them – was he responsible? And the empty liquor bottles, were they his?

Was John a drinker, just like his daddy was a drinker – the daddy he was a whole lot worse than? She'd only ever seen him drink water, but that could be for appearance's sake. If he drank in private – drank so damned much – it would explain his continual shaking.

"What did you do to your family?" she asked, tears beginning to pool. The only reply she received this time was a howl of anguish, one so pitiful it forced her to screw her eyes shut. And then he was apologising again, a frenzy of whispers, causing Marilyn to stop her sobbing at last, and to return to a more familiar role, that of the carer.

"Caroline." David's voice was urgent.

"Okay, okay."

There were no answers to be had here, only more horrors, and more confusion. Taking a step forwards, she was surprised when David pulled her backwards instead.

"David, never mind about our coats. We can't go and get them."

"Coats?" He sounded equally as puzzled. "Why are you talking about our coats?"

"It's just… Look, we need to go towards the entrance, not away from it."

He shook his head. "Caroline, we need the light."

"The light?" What was he talking about? "But the electrics—"

"Run, run, run, y'all," Tallula interrupted their exchange, "but there's nowhere to hide, I'm telling you, not anymore. Hiding time is over." Dramatically she yawned. "Edward, I'm so bored. Let's just tell them, shall we? Get it over and done with."

"Edward…" Althea was warning him again.

Edward looked tempted to give in to Tallula, so

tempted, but then he seemed to back down, to obey Althea, albeit begrudgingly. "They'll find out soon enough."

Tallula's smug expression turned into one of fury. Edward may accept being thwarted by Althea, but she clearly hated it. "Why do you always give in to that old crone? For fuck's sake, Edward, I wish you'd man up!"

As fast as lightning, Edward's hand shot out and struck Tallula across the face. As shocking as all of this was, as shocking as seeing Elspeth again, like the architect's daughter, risen from the dead, this was worse; the sheer violence of it. As Tallula flew into the wall, a collective gasp was heard, although Althea simply looked away, not condoning but somehow accepting of Edward's actions. The shapes, the shadows hovering in the background, huddled together, as though for comfort, forming a solid black mass. Elspeth's shoulders shuddered too. Was she crying? It was impossible to see; she could even be laughing. Raquel remained unimpressed, as if she'd seen it all many times before. Caroline was beginning to think she had.

Tallula climbed quickly to her feet, one hand rubbing at her cheek. She didn't challenge Edward; instead she turned to Caroline and David, her expression, her whole demeanour very different to before. She looked beaten in every sense of the word; the porcelain of her face cracked enough to reveal the creature underneath – as scarred as any of them.

Like so many in pain she wanted to hit out, and yet again she chose them.

"You can't leave. None of us can." Spittle and blood flew from her mouth. "Are you stupid or something?

Surely you realise that by now. All this having to find out for yourself, it's SHIT. Total SHIT!" She flinched again, as Edward stepped closer. "Don't worry," she said to him, "I'm not going to say anything." Her ice-blue gaze back on them, she continued. "Go on then, find out for yourselves what hopeless company you're in. A drug addict, the suicidal, an alcoholic, and me. Some might have called me hopeless too, but I enjoyed what I did, who I was. That's what people can't understand, that there's enjoyment in inflicting pain. There's *satisfaction* in it. If that's what I truly feel, is it wrong? Is it really so wrong? Isn't it somehow meant?" Her voice cracked too, as if she doubted her words, despite expressing them so ardently. "There's no hope for any of us. She," – although she didn't dare to look at Althea, she thrust a hand in her direction to show who she meant – "likes to peddle hope, but I know different. We know different, don't we, Edward? In here, out there and beyond, it's all the same. It's all just…shit."

"We have to go." David's fear was infectious, but Caroline gave it one last shot.

"Tallula, tell us what this is all about."

"I can't!" she screamed. "Don't you ever listen? It's the rules, the fucking rules!"

Althea, it seemed, had slumped further, whilst Edward had his hands balled, as if he wanted to strike out again; as if any minute he was going to pummel Tallula into the ground, finish off what he'd started. And ordinarily David would step in, *she* would step in, but there wasn't anything ordinary about this instance. They had to keep their distance – from all of them. Their sanity depended on it. And yet, still they were backing away from the entrance, inching past the lobby desk, past the elevator, towards the stairwell.

"David, why are we going this way?"

Instead of answering, he reached out, pushed the door open, and almost dragged her to where the stairs veered upwards…or downwards even, deeper into the darkness. *Staff Only.*

"Okay fine, we'll go up, but to my room, barricade ourselves in, sit tight 'til morning. I don't think they'll harm us. No one seems out to harm us. Not physically. It's our minds they're messing with. We'll leave at dawn. It's probably best we leave then anyway. It'll be easier. David… David… Are you listening? Let's go to my room. Get away from them."

She knew she was babbling. But could she be blamed for that? Elspeth was dead, and yet she'd been standing in front of them, her shoulders shaking, her chest heaving.

"David!" she screamed his name at him. "Let's go to my room."

At last he acknowledged her, but instead of agreeing, he shook his head. "We can't."

"But we have to go somewhere!"

"Not to the eleventh floor."

She'd learnt to read him so well in the short time they'd been together – knew he was keeping something from her again. "Why not?" Her voice was calmer, sterner. "David!"

"Because… There is no eleventh floor."

It was some seconds before she could muster a reply. "I know you're scared, I am too, but—"

His hands grabbed her, forcing her to listen to his next words – *truly* listen. "Caroline, I told you I did some research on this place?"

She could only nod.

"I remember reading that it only had ninety rooms, over nine floors."

"Where? Where did you see that?"

"On the Internet. The Egress is listed on various hotel sites, you know *TripAdvisor*, *Hotels dot com*. I could never check the official site. Every time I tried it was down, undergoing maintenance, but the other sites, they all had it listed as a ten-storey hotel; lobby and function rooms on the ground floor, and bedrooms on the other nine floors. When I got here, I found out there were *eleven* floors, that's one hundred rooms as opposed to ninety. I didn't think too much of it. Why would I? Sites like those always get the finer details wrong, but..." Again David shut his eyes briefly, as if trying to come to terms with what he was going to say too. "I think they were right, after all. Every time I'm on the eleventh floor, I start to feel drained, ill even, except...except when we first made love. Then I felt invincible." His voice cracked as he recalled. "We can't go up, Caroline, we have to go to the basement."

"David, let me say something. In Althea's room there was a promotional poster for the hotel, I remember studying it. It said there was going to be eleven floors."

"That's right. There *was* going to be. But it was never completed."

"But..." And then it hit her. "Because of the architect's daughter."

"Because of her. Her death, and the death of the second architect, cast a shadow over the hotel, one that refused to budge. I've said this before, but people must have thought the hotel was cursed, the investors included, pulling the plug, quitting whilst they were ahead. It was a hotel drenched in blood from the start. Caroline, I know it sounds as if I'm speculating again, but I think I'm right. It makes some sort of crazy sense. One thing I am certain of is that *nowhere* did I ever find mention of an eleventh floor."

Having hung on his every word, Caroline turned her head to the side and looked into what could only be described as a chasm. "It's just so dark," she whispered.

"No, Caroline, that's where you're wrong." Once again, she could sense his desperation, almost smell the sourness of it, oozing from every pore. "It's where we'll find the light."

Chapter Twenty-Seven

There was no one following them, not yet. Even so, the trepidation that gripped Caroline as she and David made their way into the basement of the Egress threatened to overwhelm her. The darkness was as thick as syrup, as cloying too; the torchlight on her mobile, which David had taken from her and which was fast running out of battery power, barely able to make a dent in it. They had no choice but to feel their way, their hands outstretched, taking pains to tread carefully, especially on the steps; neither of them wanting to fall and injure themselves, to make a horrendous situation worse.

It was colder still in the depths; it smelt musty, of things abandoned and left to rot. Several times she placed her hand over her mouth and nose to try and blot out the smell, the memory too, of the man it reminded her of – Edward. She didn't want to think about him, about Tallula, Elspeth, any of them, but it wasn't as if she could forget them either. They might not have followed, but they were close.

It's almost like you're a part of them. They're a part of you.
She shook her head, denied it. *I'm not like them. I'm not!*
So why did the thought persist?

"David, this isn't a good idea… David."

But David was distracted.

"Where is it? Where the hell is it?" he kept muttering.

"You're looking for the electrics, right? That's what you meant by the light?"

He replied this time, but it was half-hearted. "Yeah, we need to find the electrics."

"They'll be here somewhere." She looked around, her eyesight beginning to adjust, registering a vast space ahead of her, various shapes within it but so far resembling inanimate objects: tall cupboards, items of furniture, and spare beds stored upright.

"It's not so dark anymore, is it?" she commented, at the exact same moment he walked into the side of one of the objects.

"Fuck!" He rubbed at his thigh. "Where's the damn fuse box?"

"Why are you so fixated? If you won't go back to my room, or yours, why don't we just get out of here?"

She was stunned when he almost growled at her. "We need the light, Caroline! Don't you understand? *I* need it."

Her hand shot out, landing on his forearm. "Okay, okay, calm down. Look… I'm scared too." Her voice cracked, but she fought to gain control. "Really scared. *You're* frightening me, the way you're acting." It was an admission that startled her, but ever since he'd seen Elspeth, he'd changed. Then again, perhaps she'd changed too. "Tell me you're alright. I need to know that you're alright. What we've seen is…it's mad, it's terrible, but—"

"You have to let me find the light."

Removing her hand, she sighed. There was no point in arguing further.

Again, he walked into another object, the light from her phone waning as the battery ran even lower. Still with his hands in front of him, he proceeded more cautiously.

It's only my eyesight that's adjusting, she realised, able to make out something else in the darkness too, something in a room beyond, one that was separated from the other by a low arch – a figure that was neither bulky or boxlike, but similar to her own...

"Caroline, I've found the fuse box. Damn it! Your cell's going to die in a minute. Hurry, help me."

It was hard to tear her eyes from what was waiting but she forced herself, taking her phone back and holding it up as he struggled with the metal casing beneath which various fuses and switches were buried, swearing again, over and over.

"Caroline, hold it steady, will you? I need a crowbar or something. Look around, there's got to be something of use in this pit."

"Over there, there's some kind of rod."

"Where?" he said, looking at where she was pointing.

"I'll get it," Caroline murmured, hurrying over, grabbing the rod, which was long and thin and made of steel. Bringing it back to him, she handed it over.

"Excellent," he enthused. "God knows how you spotted it there. You must have night-vision. Don't worry, I can do this. I can get the light to come back on."

"I'm not worried," she assured him. "I can see well enough already."

Putting all his might behind it, he eventually levered the doors open, to reveal a bewildering array of all things technical, plenty of danger stickers adorning them.

"David," she said, "do you know anything about this

stuff?"

"I know enough. Bring the cell closer."

"I don't think it's any use—"

"Caroline, will you help me! Please."

She stared at him, realised how much his hands were shaking, making it impossible to clutch at anything, let alone delicate switches and wires. One other thing: he hadn't noticed the mobile had switched itself off. He was too focussed. Either that or deluded. She took a step back, assessed him again. It was as though he were caught in the throes of panic. "These fucking wires," he was saying. "God damn these wires."

The odd thing was he was tearing at his arms rather than the electrics in front of him.

She continued her retreat. For the moment he was beyond her reach. Turning, she stared at the figure again. It was becoming more defined, just as everything else was around her. A female figure, albeit still heavily in shadow.

Although no finger beckoned her onwards, Caroline felt compelled to draw closer. Perhaps it was the key to this; it might help her understand their situation. Such hope obliterated fear. If she understood, she could help David; bring him back from the abyss.

"I'll be back, David," she promised, but the darkness seemed to eat her words. "I'm not leaving you. I will *never* leave you."

In all of this, that was the one thing she was certain of.

Walking forward, the same thing happened here as it had happened so often on the eleventh floor – the distance between them took more time than it should to traverse.

It's an illusion.

Someone whispered those words into her ear. A voice

she recognised. Quickly, she turned her head to the right expecting to see Althea, materialising out of nowhere, but there was just an empty space.

On the contrary, Sweet Caroline, this is the only reality that matters.

This time her head whipped to the left. That voice was Edward's, smooth and arrogant. He wasn't there either, but still the bickering continued, she caught in the middle of it.

Why does it have to be like this, Edward? Why do you persist in tormenting?

Because, dear Althea, it's fun. It's what I do. What I'm meant to do.

I wish you'd go.

I know, but I'm here to stay. It's the rules, remember?

There was a brief silence before Edward started again.

You're growing tired, aren't you, dear Althea? Weaker too.

I've told you before, Edward, don't judge me by my appearance.

But you're weak. That's why you have Jenna. Why you lean on her.

Just as you lean on Tallula.

That's right, I do…for now. At least she's attractive to look at.

Jenna's worth a thousand Tallula's!

Ah, yes, she's the strong, plain and silent type, isn't she? Not like my mouthy little Tallula, but I can see that she's tired too. She doesn't want to be here, not anymore.

Althea seemed to falter. *Jenna won't go, not yet.*

But when she does, oh Lord, Althea, when she does…

"Stop it!" hissed Caroline. "Back off, Edward, and leave us alone."

Us? Once again Edward was mocking her. *So you've chosen sides? What a pity. I almost had you, Caroline, didn't I? You almost succumbed.*

"Never!"

Poor David, I'd congratulate him if it weren't such a hollow victory.

Edward, enough!

There you go again, Althea, spoiling my fun.

Turning back to the left, staring into the nothing that was there, Caroline snarled. "There is nothing wrong with me, Edward."

Oh, but there is, there really is.

As his laughter echoed through the chambers of her mind, one hand came up to wipe at tears that were spilling onto her cheeks. "I hate you, Edward. I hate you so much."

Don't hate.

It was a warning from Althea, one that Edward overrode.

Hate me all you like, Caroline. Hate is good. Hate is exciting. Don't you feel just a little bit excited when you hate someone?

"Get out of my head. Go!"

Only Edward answered.

Calm down, relax; I'll wait for you upstairs. Meanwhile, have fun with Helen. I know I did, although I have to say, she's a little more staid than Tallula. My Tallula, she's not staid at all; she's quite the adventurer. Ice-cold Tallula you call her, don't you? Apt, that's very apt. I swear that girl's heart was frozen at birth. That happens sometimes, you know. Sometimes I don't have to persuade a person to surrender; they're mine from the start. But she'll tell you all about me, won't you, Helen? Still hiding are you, down in the depths?

You can't hide forever, though, no one can. We have to face the truth one day.

Caroline inhaled sharply as Edward left her too. She was herself again, no warring factions dominating her mind. But she wasn't completely alone, and she'd come further than she thought. She'd passed under the arch and was in the second room which was as vast as the first and furnished with what seemed to be several rows of beds – the kind you'd find in a hospital, a thin mattress on a cart of sorts, blankets on some of them, no doubt mouldering. She was tempted to turn and run. This was a room that was out of time, she realised, a room *in between* time. One she wished she'd never discovered, just as she wished she'd never heard of the Egress; that her parents had never spoken of it to her; that her mother was wrong about her having been conceived here. Oh God, she wished she didn't belong. But her feet refused to carry her anywhere – only the figure moved, standing beside one of the beds. She came forward and closed the gap between them, the smell of decay becoming more pungent as she approached.

Caroline closed her eyes but only briefly. As much as she was loath to admit it, Edward was right about one thing: she had to face the truth – her truth, Helen's, and that of everyone around her.

The girl who stood before her was no longer a mere figure, a shape, or a shadow, someone in the dark who was anonymous. Caroline recognised her straight away from the photo David had shown her. It was, as Edward had inferred, Helen; young and fresh, no evidence of decay at all, her strawberry-blonde hair abundant. She was just a young girl, out to have a little fun, last spotted in a Williamsfield bar in the company of a tall, blonde man, who had left to spend the night at a local hotel, perhaps at his invitation, who'd reached it one way or another, and who was still there, hiding in the depths.

Helen raised her hand, an invitation for Caroline to take it.

Remember what Tallula said. There's nowhere to hide. Not anymore.

Deep down she knew that was the truth, which is why she took Helen's hand, inhaling deeply as their fingers entwined, as cold sank into the marrow of her bones.

"There was no tick beside your name," she whispered to the girl, "or mine."

Helen grasped her hand harder.

This was it; this was when Caroline would learn what had happened back then and what was happening now. Was she strong enough to bear it?

Chapter Twenty-Eight

Lucky. That's what she was. So lucky to have the parents she did, to live the life she was living, to be young, to be pretty, to be raised in California, to be free to travel the world… Okay, not the world, not just yet. Her father had insisted she explore her own country first. 'It's wonderful, Helen, so diverse. Spend a few months getting to know it. After that, come back, get a job, save up some more money, and then you can take off again, to Europe this time, or wherever it is you want to go. You know what I've always said.'

She did – travel was the best education a person could have. Although to be fair, she'd had a university education too, studying for a BA in Creative Writing at San Francisco State University, not quite gaining a first, but described as 'having flashes of genius', not by one tutor but by several over the years, and 'a real boon to the writing world.'

"Make like Jack Kerouac," her father had said, both laughter and longing in his voice. "Write something to rival him one day."

She'd laugh at that and roll her eyes. "Daddy, Kerouac was an icon."

"What are you saying? That Helen Ansell can't be? Why not? Give me one good reason."

"Because—"

"There's no reason," he'd interrupted, taking her by the shoulders and staring into her eyes – the same shade as hers, cobalt almost, she was lucky to have inherited them too. "Jack Kerouac, Allen Ginsberg, William Burroughs," God, her daddy had a thing about Beat Generation writers. "They're only human, not superhuman, and that's what made their writing great – the human element. Get out there, baby, live life to the full, and then infuse your writing with it. You've got a great career ahead of you and we stand behind you all the way. Start a new literary movement even—"

"Daddy!"

"Okay, okay, just write, Helen, because that's what you're good at, what you love to do."

She also loved to party, but the less her daddy knew about that the better.

So off she'd gone, leaving the west coast, heading to the mythical Deep South, the home of other writers she admired, including Harper Lee, William Faulkner, Tennessee Williams and her personal favourite, Truman Capote. A man who could write works as diverse as *In Cold Blood* and *Breakfast at Tiffany's* was nothing less than a hero to her. New Orleans had spawned or attracted a lot of those writers and, boy; she could see why – what a place it was, full of culture, variety, and atmosphere. Wow, the atmosphere! Especially in bars and clubs where, to be honest, she'd spent most of her time, drinking, smoking, dancing to live music and meeting some great people. The Southern accent made her swoon every time. Not just that, the way Southern men took their time with you, especially in bed, as if they had all the time in the world. To be fair, it was laid back where she came from too, but Southern men were less – how could she phrase it? – self-obsessed. She'd swear home-grown men were more concerned with their looks than the girls were, at least the men she'd kept company with. In New Orleans, in the Carolinas, in Nashville, Memphis and Georgia, they'd been a different breed entirely, the heat of long hot summers running through their veins, lending a sultriness to proceedings that she'd thrived on. The Dirty South, indeed.

She hadn't travelled alone at first; Kate had been with her, a fellow Creative Writing student who had happened to be a bit of a wildcard. She wasn't as passionate about literature as Helen was, she just happened to be good at English, had studied it because it meant she could put off having to find a proper career for a while longer – she could focus on the fun aspect of life instead. As she said, a wildcard, someone who was unpredictable, who grasped life with both hands, was greedy for it. Daddy hadn't really approved of Kate but acknowledged the irony after everything he'd said. Certainly Helen hadn't predicted Kate falling in love with a Latin waiter in Dallas of all places, and not only that, but staying on there too, leaving Helen to continue alone. Her daddy would have a fit if he knew, her mom too; she'd insist Helen return, but no way. She had another three months ahead of her and she was going to max it to the full.

Having left the Deep South – reluctantly – she'd gone to Washington DC (of course), and New York. The latter she wasn't as fond of as she'd thought she'd be. After New Orleans, it seemed a little soulless, lonely. Even without Kate, she'd never felt alone further south, whereas in New York she was one of the anonymous millions, all milling about in an endless ebb and flow. She'd left sooner than she'd intended, to make her way upstate, and then dropped a little south. Pennsylvania was a state she fell in love with straightaway. How green it was! And the Amish people fascinated her, driving their ponies and traps on the roads, alongside the regular traffic. The people were back to being friendly too. 'Real apple pie people' she'd heard them described as, as welcoming as their counterparts a thousand miles away.

How she'd landed in Williamsfield was another matter. She hadn't been intending to stay there, she'd wanted to push on to Pittsburgh, another four hours' drive away but bad weather had stopped her – the biggest storm she'd ever seen, rain lashing down from the heavens above, thunder and lightning; dramatic, beautiful but so dangerous to drive in. And so she'd pulled in, found a bar, ordered a Coca-Cola, decided to wait it out.

A couple of hours later, she was sick of Cola. In fact, if she never saw another glass of the brown fizzy stuff again it'd be too soon. She was going to have to bite the bullet, order a glass of wine – a Californian Shiraz, of course, a drink she'd developed a taste for at her parents' dinner table that would comfort her with thoughts of home while feeling temporarily, helplessly, stranded. Thankfully, what the bar lacked in people it more than made up for in drinks. There was just her and a disgruntled bartender with acne and glasses who, frankly, looked as bored as she was.

She was ruminating on where to stay in Williamsfield – the storm showed no sign of letting up – when another man entered the bar, not windswept and wet through as she had been, even though it had been such a short dash from the car. His hair was blonde, perfectly styled, and his clothes – a razor sharp suit, shirt and boots – were immaculate.

Well, well, well, things are suddenly looking a whole lot brighter.

He noticed her immediately. How could he not? She wasn't modest but between her and the bartender, she reckoned she'd win every time. Unless the newcomer was gay of course, which he obviously wasn't from the way his face lit up when they locked eyes.

Nonetheless, he played it cool, ordered a drink from the bar – Maker's Mark and ice – clinking the amber contents round and round in the tumbler before draining it at a pace that was tortuous. Then, and only then, did he turn to look at her more fully.

Travelling on her own had taught her to be less shy, besides, her drink was empty; it was the perfect time to head to the bar again. She rose from the booth she'd been sitting in and closed the gap between them. About to open her mouth, he spoke first.

"Another glass of Shiraz?"

She gasped. "How did you know?"

He smiled again, showing perfectly straight teeth. "Relax, I'm not a mind reader. I checked with the man here."

"Oh." She burst out laughing. That was smooth of him, very smooth. Handing her the glass of wine, their fingers brushed, the electricity between them causing her to jolt.

"Shall we find a seat?" he suggested, not waiting for an answer but leading the way to the farthest, darkest corner of the bar, wanting their privacy as much as she did.

She loved his confidence, the way he walked, no...not walked, he *strode* – like he owned the place – and she followed like a lost lamb, desperate for him to bestow on her more of his smiles. How old was he? she'd wondered. Older than her, that was for sure. In his late thirties, early forties. It was difficult to tell. There was something ageless about him, and certainly no lines or wrinkles marred such perfect skin. It was his confidence that really suggested maturity but whatever; she had no problem with older guys. On the contrary, she'd developed a taste for them recently.

Carl, his name was. A strong name, she liked it.

"And you are?"

"Helen."

"Not from these parts, are you?"

"I'm from California."

"Travelling?"

She'd nodded.

"On your own?"

"Up until recently. My friend, Kate, well…she met someone, in Dallas. She stayed on there."

He'd flashed her that smile. "That's the trouble, isn't it, meeting someone you like. It can interrupt plans."

"It's okay, I don't mind. It's fun being on my own, a real experience."

"How long have you got?"

"Tonight?" She'd shrugged. "All night."

A small burst of laugher. "I meant before you head home to California, but believe me," – he'd moved closer, snaked one arm around her shoulders – "I'm glad you're in no rush."

She'd blushed, both euphoric at his touch and a little nervous. "Hard to rush anywhere in this weather," she'd said, just as another bolt of lightning illuminated the night sky.

Carl had glanced over at the window but only briefly. In the main, he never took his eyes from her, devouring her almost, with intent. "The weather sure does suck in these parts," he stated, looking nothing less than delighted about it. "Where are you staying?"

"I don't know, I haven't decided yet. Know any good hotels?"

"A few."

"Where do you live?" She couldn't believe she'd asked, been so bold. It was obvious what she was inferring. Strangely he recoiled.

"Can't go to my place, I'm afraid. It's...difficult."

Her heart sank. He was married then, despite no wedding ring on his finger. "It's okay, don't worry, I under—"

"My sister's staying with me at the moment," he hurried on, "her two kids as well. Bad divorce." He leaned closer, a smell on his breath as heady as the weed she sometimes liked to smoke, "You see I'm a free agent too, and as soon as there's a break in the weather, whaddya say we split, get out of here, find somewhere to shack up?"

"I say we go for it," she said breathlessly, her head swimming, not just because of the wine but because she was finding him intoxicating too.

Closer still, his lips brushing hers, causing tingles to race through her again, he murmured, "Good, because I know a place where I think we're gonna be very happy."

* * *

How long had she been at the Egress?

She had no clue. She remembered leaving the bar and

279

running to her car with Carl, handing him the keys because he wanted to drive. A good idea she'd thought at the time, he seemed less tipsy than her, more able to handle his drink. As soon as they were in the car, he'd lit a cigarette, not the ordinary ones, the special ones, and she'd giggled, taken it from his long, elegant fingers, and dragged deeply on it. His smile when she'd giggled again was indulgent. He leaned over, kissed her much harder this time, his hands riding higher up her thighs as the thunder crashed overhead, making her long for him, for the journey to the hotel to be a quick one in case she ripped off his clothes and hers right there and then, on a rain-soaked empty street in the middle of Williamsfield, Pennsylvania.

The journey had in fact been a blur, as had first entering the hotel, a bit of an odd place, not many people around, and a receptionist that clearly thought she had better things to do. It was grand, she supposed, in an old-fashioned way, different to the hotels she was used to. She was sure he muttered something to the receptionist about his usual room, and anger had flared within her. She'd talked herself down, though. So what if he'd done this countless times, if she was one of many women? She wasn't looking for a significant other, as much as she liked him, she just wanted to have a little fun, to live a little, and that was the thing with him, he made her feel *alive*.

They didn't have his usual room, though, someone else had intervened, had said no. She couldn't remember who, but it was an old person's voice, authoritative. There was a mention of renovation, she was sure of it. 1104 was the room they were given, a big room, with a separate living room, but the bed, oh the bed, that was all she was interested in, and Carl in it.

Hours passed; a day or two, perhaps more? His stamina amazed her for an older guy. He was a stallion, a stud, his appetite voracious, making her scream with delight, beg for mercy on occasions, when she was tired, sore, when she needed to sleep, and he'd let her, for a short while, before starting all over again. She must have eaten, but she couldn't remember what. She'd definitely smoked. Carl had a never-ending supply of weed – 'colitas' he called it, blowing smoke rings into her face, causing her to giggle again.

"You're a devil," she'd say. "A little devil."

"Not so much of the little," he'd reply, grabbing her again and making her squeal.

Incredible times, amazing, the time of her life. And then one morning she'd woken, her mind no longer hazy, but much clearer, to find she was alone. Immediately, she was bereft. Where was he? Swinging her legs over the side of the bed, she'd grimaced. She felt bruised everywhere. It was rough sex they'd had, that's the way he liked it, and she'd gotten used to it, but that rough? She looked down and saw big splotches of colour on her skin, purple, red, and black, as though some mad artist had painted her.

"What the fuck?"

Looking around her, she was struck by how silent it was. Without her giggling to fill the air, her cries, her screams, it was nothing less than eerie. *Screams?* Helen swallowed. Yes, she'd screamed, but they'd been screams of delight, hadn't they?

Quickly, she padded over to the window. The storm was long over, but the sky was still grey, the horizon too, barely defined. In what part of Williamsfield was the Egress? She tried to remember the journey again, but she couldn't, not one single thing.

She needed her cell. Where was it? Spying her clothes on the floor, no doubt lying where they'd been ripped off, she knelt and started rifling through her jacket. Panic started to get a stronghold. She wanted to call her parents, let them know where she was, let *someone* know. That longing to hear their voices as desperate as the longing she'd had for Carl when she'd first met him. Outstripping it. There was something wrong here, something very wrong. She shouldn't be as bruised as she was, she shouldn't ache as much, and her head, it was as if it was going to explode.

There it was! Her cell, she'd found it.

Breathing a sigh of relief, she prayed it still had some battery left, if not, she'd have to find her charger. Where would that be? Had she even brought her backpack up to the room with her? Again, she looked around. It didn't look like it.

Please, please, have some battery left.

Miracles of miracles, it did – twenty per cent, but that was enough. She'd try calling first, if they weren't in, she'd send a text. Perhaps she'd even head home. She was tired of travelling suddenly. She could leave her car at the airport and fly, sort out retrieving it later. It would save so much time. California – where the sun always shone, where the people were her people. She might find Carl exciting, but she wasn't into sado-masochism, not in the bright light of day, not when she'd sobered up. The things he'd done to her, it was only now becoming clear.

Shame began to flood her. Her hands were shaking as she punched in numbers, almost completing the dialling when she heard movement in the bathroom – a shuffling. She wasn't alone, after all. Carl was still with her and about to come back into the bedroom at any minute.

Still clutching her cell, she jumped into bed, unable to face him. She'd pretend to be asleep still, give herself a few minutes to think about what she was going to say to him, an excuse as to why she needed to leave – soon, today, in the next hour. But she needed to think first; her mind had gone blank, fear clouding it.

The sheet over her, she screwed her eyes shut. He'd left the bathroom and was in the room now, still shuffling, grunting too; strange noises for someone as agile as Carl, but she daren't look, she daren't let him know that she was awake; that the spell he'd cast over her was broken. She didn't want any fuss, no goodbyes, she just wanted out. Maybe he did too, he was gathering his clothes and he was leaving. Her heart leaped at the prospect.

Just a sneak peek, she thought. *I'll open one eyelid. If he catches me, so what? I'll tell him straight, I'm leaving, thank him for his time... For the bruises...*

An eyelid opened, scanned the room, coming to rest on the man in front of her.

How she stopped from gasping, from screaming out loud, she'd never know. It wasn't Carl; it was someone old, hideous, his back stooped as he zipped his pants, his hair: white hair, mere strands plastered across his head. Perhaps she *had* gasped, because the man turned and stared at her.

"Helen!" he said, as if thrilled to see her. "How are you, darling? Oh, what is it? Whatever's the matter? Don't you like what you see? I admit I'm not looking my best, but that's your fault. You've worn me out. I feel as though I've aged a thousand years."

Instead of answering, she backed up against the headboard, still clutching the sheet, trying to cover herself.

She didn't know this man, she didn't! He wasn't Carl!

The old man chuckled. "I can see you need time to yourself. I'll leave you now, but I'll see you downstairs, there's a ballroom, breakfast is served there. Don't be late, will you? I hate to be kept waiting."

Turning from her, the man left. Although quivering with terror, she remembered the cell. It was beside her on the mattress. Grabbing it she redialled her parent's number, surprised she was able to as she was shaking so much, desperation driving her on.

The line connected.

"Hello, hello, Mom, Daddy, can you hear me? It's me… Helen."

"Hello, who's this? Is someone there?"

It was her father's voice, her dear father, but what was wrong? Couldn't he hear her? "Daddy, it's me. I'm… I'm at this hotel, the Egress, near Williamsfield, in Pennsylvania. Something strange is happening. I think I need help. Oh, Daddy, I do, I need help."

"Hello, hello. I'm sorry I can't hear you, there's too much interference on the line."

"DADDY!" Helen screamed, just as the line went dead. "Shit! Shit! Shit!"

The battery was draining fast but there was still a few percent left. She'd text where she was instead; ask them to send help. Her mind on the old man again, she shook her head in denial. There was no way that was Carl, no way.

Daddy, this is Helen, I need help. I'm at…

The cell died.

For a second she could only stare at it and then, fury overcoming her, she threw it against the wall; shut her eyes as the screen shattered.

Once again, time passed in a daze.

She didn't know when she finally summoned up the courage to leave her room. It could have been hours later; it could have been the next day. It was dark, though, both outside and inside the hotel, only a row of red lights in the corridor leading all the way to the elevator, which was waiting for her, its doors open; a light in there at least.

After pressing the button for the lobby she stood still, the elevator creaking and spluttering before finally starting to move. He'd said not to keep him waiting, that he *hated* to be kept waiting. Would he hurt her some more because she'd done exactly that?

Finally she reached the lobby. It was dark too, with no one at reception.

Leaving the elevator, she seized her chance and made her way over to the entrance instead of the ballroom, only skidding to a halt when she caught movement out of the corner of her eye: a shape, a shadow.

"Carl?" she whispered. "Is that you?"

"SURPRISE!"

It wasn't him; it was a woman who'd shouted, tall, beautiful, and pencil thin. It might be dark, but she could see her perfectly, her close-cropped blonde hair, ice white in colour, a smile on her face, but a glacial smile, nothing warm about it at all. There were other figures too, but none that she recognised, not even the tall blonde man that stood beside the woman, although certainly there was something familiar about him. It was that smile of his, a *wolfish* smile, the same smile that Carl had. That the old man in her bedroom had. That same horrific smile...

"Where d'ya think you're going?" It was the woman, her Southern-tinged voice cruelly taunting. "You can't leave, none of us can. Are you stupid or something? Surely you realise that by now?"

No, no, no.

The woman took a step forward and gestured towards the entrance.

"There's nothing out there for you, not anymore. Perhaps the basement is safest. He won't go down to the basement, will you, Edward? You don't like it down there, it reminds you too much of where you came from, doesn't it? The depths, the pits, the slurry, the shit at the bottom of the sewer. Funny you don't like it, that you shun it, it's so fucking funny. Go there, Helen, you'll be safe there. He won't *claw* at you there."

The man she'd called Edward stepped forward too, his eyes not on Helen, but on the woman beside him. Raising his fist, he smashed it into her face, no doubt bruising her too.

No longer rooted to the spot, Helen turned and ran in the direction she'd come from, trying to get as far away as she could from these people. The basement... Could she trust what that woman said? Was it true she'd be safe there? What choice did she have? Finding the stairwell, she smashed open the door, almost tripped as she flew down the stairs. The darkness welcomed her, seemed to stretch out its arms to hug her close. There *were* arms, so many of them, hands that were eager, that were grabby. So many people, some on beds, others were standing, greeting the new resident.

What is this place? Who are you?

It was a morgue, she realised. And these people, like her, were dead.

Chapter Twenty-Nine

Caroline almost doubled over as Helen's hand fell away. At the same time the lights came on, throwing everything into sharp relief. Helen was gone but the gurneys were still there. A morgue? This was once a morgue? And what had happened to Helen? Had Carl or Edward, or whoever he was, the old man even, killed her? Beaten her to death? And if so, was it before she reached the Egress, or after, in her room on the eleventh floor? There were still so many questions crowding her head, so many answers that she needed before she could draw any conclusions about what was happening.

Something on one of the gurneys moved, something covered by one of the sheets. There was more movement from a bed further back and then another to the left of her.

My God, the room's alive!

Or if she were to believe Helen, it was very much dead.

"David! David!"

The lights were on, he'd got what he wanted, and now they had to get out of there.

But it's safe in here, remember? Edward won't follow. He doesn't like it in the pits.

He could still reach her, though; he'd already proven

that by invading her mind. No, she wouldn't hide, not like Helen. She'd go mad if she stayed in the basement a minute longer than she had to, especially with those…those things writhing in front of her.

"David!" she screamed again, turning and running to where she'd left him. She half expected him to have been spirited away or an old, old man to be in his place, stooped and naked, with white hair plastered across his head, but thankfully it was just him, looking from side to side, blinking, as if he couldn't quite believe there was light again. Reaching him, she said, "You did it, you fixed the electrics!"

"I… I didn't," he replied, still bewildered. "They just came on."

"Okay, but it's a good thing, isn't it? You wanted there to be light. But now we have to leave, we have to go back upstairs and walk out of that door. I don't care what the weather's doing, about our coats, about anything. We've just got to get out of here."

He didn't argue this time. "We do." Looking beyond her, he said, "What's that noise?"

Noise? Could those creatures be making their way towards her? As quick as she could, she tried to explain. "This was once a morgue, and in that room over there are the gurneys they used back then."

"Yes, that's right, it was a morgue."

For a moment she couldn't move, couldn't speak. "You knew?" she finally managed.

"This was where the city morgue used to be, on the outskirts of town. You were the one who prompted me to find out, when we were looking at the photos in reception. You pointed to the construction shot, and you said you wondered what had been here before. *This* was going to be the new centre of the city, this hotel, so they moved the morgue into what was going to become the old town area. They were going to switch it all around. As we now know, the death of the architect's daughter and all the shit that went down afterwards meant none of that ever happened. The new downtown idea was abandoned."

Still she was incredulous. "Why didn't you tell me?"

"I was going to, but… I thought it would freak you out."

"Freak me out?" she yelled. "More than I am already, you mean? You know what, it might have helped me piece together more quickly what's happening here."

"I was trying to protect you," he explained.

Remorse flooded through her. "I know, I know you were but, Christ, no wonder people thought the place was cursed."

"Caroline, what *is* happening?"

"I… I…" Should she tell him about Helen, about what had happened to her? She would, but not now, not with those things behind her. When they were out of here, when they were long gone, she'd tell him then. She grabbed his hand. "Let's go, quick."

She started to pull him, fearing resistance again, but she needn't have worried. He soon took the lead, pulling her instead, up the stairs, through the doors and back into the lobby, both of them coming to a standstill, breathless from the exertion, but also because of something else.

The lobby, the entire length of it, was busier than she'd ever seen it. So many people were milling about, and in the floor space just in front of the lobby desk – no longer carpeted but covered in the fancy tiles she'd seen in the black and white photos – couples were dancing to music played on the piano, elegantly gliding along the floor, others more lively, their heads thrown back in laughter. Only a very few were in modern dress. Instead, the women wore tea dresses and the men suit trousers and jackets. Above them the chandeliers blazed more fiercely than ever, and on tables dotted around, in dramatic Grecian-style urns, there were plants that were more dramatic still. She glanced over at the lobby desk – still in situ – and sure enough the clock with its oak surround was on the wall above, ticking away. Grand. It was all very grand; as grand as originally intended. Dragging her eyes to the left, the doors to the ballroom were wide open – people were dancing in there too, whirling around and around, including two figures she no longer had to struggle to recognise: her mother and father, the newlyweds.

She started pointing frantically. "Look, David. That's my mum and dad!"

He looked to where she was pointing but instead of answering, he frowned.

"David, look, it's them. Oh my God, it's them! Let's go to them, they might be able to help us. You can see them, can't you? You can see everyone that's here?"

Still he didn't reply.

"David!" she said, her elation dwindling. "Tell me what you can see."

"Shadows, shapes. But they're fading."

"No, they're not shadows, they're not shapes, they're people, as real as you and I." She swallowed before continuing. "Can you hear the music?"

"There's no music," he replied.

She turned her head from side to side, her eyes

frantically searching. "There they are! There's Edward and Tallula. Surely you can see them."

The pair were leaning casually against a far wall, each with a glass in their hands, a cocktail of some sort, glancing their way every now and again, their heads, as usual, close together and whispering conspiratorially in between bursts of laughter. She had to look away, not wanting to witness further how much their confusion, terror, and upset delighted them. "There's Althea too, and Marilyn's dancing with John. They're so sweet, aren't they? I know they're troubled, but I don't think they're bad people, not at heart. I'm so glad they've found each other, that they can comfort each other. Don't tell me you can't see them either."

David squinted, as though he were trying to see something, as if he wanted to please her with the correct answer. "I'm sorry, I—"

"Elspeth! There's Elspeth!" Caroline's voice had risen. "You have to remember Elspeth!"

"Caroline, I think I was imagining things when I mentioned shadows. I don't know where everyone is, but the way ahead is clear, so we need to take advantage of that."

Her heart started banging against her chest wall, as if seeking an escape of its own. "It's not empty," she whispered. It was far from empty. "David..." She wasn't sure she could bring herself to ask. "What about me? Can you see me clearly?"

"Caroline, yes!" His movement swift, he grabbed her by the shoulders, his eyes brighter than any chandelier. "I can see you. I can hear you and I can feel you."

She stared back, angry that tears were blurring her

vision. She wanted to see him clearly too. "We have to leave."

"Yeah, yeah, we do, right now. This is one hell of a place, but don't worry, I'll manage to get the car started, yours, or mine. We'll be in Williamsfield soon enough, then we can find ourselves somewhere to stay until you catch your flight home. I'll finish work on this Helen case and then I'll come over, I promise. I'll come to England. This isn't the end."

She nodded. "It can't be the end, not for us, but... Helen's dead."

He reared back slightly. "Dead? How do you know?"

"Call it a gut feeling."

His jaw clenched, briefly he screwed his eyes shut, his agony at her fate etched all over his face. "I told you, that was my gut feeling too."

"She did come here, we know that, because of Althea's register."

"Althea?" Confusion reigned once again. "You just mentioned her. Who is she?"

She shook her head, unable to believe her ears. "You really don't remember, do you?"

"Caroline, we can talk about everything later. While there's no one here we need to take advantage, come on."

"But, David, do you even know why we're running? Why we're leaving behind our clothes, our belongings, my passport even?"

There was the slightest flicker of memory in his eyes, an echo, and then it was gone. Fear gripped her, darker and colder than anything she'd encountered, at the prospect that soon she'd become an echo too, that despite what they'd said, what they'd declared, it was the end – but it was also a kind of beginning, for her anyway. *Another beginning.*

Together they walked, the dancers parting before them, and only her able to witness it. For once she wanted the path in front of them to run on and on, as it had done so many times before at the Egress, never to end. She wished she and David could lose themselves for all eternity, defying the fates. But all too soon they reached the main doors. She peered outside, at the whiteness of the land.

"It looks better out there, doesn't it?" said David, so much hope in his voice. "Sure, the ice is going to be a bit treacherous, but if we take it slowly, we'll make it to Williamsfield."

If we take it slowly…

"You'll be careful, won't you, David?"

He turned to her, his hope almost blinding. "I won't do anything to put us in danger."

She gripped his hand harder. "I want you to be safe."

"We will be, I promise."

Standing on tiptoes, she brushed her lips against his, savouring how soft they were, his clean soap and water smell. "Thank you," she said, having to force herself to withdraw.

"What for?" He looked part amused; part bemused.

"You showed me what life should be like."

"Caroline—"

"Here, let's get this door open." Releasing him, she placed her shoulder against the glass and pushed, David joining in and helping her. "I've got it, it's not as bad as it was before. You go first."

"Okay. God, it's cold. We haven't got our coats," something else that bemused him. "Why haven't we got our coats, Caroline?"

"Because there was no time," she answered, stepping backwards, not forwards.

His face crinkled. "No time?"

"That's right, it just…ran out. Take care, David."

"I've told you, I'm going to be careful."

"And believe."

"Believe in what?"

"In me at least."

"Caroline?"

Before either of them could say another word, she closed the door on him, swiftly sliding the bolt at the top into place, as well as the bolt at the bottom.

Immediately David began banging on the door, his fists hammering away at the glass. "Caroline! Caroline! What do you think you're doing? Hey, come on, let me in! Caroline?"

Again and again he struck the glass, but there was less and less strength behind each blow. What did increase was the puzzlement on his face, almost comical if she had the will to laugh. She cried instead, tears racing down her cheeks, to splash on the floor below.

"Caroline!" Still he was calling her name, but he'd stop soon, she knew that.

Someone had come to stand by her – Althea, gliding on silent feet.

"I'm dead, aren't I?" Caroline said, not turning her head to the side, still staring at David.

"Yes," Althea replied.

"And David isn't?"

"I suspect he had an accident like you did and was in a coma."

"But now he's waking up."
"Yes, he's beginning to wake."

Chapter Thirty

She was waking too, but to a different reality, just as Helen had done. The light David had wanted so badly must have been the light in the hospital, and the wires he was complaining of in the basement were those he was attached to.

Her eyes still on David, he was faltering over her name, just as she'd predicted, looking to his left and to his right, up and down, clearly wondering what he was doing there, outside a hotel, in the snow, in the middle of the night, banging on a door and shouting.

"He'll think it's a dream," Althea stated.

"And me," she whispered. "Will he think I'm a dream too?"

She paused. "Maybe. Maybe not. I think the memory of you will run deep."

As David scratched at his head again, turned, and wandered away, Caroline's heart – if it could be said that she still had one – seemed to convulse. She couldn't drag her eyes away to look at Althea, not yet, but she had to ask. "How did I end up at the Egress? If I crashed my car, surely that's where my body is, out there, on that highway."

Althea placed a hand on her arm. "You lost control, your car span, not into a bank of snow – that was just what you told yourself. It was a metal gate. Your death was sudden, wholly unexpected. When death is like that it can take time to accept. You were young and there was so much you wanted to do still, and so you carried on, you *forced* yourself to, arriving at the Egress, because that was where you intended to go." She took a brief pause before continuing, allowing what she'd imparted to sink in. "The snowstorm, it's not as bad as the one in 1950, despite all the scaremongering, but that's what you'd heard on the radio and that's what your subconscious created – a barrier between you and a world that you knew, deep down, you no longer belonged to. In a way it's a safety mechanism, you were giving yourself time to adjust, but there's only so long you can fool yourself."

Although she was listening, Caroline continued to stare outwards at the receding figure, refusing to take her eyes off him. "Are you telling me that what happened between me and David wasn't real either?" He was becoming so small, a distant figure, soon to be consumed by the surrounding landscape. *How am I going to manage without you?* She knew grief well enough, but this was it at its ultimate. "It felt real," she managed. "So real."

"Darling, look at me. Take my hand and squeeze it."

"What?"

"I said squeeze my hand."

David had gone. He'd disappeared.

Choking back a sob, she reached out, blindly at first, but soon felt Althea's fingers wrap around hers.

"Squeeze, Caroline, harder. I'm not as frail as I look."

She tried her utmost to obey.

"What can you feel?" Althea asked.

"Flesh. I can feel flesh."

"And warmth?"

"Yes, you're warm enough."

"Because I'm real too. You're real. There are so many of us at the Egress that are real. Just because you're dead, doesn't mean it's over. Death isn't the end."

"It's the end of something."

"Caroline, please, will you look at me. One leg of the journey is over, that's all. Another awaits."

She only half turned. "But I'm stuck here."

"No, you're not," Althea denied.

"I don't understand."

"You're beginning to. Come on, let's move away from the door, and sit down."

"But David…"

"You know he's not there anymore."

No, he was on the road to recovery.

Althea had to guide her away, Caroline stumbling blindly otherwise. Her head rising just a little, she pointed towards the ballroom. "In there…my parents."

Althea stopped to look. "Darling, I said many of us at the Egress are real, but there are plenty of shades too, or shadows as you call them. A part of them lingers still; their hearts possibly, but not their souls. That's the difference you see, your *soul* is here."

"So my parents…"

"Had a magical time, didn't they, on their honeymoon? They laughed, they loved, they danced, and they conceived their first child. Experiences like that are special and they tend to imprint themselves on the atmosphere, playing on a loop over and over. As much a part of the building as bricks and mortar, they *define* the Egress and make it special too." After walking a few more paces, she seated both of them on a small sofa. "But not all memories are good, of course. This is neither heaven nor hell, but it can feel like both at times."

A thought that had already occurred to her. Taking several deep breaths, Caroline tried to compose herself. "Does this hotel even exist? In the world I left behind, I mean?"

"Oh yes, yes, despite its rather…sorry reputation. It still exists and we exist right alongside it. In the 'real' Egress, people check in and out on a daily basis, the numbers not great, you can't expect them to be as we're off the beaten track, but still people come. I tend to think they always will. The shadows that you see? They're not all made up of the dead."

A glimmer of wonder tried to skirt around despair. If she was to believe what she was hearing, the shadows and the shapes were a mix of the living *and* the dead. She remembered interrupting David when he was speaking to someone, someone that had seemed vague to her, one of the people that hadn't quite stood out – a shadow. "David could interact with the living as well as the dead, because he had a foot in both worlds."

Althea nodded, a semblance of relief in her smile.

"And he could also connect to the Internet, whereas I couldn't, because literally, he was connected to the outside world, whereas my connection had been severed."

Again, Althea nodded.

"But not all memories are good, as you said," Caroline continued, explaining in brief the dreams she'd had, and what she'd experienced in the corridor outside Althea's room.

"That's right, they're not all good, but what you saw in your dreams, maybe even in the corridor, is most likely to be facets of your own personality; the demons in your head, if you will, seeking release. The shadow side of you, all the thoughts and the feelings you've accumulated which never entirely sat well with you, which in death rise to the fore."

Again Caroline had to breathe deeply. "But the emotions, they were so *powerful*."

"Which is why we suppress them, because they're exactly that. They're our driving force."

"The architect's daughter, what about her?"

Althea nodded, clearly expecting some reference to her. "Ah, the architect's daughter. Now there's an example of emotions running high."

"Is she an imprint or is she real?"

"Oh, she's real enough. She can't move on. *Won't* move on, poor girl. She insists on reliving the moment of her demise."

"What's her name?" Caroline asked.

"Martha Bergstein."

She'd been the very first entry in Althea's ledger, the girl with no tick beside her name. "And the second architect, the one who was murdered?"

"Ronald Greaves."

"You ticked his name off," she responded.

"Because he left the Egress, straight away, despite the shock of his death. Some do, some don't. Darling, when you die, you have a choice: you either accept what's happened to you, or you don't. Greaves clearly did. Others simply carry on, trying to live. If that's the case, if that's you, and you passed either at the Egress or it was your intent to come here, then here is where you'll find yourself." She stopped to consider her words. "I have to say, the hotel does tend to house a lot of lost souls, but then there's always been death here, and where there's death there's an attraction. It opens up a gateway."

"What about Helen?" Caroline asked. "She's not just a shadow."

"No, she isn't. I wish she'd come up from the basement and stop being so afraid."

"Did she die here?"

Althea shook her head. "I gather she was driven somewhere nearby, beaten and raped. Her body's still out there probably, lying in a shallow grave. Maybe when it's found she can start the healing process and emerge from the darkness that hides her."

Caroline swallowed. "Was it Edward who murdered her?"

Althea glanced briefly over at Edward. "No, not him, but certainly he represents that type of person, and when she reached the hotel, he took advantage of her too."

"Who *is* he?" she said, glancing in his direction too. "Surely, you're not related?"

"Related?" Althea shrugged, her nonchalance surprising Caroline. "In a way we are, but not how you think. We're opposites, Edward and I. We preside over what happens here. We're the managers, as you call us. It's a pity, but we both have to be on duty."

"Why?"

"As the material world is balanced, so is the spiritual world. That's the rule."

"The rule?" Tallula had mentioned something about

that; it had angered her.

"Ah, Tallula," Althea said, even though Caroline hadn't spoken her name out loud. "A woman who has never played by the rules. But I don't make them, and neither does Edward, nonetheless we have to abide by them. It's the natural order of things." Leaning forward, Althea stared into Caroline's eyes. "Darling, this is my job, to be here for souls such as yourself, and to temper other souls, those that would align themselves with Edward. We can interact with you – Edward a little too enthusiastically on occasion – but what we won't do is interfere. We won't force you to understand what has happened to you; it's something you have to come to terms with yourself. Tallula said there's no way out of here, that we're trapped. I know you've felt that way, so many do – Marilyn, John, and Elspeth, but you're trapped by your own volition. Even Tallula. Free will is something that carries on. With Tallula, it's fear of retribution, consequences to actions. In other words, she's frightened she'll have to experience all the suffering that she heaped on people while she lived, and in a sense, she will. But she'll learn from it too, that's the thing, and she'll grow in spirit, but she can't see that, not yet. She doesn't want to. And so she clings to Edward, believing he'll protect her, but of course he can't. He has no real power, not in that sense. But one thing he will do is have a little fun with her while she remains. Like a leech, he'll bleed her dry."

Edward and Tallula had finished their drinks and had joined the others on the dance floor, less than a hair's breadth between them. She stared at Edward – a man of many faces, a trickster, as devilish as they come, but still he was bound by rules. At least at the Egress he was.

"What happens if there are no rules?" Caroline asked, trembling at the idea.

"You're right to tremble," Althea replied. "Without rules, there would be no order. That's why ritual is so important, for new guests especially, it provides an anchor, and without it we risk being cast adrift, falling deeper and deeper into chaos. Do you know something? He may threaten, he may rail against me, but even Edward's afraid of that and ultimately, that's why he obeys. Beneath it all, he's a stickler for home comforts."

"What about the others?" Caroline asked. She didn't need to elaborate; Althea would know who she meant.

"I suspect Marilyn will go soon, now that she realises her husband isn't here."

"Where did she die?"

"At home, she hanged herself, hence the knotted bed sheet you found. She'd sit for hours in 1102 tying and untying it. As you know, she made her way here because this is where they spent so many anniversaries. All of you have a connection with the Egress."

"Perhaps me more than most having been conceived here."

Althea agreed. "Yes, perhaps you more than most."

"What about John?" He'd always intrigued her.

"Ah, John," Althea leaned back into the sofa. "Now, he did die here, that's his connection, he drank himself to death on one of the living floors, in room 508. After his death, Raquel put him on the eleventh floor, in the room next to me because I wanted to keep an eye on him. By the way, I must apologise for Raquel, for the persistent air of boredom that surrounds her – she *is* bored, you see. Despite her relatively modern appearance, she's been here almost as long as me; she's seen so many come and go. It could be that she's done her bit, and she needs to move on too. Back to John, he thinks he's as bad as his father, the father that abandoned him and his family, and maybe he is. Certainly he followed suit, but alcohol is a terrible addiction and it does seem to run in families, alcohol *and* drugs, as in the case of Elspeth, a woman who once spent a very happy family holiday here as a child; the last time she was ever truly happy, I think, and that's why she returned. Hopefully she'll go soon as well, once her mind's a little clearer. Doing as Martha does, dying over and over again, can be soul destroying." She shook her head, apologised once more. "I'm digressing. John keeps writing that he's sorry, scrawling the words over any piece of paper he can get his hands on, but, at the moment, that's all it is, just words. He craves his family's forgiveness – for leaving them in a time of crisis. His younger child, Ben, is ill you see, *gravely* ill – but first he needs to forgive himself, for not being a rock, for having crumbled. Only then can he find release."

There were tears in Caroline's eyes again as Althea spoke, sorrow for all of those she'd met at the Egress, for their plight. "When you say the living floors…"

"I mean floors two to ten. It's only the eleventh floor that's reserved for us."

"The floor that was never built."

"But it was meant to be built. And so, in a way, it was. It was real in the minds of many as a proposal, even if that proposal was never realised. It was born, but given over to death, the very purpose that stopped its full incarnation."

And because David was caught between both worlds, he could come and go between floors. She'd been able to as well, but only initially. As time wore on, it had become more difficult, just as it had for David, their worlds parting long before she shut him out.

"Edward was on the sixth floor, though, not the eleventh," Caroline pointed out.

"In a room that didn't exist – 666. A joke, by his standards anyway."

"The number of the beast."

"Oh yes," Althea answered, "he can be a beast at times."

"There's another thing I need to know." She had to steel herself for this answer too. "Edward kept saying I was diseased. Am I?"

Althea lowered her eyes, sombre once again. "He can see things like that much more clearly than me. He…he's not usually wrong. But remember, it's your body he's referring to, not your soul. If there was disease, it doesn't matter now."

Even so, if she'd lived, if she'd survived the car crash, it would have mattered. *'It does seem to run in families'* – that's what Althea had said about addiction, and maybe it applied to cancer too, in her family anyway. She might well have become a load for David to carry, no happy ending on the cards for them, either side of the divide.

She'd heard enough for now. Climbing to her feet, she once again surveyed the scene before her, Althea rising too, to stand beside her.

"It's not such a bad place you know," said Althea, "even without David. It has its moments."

"But I can leave if I want to?"

"You can. Simply take the elevator, that crotchety old elevator, and ride it all the way to the eleventh floor, *beyond* the eleventh floor. Have the *will* to keep going."

The will – that's all she needed – her means of escape, to whatever, whoever lay beyond, her parents even, as solid as she was, not just a hazy memory.

An idea occurred.

"What if I don't leave? What if I stay here? We're all connected to the Egress, which means David is too. It's where he came while in a coma, where he *intended* to come, investigating Helen's case. It's where we met. I know the love we shared was real, that we felt the same way about each other. In death and near-death, we were just so *alive*." Taking Althea's hands, she held them in her own. "If he remembers anything about our time together, he could come back couldn't he, one day, when he's dead, I mean?"

"There's a chance. Even if he finds love during his lifetime, it might not compare."

"All I have to do is bide my time."

"As I said before, Caroline, that's your decision. No one else can make your mind up for you. Free will, remember?"

Caroline did remember. "And meanwhile others will continue to make their way here?"

"Yes, they will. It's a heavy workload at times."

Caroline released Althea's hands. Needing a moment to herself, she walked over to the window, the piano music, the laughter, and the chatter that filled the air around her fading slightly as she pressed up against the window. Gazing outwards over the landscape, it gave no hint that David had ever been there, the snow virginal, no footprints in it at all.

She came to a decision.

I'll wait. I'll stay here, with Althea and Jenna, take over on reception perhaps, let Raquel retire. Maybe I'll go down to the basement sometimes and keep Helen company. Maybe she'll finally realise that Edward and his kind are no threat to her, not anymore and she'll venture upstairs with me to the lobby. She'll get in the elevator, she'll keep going, all the way.

Whatever happens, David, I'll wait.

And I'll hope.

The only man who could ever reach her…

She smiled.

There might be a happy ending yet.

Epilogue

"Kids, come on. Can it, will you?"

David exchanged a wry smile with the woman in the passenger seat beside him.

"Little monsters, aren't they?" she said. "It must be you they take after."

"Hey!" David retaliated. "You're the one who screams and shouts, especially in the bedroom if I recall correctly."

Melissa's mouth opened wide. "David! Don't mention stuff like that in front of the children."

David laughed. "Melissa, it's because of *that*, they're even here."

Melissa spluttered too and David carried on driving, taking his family for a weekend away, to the other side of the state, to the hills and the valleys.

God, he was glad of his family, of his beautiful wife, and his two children, both boys, Frankie and Leo, aged seven and five respectively. Grateful he was actually here to have a family. He was blessed, truly blessed. A few years previously his life had almost ended, being caught in a snowstorm in this part of Pennsylvania, that had taken so many by surprise with its sudden ferocity. He'd been driving at the time, ignoring warnings on the radio to find shelter, that it was set to rival anything experienced in the 1950s and 80s.

They always exaggerate, these forecasters, he'd thought. *There's plenty of time to reach the hotel.* He hadn't even slowed down, just carried on, trusting in his Ford to get him to where he was going. More fool him. Not only had he put his own life in danger, but also the driver of the car he'd hit, a young college grad, on his way home, sending them both careering off the highway and into a ditch. Thankfully the college grad had been wearing his seat belt. David, on the other hand, hadn't, an old hangover from his cop days when he needed to jump from his car quickly on occasions, in pursuit of the bad guys. Idiot! What a fucking idiot. He'd flown through the windshield, had an altercation with a tree, subsequently lying unconscious and bloodied in the snow while the college grad called for an ambulance, which only just managed to get through and whisk him to the nearest hospital in Susquehanna. And there he had lain for the next six weeks, the first few days in a deep coma, coming out very gradually under the control of the medical staff. The hospital bills that had mounted up were something else. But it was only money, he consoled himself, he hadn't paid with his life. It turned out that the storm had caused a fair amount of deaths across the middle states, but not as many as the 1950s storm. That had claimed over three hundred lives – incredibly – and injured hundreds too. Even if there'd been one death, it would have been one too many, but at least he wasn't counted in that tally.

"Make a left onto Highway 31 North," the Sat Nav instructed.

"What was that?" David asked. "Did she say take the

next left?"

"Damn it, I didn't hear either," Melissa responded. Turning around, she also told the kids to pipe down. "Enough already! There's a theme park where we're going, remember? If you want to reach it sooner rather than later, you gotta let us listen to directions."

Immediately, Frankie and Leo stopped jabbering, just as David made the required turn.

"See? How'd you do that, get them to obey so quickly?"

"It's called the magic touch, darling. I seem to have it too."

Again, David laughed. It was true, she did. The stirring in his loins was testament to that.

Having only met Melissa a short time before the accident, he was lucky too that she'd stood by him while he recovered, visiting him regularly, every day when he was in a coma, sitting by his bedside, holding his hand. His mom had told him that, the mom he'd been somewhat estranged from. The accident had brought everyone so much closer together, David no longer so disparaging of the beliefs his preacher father held, his unwavering faith. Perhaps because he considered himself blessed, he was more inclined to believe. 'She's a keeper,' Mom had told him, and she'd been right. After waking, it had been a while before he was back on his feet, but still Melissa was there, even when they were testing for permanent brain damage, her devotion, and her loyalty astounding.

And so he'd asked her to marry him, fast forward eight years and here they were, the two that were now four, on a weekend vacation, heading to the hills and a theme park.

"So, tell me, who's gonna ride the American Eagle?" he bellowed.

"Me!" All three of them declared.

"And the Big Dipper?"

"Me!" was again the earnest response.

"And…" he continued, but something in the distance caught his attention: a building, large red letters sitting on its roof spelling out a name – the Egress. That's where he'd been heading the day he'd crashed, investigating the Helen Ansell case.

"Isn't that…?" Despite wearing sunglasses, he could tell Melissa was squinting too.

"Yeah," he replied. "It is."

"Oh, we have come the wrong way then. We should've turned left further up I think."

David shook his head. "It's okay, there's probably a road ahead that meets with ours. Let's just…carry on." There was hesitation in his voice as he glanced at Melissa, a silent acknowledgement between them that they were close to the scene of his accident.

"Okay," Melissa sighed, a ragged sound, unease in it too. "Such a shame about that girl, wasn't it, the one you were investigating. What was her name again?"

"Helen. And yeah, but at least her body was found, a month or two after I was back on my feet actually, and her parents got some kind of closure."

"Can you imagine the pain they must have gone through?"

"I don't want to imagine, or the pain that Helen went through either."

There was a sombre moment of silence, even the kids seemed to have realised the gravitas of their conversation and barely breathed.

"Did you ever go back to the Egress?" Melissa asked, "I

can't recall."

Turning his head to look at her, he was about to answer, when she shouted at him.

"Look out!"

"Wh…?" Quickly, he swerved, there was a snake in the road – a Northern Copperhead he reckoned and venomous. What was it doing there, in the middle of a highway? Thankfully there was no oncoming traffic, and he managed to straighten up again, no harm done. "Christ, Mel, no need to shout like that, it's a snake. I could have driven over it."

"Oh, that's such a lovely thing to say, isn't it?" Mel retorted. "Just kill the poor snake."

"What would you prefer, that I kill us instead?"

Realising his words, this place, and their unease at unintentionally finding themselves here, he sighed. "I'm sorry."

She attempted a smile. "Should I turn the radio on?"

"Good idea," David said, taking a deep breath. He didn't want more tension either.

"So," she said, making conversation again, "did you ever go back?"

"Where?"

"To the Egress."

"No point, not after her body was found. And it's not a case of going back, I never got there in the first place, remember?"

Melissa swiped at his arm. "You know what I mean! I'm glad they caught her killer too."

"Eventually. Carl Warren. She wasn't his first, and she wasn't his last either. The bastard killed two more women after Helen."

"Christ! I can't understand why he hasn't been executed."

"Believe me, honey, he will be, but it's Bucks County for now while the prosecutors make their case for the death penalty."

"Let's hope they manage to pull it off." There was another brief silence and then she changed the subject. "Egress. It's a strange word, isn't it? Do you know what it means?"

He did know; he'd felt compelled to look it up one day, recently, in fact, the name popping into his head after so long. "It means the action of going out of or leaving a place."

Melissa removed her sunglasses and rubbed at the bridge of her nose. "So, it kind of means transition. Pretty apt for a hotel, I suppose."

"I suppose."

They drew ever closer to the hotel, a lonely building, pretty much nothing else around it.

"There were such great plans for this area," he continued, having read that too, once upon a time. "But it never really took off. The hotel had some bad luck right from the start, the architect's daughter died there, and then another architect, the one who took over from him, in some sort of gambling dispute. Plus, it was once the site of the city morgue."

Melissa pulled a face. "I wouldn't want to stay there, knowing all that."

"I don't think many do."

"It looks derelict to me."

"I don't think it is. I think it's still limping on, doing a little business here and there."

He started to lean heavily on the brake.

"Why you slowing down?" asked Melissa.

"I just want to see," David replied.

"See what?"

"I don't know, I… Hang on a minute, Mel."

Was that someone at the window, to the left of the entrance, staring outwards? He slowed further – almost grinding to a halt, careful no one was behind him, although it was unlikely on this lonely road. There was someone at the window, staring right back at him!

"David…"

He realised Melissa was talking to him, but her voice seemed so far away, unreal even. What was real was what was in front – the person, a female, he realised, who'd caught his eye. There was something…familiar about her. How come? Why on earth should a woman in a window of a building he'd never set foot in be familiar? And yet, he knew what it would look like inside; the piano that would be to the right of the entrance, the lobby desk, the bored receptionist, a ballroom, in which dinner was served every evening, the guest rooms even, unusually large for this area. A grand place, or at least it was meant to be, that had fallen on hard times, which had never fulfilled its potential, its dreams; that was seen as cursed… But it wasn't cursed, not really. It was special.

Sweet Caroline.

That was the song playing on the radio, courtesy of some country station Melissa had tuned into.

Good times never seemed so good.

His heart both ached and soared.

Who are you? he wanted to ask. *Why are you so familiar?*

"Daddy, come on," a voice behind him started whining

again. "We want to go on the water slide!"

"The water slide?" For a moment he didn't know what that was, who was speaking, or why he was having to wipe away a tear that luckily no one had noticed yet. *It's your son speaking, David. How can you forget your son?* "Oh, the water slide. Yeah, yeah, okay."

"Oh good, you're speeding up again," Melissa seemed relieved. "I thought you were going to make us go in there for a minute, take a look around. You know, I don't think you're right, I don't think it is in use anymore. It really does look abandoned to me."

As the Egress fell out of sight, he glanced at Melissa. "But didn't you see her, the woman in the window, the one who was staring?"

She shook her head. "A woman in the window? What did she look like?"

"Look like?" he repeated. "I...don't know. She was a shadow, a silhouette."

"Maybe it was a guest then, admiring what a gorgeous day we've been blessed with."

"Maybe."

She started to sing along to the tune still playing on the radio. "I love this song," she declared happily. "Neil Diamond's got the most amazing voice."

The ache in him increased. "Yeah," he replied. "I love Sweet Caroline too."

A note from the author

As much as I love writing, building a relationship with readers is even more exciting! I occasionally send newsletters with details on new releases, special offers and other bits of news relating to the Psychic Surveys series as well as all my other books. If you'd like to subscribe, sign up here!

www.shanistruthers.com

Made in the USA
Las Vegas, NV
23 September 2022

55875485R00179